SYBILLE BEDFORD

was born in Germany which she left for good in her early childhood. She was educated privately in Italy, England and France. Sybille Bedford started writing at sixteen — literary essays, critical work and fiction. Her first book, *The Sudden View: a Mexican Journey*, was published in 1953 and later republished as *A Visit to Don Otavio*. Her first and most famous novel, *A Legacy*, was published in 1956 and televised in 1975. *The Best We Can Do*, an account of the trial of Dr Bodkin Adams, was published in 1958, followed by *The Faces of Justice* (1961), a report on law courts and judicial procedure in England, France, Germany, Switzerland and Austria. The novels *A Favourite of the Gods* and *A Compass Error* appeared in 1963 and 1968 respectively, and her two-volume biography of Aldous Huxley was published in 1973 and 1974.

A distinguished literary journalist and law reporter, Sybille Bedford has covered the Auschwitz Trial at Frankfurt, the trial of Jack Ruby at Dallas and the Lady Chatterley and Stephen Ward trials at the Old Bailey, London. She has contributed to numerous magazines and papers both here and in the United States, and as a journalist and critic is most famous for her travel writing, her articles on wine and food, and for her book reviews. A Fellow of the Royal Society of Literature, an English Vice President of P.E.N., she was awarded the O.B.E. in 1981.

Sybille Bedford married in 1935 and has lived in France, England, the United States and Italy. She now lives in London where she is working on a new novel.

D1149947

A Favourite
of The Gods

SYBILLE BEDFORD

With a New Introduction by
Peter Vansittart

Virago

TO EDA LORD

Published by VIRAGO PRESS Limited 1984
41 William IV Street, London WC2N 4DB

First published in Great Britain by Collins 1963

Copyright © Sybille Bedford 1963

Introduction copyright © Peter Vansittart 1984

British Library Cataloguing in Publication Data

Bedford, Sybille
A favourite of the Gods.
I. Title
823'.914 [F]   PR6052.E/
ISBN 0-86068-387-7

Printed in Finland by Werner Söderström Oy,
a member of Finnprint

CONTENTS

Introduction

Sybille Bedford is an authority on law, a connoisseur of unusual houses and families, of manners, wit, social rituals, food and drink. She will not fob the reader off with "they sat down to a meal, and afterwards . . ." but will usually describe the dishes, affectionately and precisely. Few writers have been less tempted to disregard Dr Johnson's injunction not to cant in favour of savages. If chalices of Margaux and Lafite are on offer, one does not readily envisage her demanding mouldy beer or muddy water out of somebody's toothmug for the good of the soul. This does not make her a solemn snob, she can lightly mock her most cherished pleasures and friends. It is agreeable to learn from her of the fastidious Huxleys, in India, offered a meal of chocolates, ice cream, hot dumplings stuffed with curried mice. She has written the standard biography of Aldous Huxley and one of the wittiest of travel books, *A Visit to Don Otavio* (originally *The Sudden View*).

None of this inevitably makes an exceptional novelist, but it does indicate something of her flavour. It derives from a European imagination, cosmopolitan yet with very strong local roots, far-reaching in *A Legacy* but never losing a very personal richness of texture. It is part of an old, multi-lingual society with sub-divisions, feuds and alliances, cohesive culture, vestigial feudalism, and the flaws of complacency and arrogance that assisted its destruction. In this novel she writes:

Obviously their marriage was a failure but that was something both were able to set aside, and if they had little else in common, they shared at least two things — a belief in the importance of society and the habit of being rich. Both were at home in their time.

Sybille Bedford herself is at home in rather more. She is an historian, not only in her grasp of events and movements but, more important for a novelist, of the *mores*, the nuances of vanished classes, their codes and passwords, their élites, their scents and dresses, their style, their singular households, private trains, pleasure-domes and spas . . . Hamburg, Carlsbad, Baden-Baden, Marienbad, Monte Carlo, that roll call of the opulent, the aristocrat or flashy. More than many professional historians, the novelist senses the implications lurking within the hush of a mid-afternoon in the eighties, the enormities astir within a crack Prussian regiment. Like the Russians, she has a pronounced feeling for time, of long moments and brief, exquisite hours, for

the kind of morning when one cannot bear to be in bed, when numbed insects stir to a new lease and one picks up one's tea cup and walks out into the garden. Here the unexpected gift comes every day. Breakfast is laid on the patio: there is fruit, the absurd goldfish are swishing in the fountain and everything smells of geranium; warmth lies gently across one's shoulders; E has ceased to talk politics, the housekeeper stops to chat, the boy comes running with hot rolls and butter . . . it is good to be alive.[1]

It belongs to what she calls "that sense of lighter heart, of deep-grooved pleasures, daylight, and proportion". All her novels contain sadness, even tragedy, but never fail to convey the desirability of existence, despite the ambiguity of its goals and rewards. Characters may suffer, but not through boredom or ingrained glumness. They have tasted life's variety and demand more, or lament the treasures that seem lost.

Nostalgia seeps through Sybille Bedford's work but within rigorous unsentimentality and irony. Life flows on, probably for the worse but without rigidly controlled objectives, and indeed these can be diffuse or contradictory. Opportunities exist for choosing, and if the choice is mistaken, even fatal, it has nevertheless generated adventures, wayward delights, memorable occasions. In one novel she declares

The perceptions, pointers, flashes that shape a work of art, or shape a man, are infinite and swift. All one can do is to attempt to trace some kind of pattern.

After 1918, travel, literal and metaphorical, is in diminished style for all but the few, but the unexpected, bizarre, and unrepeatable still occur, to be the more deeply cherished. In wild Mexico there was "a hazardous journey with half a ton of sculpture in the car and a difficult boy for escort, a beau of Sylvia's who had turned Buddhist and refused to consult a map".[2]

Such a passage, very typical of Sybille Bedford, suggests a cool gaze, reflective, slightly amused, sceptical about human perfect-

[1] *A Visit to Don Otavio*
[2] *Ibid*

Introduction

ability but alert, even in adversity, for personal oddity, for some "mad, enchanting detail". A critic has mentioned her awareness of the significance of trifles. They stick to the imagination. "The banknotes were new. Money, like animals, was not hygienic, and no one employed in the house was supposed to handle new notes." *A Favourite of the Gods* is filled with "the unfathomably queer and complex facts of human existence". Reading, I remembered the effect on the young Dickens, when he saw from outside, "Coffee Room" spelled backwards on a windowpane. Here was the queerness of things reversed, his "romance of common things". One of those sudden, brilliant incidentals that illuminate a grey street, a grey spirit, or freeze a glittering ballroom.

In terms of political gangsterism and dogmatic zealotry, Sybille Bedford is "uncommitted". A party slogan is not imaginable in her work save in grave or sardonic irony. It should, perhaps, be added that she was already passionately anti-Mussolini when Churchill, Shaw, Ezra Pound were loudly supporting him. She is of course deeply committed, to matters more important than the noise of bullies, know-alls, and buffoons. More than mild curiosity impelled her to probe legal history and individual cases with a concern for justice. In *The Faces of Justice*, she reported on the trial of six Algerians for mass murder. She covered the trials of Dr Bodkin Adams and *Lady Chatterley's Lover*, has expert if contrasting knowledge of both Captain Dreyfus and the Ogre of Didier-le-Marche. The core of *A Legacy* is scandalous injustice encased in a Prussian cadet institution, "organised hunger, brutality, and spiritual deprivation".

Sybille Bedford's temperament enforced a need to explore not only the chasms and oasis of human relations but the physical challenges of Mexico and its people. What lies behind the impassive face of the Indian huddled on the street, what moves in the shadows of a sunbaked hut? This search for answers, neither ponderous nor preaching, never deserts the brilliant, surprising, diverting surfaces of life. All her books contain comic anecdotes, sharp insights particularly of those who fancy themselves unobserved. Whatever her remoter political allegiances, she can present curious international social trends and dire class structures, and make many more fashionable writers seem drearily insular. Her imagination incorporates the republics of Cicero, Cromwell, Stresemann as vividly as it does a contemporary love affair or family disgrace, but is always

Introduction

subordinate to the personal and felt. In E.M. Forster's words "Arguments are only fascinating when they are in the nature of gestures and illustrate the people who produce them." In this area, an indiscreet cough can drown the thunders of Nuremburg, a witticism demolish a resplendent uniform. This can be unwelcome to an age disposed to prefer sociology to history, generalised rant to reasoned argument and recognition of human complexity. Suffice it that the most jealous sociologist will discover that forty years of close friendship with Aldous Huxley has not left Sybille Bedford ill-informed about the world, the multitudinous processes of living, the fruitful contrasts of sophistication and simplicity, the dark and the light. She will note the coexistence of airy Impressionism with top-heavy mahogany furniture, make a casual observation on the literary pitfalls offered by the story of Maximilian and Carlotta of Mexico, then deftly pass on, though leaving a small ripple behind.

Even today, some readers are wary of feminine intrusions into quarters traditionally masculine. Even so intelligent a critic as Philip Toynbee was puzzled that Susan Hill could so realistically describe the trenches of the Great War. Occasionally I have heard something of this perplexity, about Sybille Bedford. She could be expected to portray a Prussian drawingroom, a Belle Epoque salon, Edwardian picnic or hunt, but the Kaiser's officers in a Mess, a military prison, the private ruminations of an ambitious Jesuit politician might, perhaps, be better left to a man. This, it scarely needs saying, is to undervalue the imagination and ignore the matter of craft. Imaginative transformations of time, place, identity probably make the novel's most popular attraction, but are not its supreme virtue and are not unusually difficult to achieve. Competent novelists of any sex or none can render convincingly enough a Renaissance orgy, Lithuanian siege, Victorian nursery — the last might prove the most exacting — but these are backgrounds or set pieces, and a novelist who can do no more has failed. In a novel, people must move, not always in the direction originally intended. The author may be a god but, on evidence, few gods, perhaps none, are either omniscient or omnipotent. Meanwhile, motives must be explored, definitions attempted, misunderstandings dissected, character suggested if not finalised. Daydreams, the dead, the personality of locale — Rome, a garden, a seashore — have their significance. And, however powerful the houses, adroit the conversation, beautiful the speakers, there can yet be, offstage but inescapable, "great lost forest howls of rage and pain". Greed, pathos, absurdity.

In each novel, in the present one as much as any, we are not told too much. Life is mysterious, let some of it remain so. Sybille Bedford knows when to explain, when to conceal, when to cut a dialogue, description, confrontations at the electric point which compels reading further. Loose ends can stimulate, and paying readers the compliment of assuming they possess imagination, she creates gaps for that imagination to fill. Attention is crucial, one is following more than a story and must read fully, pause to savour and, pausing, may discover clues easily missed by too much haste. She dislikes the blatantly schematic, the too obviously contrived. Not even the last page will present complete truths about people and situations. How seldom in life can we be absolutely sure even of our closest friends: their essential vision, the springs and coils of their nature, their reliability when this most matters! Truth mocks. Even shared memories can be grotesquely divergent, and the Russians have a proverb, "He lies like an eye-witness." Time can drop a kindly haze over a dreadful childhood, the past be altered by self-interest, turn traitor through revelations tardily recognised. Time transforms hope to cynicism, despair to delight, and raises questions of degrees of truth — about a failed relationship, an outbreak of war, an adultery — in which someone can speak untruths without lying, and in which three people may utter an identical sentence yet with only one speaking truthfully. A reminder of Erich Heller's remark that Oswald Spengler's *History* must be rejected, not because it is incorrect, but because it is untrue. In *A Favourite of the Gods*, from a tissue of absurdities and evasions, certain truths, though probably not truth itself, may conceivably emerge. The oblique, so central to Sybille Bedford's art, can be more trustworthy than the candid camera and — I am thinking of bedroom scenes — frequently more entertaining. Much, even between the highly literate, fiercely articulate, sometimes especially between them, cannot be exactly communicated, and all human relationships carry reminders of Tallyrand's saying, that we are given speech in order to conceal our thought. But, and I cannot stress this enough, the oblique, the suggestive, the allusive, is not, in this novel, vague, obscure, dense, for it comes from a narrator who knows what she is doing. Words from *A Legacy* apply here too,

Introduction

What I learnt came to me like everything else in this story, at second or third hand, in chunks and puzzles, degrees and flashes, by hearsay and tale-bearing, and being told, by one or two deceptions that meant everything to those who gave them. Also, by putting two and two together.

An honest admission, conforming to the facts of life.

The reader will note a deft use of dialogue, to advance the story, suggest character — the silly, malicious, conspiratorial, questing — yet also to convey the bewilderments and incomprehensions between those who think themselves intimates. There is a story of Napoleon and Madame de Staël meeting for the first time, eventually separating, both convinced that they had been unable to get a word in. A Bedford situation! In her dialogue, an inflection, a pause, an emphasis, a *non sequitur*, allows us to see a complex personality or event — a man taken ill, the dissolution of love, the fate of a marriage on which the percipient reader would not have placed a substantial bet — as it probably is, unimpaired by description or comment so precise that it becomes implausible.

Throughout her work, the writing, sentence-by-sentence, is very sharp, very visual. Travelling through Mexico to see Don Otavio, she saw "In the kitchen doorway a very old white-bearded man was improvising poetry — sometimes sentimental, sometimes heroic, sometimes obscene — to a huddled and enthralled audience all big hats, crimson blankets and beautiful eyes." She has marked comedy, even fun, though not that of the stand-up comic, rollicking or quick fire, nor will she introduce some roaring Ginger Man or a boozy, mendacious clown demanding drinks on the house for once having met Dylan. Her comedy is not broad or fantastic, but sly, impish, observant. A bossy donkey, sufficiently a connoisseur of pleasure to enjoy counting people's money, wanders into a mansion, stops a servant and insists he strap on her over-hooves. There are authoritarian, smilingly insolent servants and alarming secrets, unusual situations and verbal play, casually introduced and not pushed to extremes. In *A Legacy*, we must wait several pages before realising that Robert and Tzara, first reported as enjoying a picnic, are chimpanzees.

Robert poured Madeira, and Tzara showed an interest in the old gentleman. He gave her a gold piece and he went home impressed.

From different books I have stored remarks, typically unsensational, calculated to elicit not ribald mirth but a nod, perhaps a smile.

"Nannies," a child says, "are a kind of grown-ups." From another, "Don Otavio realised that he was confronted by that unfamiliar thing, a joke." A simple statement, yet it illuminates the past and delineates a future.

To marry into an aristocratic family, one character, a Jewish girl, must get herself baptised, but carelessely, to outrage and dismay, selects the wrong denomination. Humour can emerge quietly through direct speech.

"They have nine children. Nine alive, I mean." Or "Hear you had quite a rumpus yesterday. Gardener killed his wife and two of the *mozos*, and wounded some of the housemaids. If I were Otavio, I'd make it an excuse to sack the man." Straight description will contain some small but quicksilver word to quicken the whole, such as "shorter" in the following:

Supper in the provinces is at nine, and a shorter meal — chicken broth, omelette, a hot vegetable course, beefsteak or cutlets, a salad, beans, fruit, breads and chocolates, perhaps an extra piece of cake for the children, but you may ask for many things that aren't on the menu.

In *A Favourite of the Gods*, important revelations are made almost as if in afterthought, yet perfectly placed, forcing the reader to ponder, assess, reconsider. Constanza and Flavia, mother and daughter, are on a train. Only a dozen pages further on is it revealed that Constanza is journeying to her own wedding. Through carelessness, they suffer a minor hold-up, a night's delay, which will in fact endure eleven years. These years are not spun out in detail. I have said earlier that Sybille Bedford richly appreciates Time. Time is not consistent in pace. One understands here, as one does with Proust, a difference between *minutes* — the chronology of the clock, programmes, public events — and *moments*, those flashes of joy, horror, crisis which can swiftly dazzle, then vanish like a rocket which yet remains unforgettable, reverberating forever, exposing the flaws and assets, the options, within life itself.

The moment of the rose and the moment of the yew tree are of equal duration.

The distinction between minutes and moments helps condition the Bedford technique. Notice the organisation of chapter, its rises and falls, its movement between brightness and shade, its shape. Longish chapters may break up into short scenes, often in dialogue, erected, block by block, each block at an angle very slightly different from the rest, to create a many-sided impression of a situation or sequence. Yet readers of this novel will find the narrative, though subtle, firm enough to please the most exacting demands for "the story". It can certainly be read for its story, though not re-read for that alone. The test of a book is in its re-reading, and we do not re-read *Hamlet, Cousin Bette, What ho, Jeeves*, to discover the endings. In this novel, we are invited, as it were, into a rambling house, palatial though not quite a palace, where ample rooms are crowded with hedonistic guests, servants, parasites: also with marked details of dress, furniture, physiognomy, with people rather deliberately sited as if suggesting long-finished love affairs, money affairs, dynastic affairs, with formal good manners covering unspoken antipathies, covert rivalries, secret loves. Voices are courteous, but almost every eye is an innuendo. It is the start of some old-fashioned dance, most probably a minuet not quite perfectly remembered. Soon, however, we are aware of a further dimension, of shadowy corners easily overlooked, small hushed arbours, remote conservatories, gardens, a terrace, a lakeside where more natural dramas are occurring perhaps more easily accessible: quiet tears, muffled laughter, small but fateful exchanges, youthful repartee. I never re-read a Bedford novel without discovering some small display of character, some overheard remark, some off-shoot of the main narrative previously missed.

The story here includes the intricacies of the mother-daughter relationship, marriage, self-discovery and self-evasion, the elusive nature of happiness, the instants of sheer delight which yet reveal conflict and dismay more sharply. The mother is Anna, beautiful American heiress married to an Italian nobleman. The settings are pre-1914, aristocratic Rome and the Italian countryside, and London, with the disruption of the Great War and the rise of mountebank warlords throughout Europe. The first part depicts, if not total society, at least a ruling caste of immense self-confidence which, with hindsight, can be seen provoking retribution. It contains many gifted, vigorous women who are allowed too little to do. Some are beginning to revolt. Anna herself is not a natural rebel. She prefers to play, unconventionally, yet by the rules, but seems

Introduction

insufficiently aware of what Roman rules actually are. I use "seems" for, as ever, Sybille Bedford is knowledgeable but not a know-all.

It was in the autumn following the old principessa's death that Anna became involved in the rather mysterious episode that is said to have affected her so much. What exactly happened nobody does know as Anna never told the whole truth to anyone.

It is doubtful whether Anna, even to herself, recognised a consistent concept of truth. This permits the novelist digressions, absorbing speculations, extended jokes, obstructive in a thriller but conforming to the leisurely proportions of the lives discussed and which cannot be tailored to the streamlined and masterminded. The mysterious episode causes Anna's tearful, unforgiving yet half comic-opera separation from the Prince and her departure to England with young Constanza, who will watch with curiosity, fascination, occasional distress or rebellion, Anna's alternate fits of grievance, frustration, disillusion, self-delusion, idealism. Many questions will be unresolved. Was the Prince's flagrant infidelity, common knowledge for years, really a surprise to Anna? Certainly there were primal misunderstandings. To say that the Prince had only married for money would not be quite true, but for him and his peers marriage was not the ultimate goal of life or even love. Probably, though inadmissably, it was not for Anna either. She loved him but also Rome, Italy, Europe, which beckoned her away from the accepted role of woman as mere custodian of the home overcrowded with tiresome in-laws and hangers-on. Something in her lively Yankee nature must have rebelled against Roman High Society, that "twilight element of forgotton rancours, casual tolerance and resignation". Suffice that she is always deceived, not least, though it would have astonished her, by herself.

The Favourite of the gods is not her but Constanza, whose fortunes appear enviable, perhaps too enviable.

Her first English summer was nearly as exciting, as delirious, as had been her winter. It was made by people — every kind of people, new people, points of view, tones of voices: undergraduates, riding partners, authors in their prime, colonels who had loved her mother, young men who went off to work in the City and young men who already spoke of nursing a constituency, K.C's, radicals, fast girls, spectactular old women, aesthetes, dons. At odd moments Constanza missed her father and thought of him, affectionately, ruefully, as a child might think of a nanny during a wild and glorious party.

Introduction

Her's is the London of Asquith and the suffragettes, Bennett, Wells, Henry James, the *Chapeau de Tricorne*, the Grafton Galleries, Fabianism, the young radical Winston Churchill, the young T.S. Eliot, the Sitwells and "a magic girl, Virginia Stephen". This is mostly suggested, rather than described in the leave-out-nothing manner of, say, Bennett. Constanza, more unconventional than Anna, is more thorough in the quests and experiments. "The men who attracted her were vigorous, detached, subtle, gay, whose spirit matched her own. A rake herself, she looked for brother rakes, and even in that England found them."

She will grow from sensitivity to perception, from perception to understanding, and the cost will be exacting, sometimes painful, at times exorbitant. Meanwhile, "she was seldom without what is called a man in her life. she was slightly in love or much in love, once or twice very much in love. But it always ended. It was not what in the last resort she wanted: it was not enough."

What would be enough? this will be the leading theme. The going is not as smooth as it promised. She belongs everywhere, yet nowhere, save somewhere in herself. Italian, American, English, she is all, she is none. A modern shrugging off religion, she is yet fitfully superstitious, inheriting more from Anna than she welcomes, so that her adventures tend to be unexpected, in tune with her real nature. The reader can be grateful.

Like Anna, like her own daughter Flavia, like Sybille Bedford herself, Constanza had the inestimable advantage of not having suffered school, and is thus immune from parrot responses, stock information, the servility to fashions — that dire phrase "with it", now superannuated in usage but not in spirit. Tutors come and go, but these are mostly young, amusing, themselves willing to learn and indeed needing to.

If the Prince, by saying that education did not seem to be doing the child much harm meant that it did not take up all her interests and time he was quite right; Constanza always had a good many things up her sleeve. When she was little she played, and she played very hard. Seldom with toys.

Country matters, Roman streets with their smells, sounds, brazier-lit sights, homely and bizarre, her small submissive gangs, lively talks with adults, seldom one-sided, slow moments of solitude to savour the day with its countless shifts — the surprises, heart-felt expectations, false starts, unsought prizes, blazing rows — prepare for the years with their emergent patterns. So far, good. Years later:

Life was still good to her, exceptionally good. She had what all mortals pray for and unfortunately few are given. She had health, she had looks, she had money for her needs. If she was free, it is too large a question, but it can certainly be said that in terms of our own common lot she was her own master. She was equipped to appreciate, to derive entertainment, connotations, pleasure, from almost any situation she happened to find herself placed in. She had the power to inspire love. And she was not unhappy: there was only a vague disquiet, a nagging question: What is it for? What have I made of it? Where is it going, where can it go?

It is a continuing situation, there from the start, made for danger, gamble, excitement, anything save boredom and stodgy despair.

Anna has assumed those permanent operatic roles which she then has to justify, however ludicrous the consequences. Amusing to the reader, she cannot forgo tragic poses, arias of lamentations, rebuke, perhaps secret remorse. Constanza has a more accessible, more definable self, with less self-deceit than her mother from whom, if negatively, she has learnt so much. She has her own code, her straightforwardness, often disconcerting to older people:

"So you believe in lies, Constanza?"
"I have never been able to see how one can manage without them. We can hurt *too much*. I lie like a trooper; and for my own convenience. The thing is to remember one's lying. The truth is safe enough as long as one does that"

Constanza's youthful arrogance is streaked with the humility of the intelligent. People, nevertheless, whatever their public behaviour are seldom in essence consistent. They are bundles of barely-definable opposites. Constanza makes a false step, or seems to. She marries a charming, intelligent grabber, who begins as a rebel, cheeky and amusing, then, acquiring political importance becomes pompous and ordinary. Constanza has betrayed herself, by loving without admiring him, not the recipe for a successful marriage.

With the Great War, fine schemes and high hopes go awry. Throughout Europe, socialists forswear their vaunted general strike and vote the war-credits: modernists flock to the colours or win profitable jobs behind the lines, a few clever ones contrive to dodge the whole thing. Virtually unknown, Mussolini is already in the wings. Whatever the outcome, nothing will be the same again: not for the Prince and his world, not for Anna, certainly not for

Introduction

Constanza. That marriage at least produces Flavia. Precocious and observant, she has her mother's curiosity and independence, and a sense of proportion far greater than her grandmother's. She will emerge fully in the sequel, *A Compass Error*, but another theme has started, the triple relationship of three remarkable women, three generations. There are tears, much laughter, nothing neutral.

As in *A Legacy*, this novel follows the momentous consequences, some of them long-delayed, of family events, often mishaps, frequently deceptively trivial in appearance. A tutor's indiscretion, a wife's instant of not absolutely sincere astonishment, an overdone outburst of hurt pride which becomes irrevocable, outraged feminine feelings sustained too long, masculine insensitivity and inability to realise that a wood is made of trees that require more than friendly glances to sustain good health.

> Flavia said, "How is one to live . . . if every step leads to another?"
> "Like that," said Constanza.

Favourites of the gods enjoy advantages — beauty, intelligence, charm, decency, though the last is perhaps the least common and scarcely the least important. Inevitably, they also risk temptations, poor judgement, gratuitous ill-will. Constanza is going to suffer, but only very slowly slacken her efforts towards fulfilment, happiness, the maintenance of a certain style. Her daughter grows up, and post-war Europe confronts novel problems, uncanny prospects, incredible propositions from uncouth political zealots of doubtful sanity. Constanza for a time, with sensations of failure, does tend to drift. She is uncertain, not about the meaning of life — life has no discernible meaning, though it is useful and diverting to behave as if it has — but about the direction of her own dwindling potential. Still young, she ransacks the past, and finds much of it missing or distorted. Adventures, however, are still possible. At last, "she was no longer searching for her past, she was meeting Lewis".

Like any adept storyteller, Sybille Bedford reserves her verdicts, the precise and the provisional, to the last pages. There remain sufficient loose ends — and is not history itself the loose ends that tingle? — to urge the reader beyond, to *A Compass Error*.

Peter Vansittart,
London 1982

Prologue

One autumn in the late nineteen-twenties for no particular reason at all, as it would seem, we began to live in France.

§

The train had stopped. My mother put a glove to the window: VENTIMIGLIA.

We each took up our book. For some time nothing happened. Then the customs were in the corridor, in pairs, in their uncouth uniforms, strung with side-arms. My mother kept them in check with a light hand. Poor louts, she said; and it could not be true that black didn't show the dirt. They went. Still we did not move. Again we tried to read. Suddenly I saw my mother's brother step into the carriage, he came swiftly forward: " Constanza! " " *You?* " she said. He put a kiss on her right cheek, on her left. She sat passive. " What do you want? " she said in her cold voice. He saw me. " *Ciao*, Flavia," he said over his shoulder. " I motored down from Sestriere to catch you," he answered her in English. I disliked him and I left the compartment; and so I heard no more.

From the platform I could see them in the carriage window —my mother sitting still with a soft and absent look on her face; my mother then was a very beautiful woman, and on that afternoon, in that empty dust-blown station, she was, as so often, like an apparition from another world. He was talking urgently, with animation, using his hands. I passed

on; and a little later I saw him jump off the train, rapidly
cross the lines and walk towards the exit. I went back to the
compartment. " Giorgio's mad," my mother said; " how
tiresome of mama to tell him where to find us." " What did
he come for? " " God knows," she said, " some hare-
brained scheme." The cast of my mother's mind was
analytical and interpretative—people, behaviour, motive—
but Giorgio had long been discounted. Nor did I insist
And soon we began to move, the train clanked across a
bridge and we were in France—all right? I said; all right,
said my mother, it wasn't anything very much this time—
and presently we began to think about getting our things
together, for we were changing trains at Nice, we were
catching the Calais Express.

We drew in and I was about to wave a porter when my
mother touched one of her hands to the other and said,
" My ring." " Which ring? " I said. " Papa's ring," she
said sharply, " the ruby! " " Oh," I said, my heart sinking.
" Did you have it on? " " You know I am never without the
ring," she said. This was true; I could not remember her
not wearing it. It was a large ring, heavy, and it had been
a present from her father, the prince in Rome. I called him
that in my mind, although he was my grandfather, because
I had never met him. We looked on the floor, we looked
under the seats, we probed the upholstery, gingerly. We
looked the way people look in such circumstances. " Think,"
I said. We went over the day. " You washed your hands."
I went to look in the lavabo, but the corridor now was full of
people getting on and the lavabo was locked. We went
through bags, pockets. " Mummy," I said, " we've *got* to
get off." Our berths on the Express were booked. Nonsense,
she said, the Express could wait, we could take it somewhere
further up the coast, it must stop at Cannes and all those
places. " I am not getting off this train without the ring."
When we got a ticket collector, he called the *chef du train*.

They looked as we had looked, only more competently. Under their hands, seats and cushions snapped apart like chunks of zigzag puzzle. Chiefly hair-clips and spent matches came to light. The men seemed as disappointed as my mother was. They seemed to be on her side.

" *Une bague de valeur, Madame?* "

" *Valeur sentimentale.*" Her French had the slight harshness with which Italians use that language. " But since you ask—yes. It's a ruby, but a rather unusual one. Oh yes, a valuable ring."

We were pulling into Cannes station when the paper-work was under way. " Stop looking at your watch, Flavia," said my mother. The ring, she told them, had still been on her hand at Alassio; she remembered touching it as we got on. The carriage had been empty. The train was an *omnibus*, a slow train, stopping everywhere, but there was in those days little local traffic into France. My mother talked; the men wrote down her name and father's name.

" *Nom de jeune fille de la mère? Lieu de naissance de la mère?* "

My mother, though impatient of most kinds of footling, was inured to this process and spelt it all out in good heart.

" *Providence?* " repeated the chief. " *Et où cela se trouve?* "

" *En Amérique du Nord,*" my mother said, smiling at him.

" *Bougre.*"

My mother now said that she was hungry. She tended her purse. Would they be so kind and get us a couple of baskets off the trolley? The men said not to waste her money on a dried-up leg of chicken, a hard peach and half a drop of wine. We had plenty of good wine, said my mother. The chief said, " *Si Madame me permet,*" and unrolled a brown-paper bundle. My mother took a large veal sandwich.

" *Et la petite?* ——*Mademoiselle?* "

I hardly thought of myself in those terms. I was tall already then and I felt—I think without selfconsciousness—a good deal older than my age, which was getting on for sixteen. My main interests at the time, or so I believed, were books and utopian politics; I hoped to go to Oxford, I hoped to be a writer, but I shared my mother's willingness to accept good things that come one's way. I reached for one of the flasks of Barolo which my grandmother's chauffeur had put in, it was loosely corked—the four of us drank.

We were moving again and it was by now quite dark outside. " *Nationalité?* " the chief resumed.

" *Anglaise,*" said my mother.

" *On ne le dirait pas. Mariée?* "

" *Veuve,*" said my mother, giving me a wink. She had been divorced, but after my father had died she sometimes used the more convenient label.

We had stopped at and left Fréjus before the men had it all pat. They chanted it back to one another with fascinated glee.

" *Veuve* Herbert " (as such my mother emerged from their inky form). . . .

" *Née à* Castelfonte. . . .

" *De paternité Italienne.* . . .

" *De mère Américaine.* . . .

" *Sujet Britannique.* . . .

" *Sans Domicile.* . . .

" *Accompagnée de sa fille.* . . .

" *Se rendant à—se rendant où?* WHERE were we going? "

To Brussels, said my mother.

" *I* am going to England," said I.

" Not tonight," said the chief.

Yes, yes, said my mother. After another look for the ring. " What is your next stop? "

" Les Arcs."

" Never heard of it."

" A junction, Madame."

" Oh good," she said, " we might as well change to the Express there."

" What express? "

" Ours." She made me hand them the sheaf of Wagon-Lits tickets.

The men became excited. " The 6.59 from Nice? But that's impossible, Madame."

" Doesn't it stop at your junction? "

" It did———"

" Oh, very well," said my mother, " let's catch it at Toulon."

" Madame! " they cried, " do you know what time it is? "

" Not exactly," she said. " If it's material, do tell me."

We all did.

" That's not so very late," she said.

" *It is the time the Calais Express is due at Avignon.*"

" Oh," said my mother : " it *passed* us. The devil! Why, of course———" She turned to me. " Why didn't *you* figure it out? "

I told her I had been taking a gloomy view all the time.

" The ring," she said quickly. " *Not* a good omen. We must not lose the ring."

The men were waiting.

" This *is* a new development," said my mother, but there must be other trains. There were. " Will you get us another pair of sleepers? " Not a chance, the men said, not tonight, not with the *Salon d'Autos*, there wasn't a couchette left either side of Lyon.

" Decidedly," said my mother, " the fates cannot be with us."

The men suggested that we get off somewhere and spend the night.

" I *am* a little tired of this train," she said, " though it appears that time has flown."

Once more I began to gather our things.

Let's get out at Hyères, said my mother. But Hyères was not on the main line, Hyères was behind us. Toulon? The men named the hotel, it wasn't very good they said, she would not like it, a murky place.

" By all means suggest somewhere cheerful."

We stopped; they told us to stand by. The chief hung out of the window and yelled into the darkness: *Mari-usse*——Someone shouted back. " The bus is gone," said the chief and banged up the window. The train moved on. We sat down again. The next stop was marked by an equal absence of life and light. This time it was my mother who peered out. " Here? " she asked with calm indecision. *Dépêchez-vous*, said the men. The train moved on. At the third, she wanted to know about the direction of the sea. " Madame," they told her, " if you don't get off soon you'll find yourself at Marseilles. " Oh, very well," she said, " Yes or no? " She looked from me to them, into the night. " Perhaps yes——? " The men fell to. Thirty seconds later we stood on a platform, our bags about our feet. The train was gone.

" And why not," said Constanza, " why not after all? "

§

My memory of the conjunction of events that followed—that night, the next day, the days after—does not stand out so clear; it has become merged with too many later memories. There was a shaky bus ride in a preposterous little vehicle along a nocturnal road that did not seem short but cannot have been more than a mile; we came out on a waterfront, tight-shut and silent. It *was* late by then, late certainly for the South of France at that time of the year. The hotel was the Hotel du Port. A woman I do not remember ever seeing again took us up.

My mother asked for Saint-Galmier water to be brought. When I was alone in my room I felt tired, dumbly depressed and went to sleep very soon. Next morning it was warm and clear. The sun shone. I found my mother on a balcony, having her breakfast. Below lay a small harbour. " This is charming," she said.

It was. The houses of the front formed two wings turned at a sheltering angle. There was a sketch of a promenade set with eucalyptus and five sturdy palms, so brief that it might have been laid out in parody. The *mairie* was blue-washed and sported a flag-tower like a minaret; the square in front of it touched the sea. The quay-side was spread with nets. It was, and it was not, like the Mediterranean ports we knew.

My mother took up my thought. " *Mare nostrum*," she said, " but not Italy, not really." For an instant she looked sad, then she rallied. " We have never been here. It is France. It is new."

I looked at the *mairie*, the four cafés almost in a row, the awnings: " I *have* seen this before," I said.

" You have. It's been painted over and over again, by a number of people. There must be three or four at the Tate. . . . I never knew where it was: now we are there. The name is on the tip of my tongue, Saint, Saint—, Saint-Something——"

I took the last peach off her tray, peeled and ate it. Then it became time to do something.

" Telegrams," said my mother. " Telegrams, first of all. One for mama. I don't like mama in on this, she always hated my wearing the ring. She won't like my losing it either. *Notre bague de valeur.* Find me a pen, my sweet, will you? At least she'll be delighted to hear I'm not in Brussels."

" A postponement," I said.

" So it is," said my mother. " Now then—one for Lewis."

"And what will you say to him, Constanza?" I had begun to call her that at times. Lewis was the man she was going to marry in Belgium at the end of that week.

" Yes, what? "

" The facts."

" Darling? That I lost a ring and missed a train? *Une bague de valeur?* "

" That's what happened."

" I don't know," she said, " I don't know." One of her flashes of frankness was upon her. " Shall I telegraph Lewis that I lost papa's ruby and got rattled? Shall I say that my mother had just made an all-out scene? Shall I tell him what it was like when she heard I was going to marry again? And what a shock this was to me as I had believed she would be pleased? " Constanza was making her voice cold, but there was an element of humility in her out-spokenness. " Shall I telegraph Lewis that pleasing my mother must have been a part of my decision to marry him? "

It was then that I felt a twinge of fear about my own future. But I also felt the surge of protective affection for my mother that came so often now that I was growing up and seeing more and loving her so much. I tried to do what she liked best, laugh at her and with her. " You know what I thought at Genoa? That you were marrying Lewis to please *me*."

She gave me a conspiratorial look. " No, darling, not to please you: *you* have your life in front of you and can please yourself."

" And she cannot? " I said, meaning my grandmother.

" Ah, I wish she had not lost that talent! " said Constanza.

" She was . . . different once? "

" She *seemed* different."

" Constanza," I said, " I've never known you actually married."

" No, not quite. Except when you were too little to remember."

" Will it make a big change? "

" People change when they know you are their wife."

" Is it the home-life? " I said.

She said, " I don't expect we shall have much of that with Lewis."

" Because he has so many flats? He has one in New York, one at Amsterdam——"

" That's more than he told *me*," she said, " I barely know his house-number at Brussels. Well then—will you write it? Say: UNPREDICTABLE DELAY WRITING LOVE."

" Lewis must be at the station now," I said.

" I can't help that," said Constanza. " I did marry to please *her;* the first time."

" Because she was so fond of him? "

" I married for love to please my mother—it does sound queer. Of course it was a great mistake: That way. For all of us."

" My father? "

" *He* got out of it. Poor Simon."

" And now? " I asked.

" Now? "

" You are marrying——? "

She hesitated. Then came an answer that surprised us both. " It seems to complete a design."

" Mummy," I said, " I must telegraph my family." My family was the tutor and his wife at Hampstead I was going to for a belated education. It was something I had wanted very much and it had not been at all easy to bring about.

" So many people at so many stations," Constanza said, " and just look at us here."

The telegrams did not get off that day. It was Sunday, as we eventually learnt, and the office had shut at eleven o'clock. " We did half our best," Constanza said, grinning at me. We still did not know the name of the place and when we asked the manager, he said: " But you *are* the lady with daughter who wrote about the villa." Not to her knowledge, said Constanza. The villa was ready for her to look at after luncheon, said the manager.

It took two days to get in touch with the outside world. When we were, it was unsatisfactory. Lewis did not take it well; he sent hourly telegrams to Constanza asking her when she was coming. She telegraphed back asking if he had never heard of the *Salon d'Autos*. My grandmother sent a brief message from Alassio telling us to await her letter. Constanza filled in time by allowing herself to be led to see the villa. Was it not in all respects, they told her, exactly what she had been asking for? They may have taken her denials for a bargaining point, for they came down a good deal with the rent, which was low. The principessa's letter arrived by express. It was one of those outpourings she had begun to indulge in at that time. She accused Constanza of levity and selfishness, she accused her of laying waste her life and mine and of wearing flashy jewellery on a railway journey. She also wrote that rings did not vanish into thin air, and were we doing all we should about it? That evening brought a milder note, asking me to keep at my mother to keep at the police; and the next day the principessa announced her coming over and seeing for herself. That was, she wrote, if the drive and back again was not going to prove too much for her man; she had heard that it was not the kind of place one would want to spend the night. By the same post came a civil note from the *Préfecture* at Draguignan asking us to call about our loss. There did not appear to be, so far, the slightest trace of the ring.

" It doesn't look," Constanza said, " does it, as if we were getting off tomorrow or the next day? " As a matter of fact we stayed for eleven years.

PART ONE

A Rational Education

&

The Story of a Marriage

Chapter I

When I was a child I thought of my grandfather as a great villain; a little later on I thought of him as a man to emulate. Still later I began to see it as what talk had made it—a part of a story. It did not concern me, it could not touch my life: there is always a point when one is newly young when one is able to see oneself detached from all that went before. I was still curious and liked to hear about it. But my mother, great talker though she was, had always seemed content to let it lie. I knew that she, also, had not been allowed to see her father at one time, until she came of age and was free to choose. She only said that he was a dear, and an ill-used man, it had all been very silly and disastrous, and of course her mother's fault, and now it was too late.

§

Constanza's early youth must have been a singularly flawless one. Born into surroundings of great physical beauty, into a society both easy and confined, well loved and splendidly endowed herself, her large advantages might have imposed curbing limitations; yet all the dice seemed to have been loaded in her favour and every discordant circumstance combined to leave her undivided, free, untouched by convention, perplexity or trouble.

She was born the first child to young parents. They were very pleased to have her but did not look on her arrival as an exceptional event. Indeed they would have regarded childlessness as a misfortune, but neither of them felt the slightest misgiving that such could be their own lot. If the prince always had a streak of tempered disillusionment, while his American wife then saw life and the world with an unbounded hope, they both shared that superb sense of personal immunity that came so easily to people like them at that time. That the child was not a boy did not bother them a scrap. The boy no doubt would come. Meanwhile, and very soon, they began to adore Constanza. They had reason to. From the first she was sound in health, equable in temper, lively and affectionate, and she showed the signs of great good looks. She appeared to have no fear and she seldom cried. She also knew what she wanted, but exercised her will with grace and what she did want amused her parents and the servants who looked after her, and when she got it she was pleased. They did not have to teach her much, she could ride almost as soon as she could stand, and read soon after she could talk. Her father greeted this youthful familiarity with print as a kind of circus trick and talked about it at his club; the principessa felt more deeply gratified. It was not long before Constanza's mind took an inquiring turn.

" Mama, is God really everywhere? "

" Oh yes, my darling."

" If he's Everywhere why do we have to go to mass? and why don't we curtsy in the houses and the street, only in Church? "

" God *is* everywhere, but he is perhaps *more* present in our beautiful churches."

" I see," said Constanza. " *Most* present in San Pietro? "

" Papa, why is it getting dark more early in the evenings? "

" Something to do with the sun, my treasure, the sun moves more slowly in winter."

Here his wife intervened. It was the earth, she said firmly, which did the moving.

" And so it does," said the prince comfortably, " so it does."

Constanza looked from one to the other. In due course she was to grow into a Titian; then she was at the Murillo stage: large dark eyes, short curls, a golden-olive skin and clothes which if not exactly rags were of becoming briefness and simplicity because her mother, though herself one of the most fashionable women in Rome, did not believe in dressing up little girls. " Why? " she said. " And why is slow more dark? "

The prince slapped his leg. " Anna," he said, " you tell us. Your mother is terrible, she knows everything."

The principessa said that this required pencil and paper, and Constanza ran to touch the bell.

" It was Luigino who told me about the dark," said Constanza, who took a detached interest in the truth of things. " He says he doesn't like it, it cuts his working day." Luigino was the prince's tenant, a cobbler who occupied a shop and living space on the ground-floor. " It's cold in the street now and it costs more in the wineshop if you sit longer."

The prince crowed. His wife looked all attention. " You should take her on your committee, Anna," he said. " What do you know about the *bottiglieria*, my ragamuffin? "

" I go there with Cosima to get charcoal," said Constanza.

" A good way to get to know her Rome," said the principessa. " She cannot start too early."

The prince did not try to take this in too much. His sisters used to be taken up the Pincio in a carriage and home again before sun-down. " Ah, well," he said, " she's your business, you're the mother."

" Papa, the Luigini have to take the soup to the *bottiglieria* because they have no chairs. There's no room to put them, the bed is so big. All the Luigini sleep in one bed. I have a bed of my own to sleep in, you have a bed of your own, mama has a bed of her own——"

The prince roared again. " That's because your mother is an American," he said, " that's the American way."

" I know," said Constanza, " because Americans are richer than Italians. I knew that. Papa, is that why we live in a whole palazzo? "

The principessa said quickly, " Your father's family have always lived in this house."

" How long is always? "

The prince hugged his daughter. " The *parroco* is going to tell you that when the time comes for you to go to catechism."

" I was only speaking of the Quattrocento," said the principessa. She was smiling but her plans were revolving round education.

Anna Howland had enjoyed an excellent New England education herself. For her time, as she would add ruefully, for she had just not gone to college. (She was born in the early eighteen-seventies.) Everything else that could be done by way of exemplary governesses, art-masters, music-masters, lectures and tutoring by her own learned father, had been done. Anna had a good mind and set store by it and very likely it would have been over-rated anywhere because she was possessed of a fine memory, inherited from her father; in the environment into which she had pleased to cast herself, she was regarded as an intellectual giant, a role which she accepted without a tremor of self-consciousness. Anna's father had been a constitutional lawyer and later on held judicial office in his own state. He had retired early to give himself entirely to writing and research. One of his brothers —they were a close-knit family—was a man of letters of considerable distinction, another held a chair of modern history. The Howlands also had some more mercantile connections and in a quiet way without making many bones about it they were soundly and amply prosperous. The white and columned house Anna was brought up in was not only architecturally full of grace, it was charming inside and had comforts and refinements such as she did not find again in her future life until she managed to introduce them there herself. The elder Howlands were liberals, Republicans (of course), inclined towards Agnosticism, Darwin, and all of them, men and women, were articulately concerned with the moral and political future of mankind. Anna was raised on Jefferson and her father's passionate devotion to the rule of law; she scarcely remembered her mother (having been a late-born child) but knew that she had done early battle for women's rights. Her father had admired Lincoln—a contemporary—known him, done work under him. When Anna was a girl, the events which gave rise to the Gettysburg Address were part of people's living memory, as close to them as the events behind Winston Churchill's speeches are still to us, and so it was that even she, a child growing up on the Eastern Seaboard of the United States in the Eighteen-Seventies and Eighties, heard a good deal about war and the threat of war.

Her father and uncles, who had seen it, came to loathe it. The American Civil War they held to have been forced upon men of good will to preserve a cause; the Franco-Prussian War that followed it so soon they saw as a cold-blooded clash of two false causes, based on despotic calculations, nationalism and mob response, and thus wholly wrong as well as of incalculable consequences. Modern war, they argued, as it was plain for everyone to see, had become so diabolical, so destructive, so incompatible with ethics, Christian teaching, Nineteenth-Century thought or mere common sense as to be as unthinkable for men to use against one another as putting one another into a pot to boil and eat. They also saw, being honest men, that very few people anywhere saw anything

27

of the kind. Confronted by the evidence of battle-ship and sabre rattling from across the ocean, they had to revise their hopes and some of their written work since both of these had been based on a belief in progress and the perfectibility of man.

In their own lives the Howlands were in most respects civilized as well as virtuous; they believed in, and practised, absolute commercial probity, tolerance, the arts, charity, good manners. They also believed in absolute domestic respectability. Yet their children were brought up most gently. Their freedom of thought and action was never questioned; the first because thought must be free, the second because their children were trusted. So Anna's youth was pleasant as well as interesting, and quite a fair part of it was skating and dancing and sailing. Anna, who professed to have worshipped her father, was always a great reader. She had absorbed a decent amount of history, but what she enjoyed most was literature: Shakespeare, some Dante, Molière, Victor Hugo, and most of all Scott, Thackeray and Dickens. Byron she condemned, though she was open to his spell; Dickens she loved placidly. She knew great chunks of all of them by heart, as did the rest of the family and in the winters they read to each other aloud. If Anna's home life lacked anything (except of course a mother after she was four or five), it was brothers. They were all girls. But her sisters—so very much older than herself—married early and soon there were brothers-in-law in the house and to visit. One sister married a man in banking, the other one in the U.S. Diplomatic Service. Anna was the prettiest of the Howland girls. She was very pretty. Very fair, with fine light hair and delicate features, small hands and feet, a fine waist, a slender figure and a graceful bearing but the overall impression she gave was one of elegance and presence. Nor did she lack in height; if she was not noticeably tall in her own land, she was to appear so in Europe.

From the first she had a very good sense of clothes. She did not spend an unconscionable amount of thought or time on the whole business—she did spend quite a deal of money—but throughout her life both people who knew or cared little about such things and people who knew minutely would remark on how well Anna dressed. With that she was never anything but wonderfully groomed, exquisitely neat, and always, as a girl, a woman, near old age, she looked inescapably, imperturbably, embarrassingly, ladylike.

If Anna's father appears to have been very much a man of a pattern of a time and place—a good pattern admittedly—it is possible that there was more to him than that. His writings for one thing, if one comes across them, are still readable. That he had a lawyer's mind is evident in every line, but if a lawyer's mind means an ability to grasp facts and their implications, a gift of exposition and a willingness to see the other side, then a lawyer's mind is an asset indeed for any writer. What is more surprising is to find, in these not very voluminous tomes, irony, an element of compassion, a curt absence of verbiage, and wit. A good deal of wit. The author emerges as a man much nearer in spirit to Anatole France than to Emerson. His daughter always claimed that he had been a most amusing man; reading him one can believe her.

There was also a hint—Anna called it a shadow—that although appearances were never as much as scratched, he had not been entirely happy in his marriage.

When Anna was sixteen she was sent to Switzerland and also for a while to Florence to be finished. She came back, beautifully polished in her languages and rather in love with Italy, and began to keep house for her papa. She did it very well.

They entertained mostly elderly men, but there were plenty of aunts and cousins and Anna did not go short of balls. She delighted in society and what it offered her:

admiration, talk, the sight of pretty rooms, clothes, lights, decorous living at a festive pitch. Anna excelled in charades, and she was also something of a flirt. One year she went to London to stay with the sister whose husband was posted there. In New England Anna had been made much of; here, she was taken up by a set and turned into the centre of a raving fashion. London made her feel that the world was at her feet. She enjoyed it vastly, but as the most natural thing; not in conceit but as part of the glory of life.

She returned the next June and the magic was unabated. After only a few years of this life her father caught first pleurisy, then pneumonia, then died. Anna was stricken. For some weeks she remained immured in the family house, refusing relatives, friends, consolation. She wrote that she was going to leave the world, she would join some missionary order. As she knew next to nothing about such organizations, the project hung fire. Meanwhile her sister succeeded in persuading her to come and make her home with them in London. Youthful resilience did the rest. A short year later Anna met her future husband by one of the Italian lakes.

She was fascinated to be meeting a real Roman, born in what she liked to call the Eternal City and to which she had never been. The prince, a very young prince then, was a handsome enough fellow and, though he did not stand much higher than she did in his shoes, he had the head of a young man of a renaissance bust, and on this occasion must have proved himself persuasive. He was his own master, his father as it happened having been killed in a shooting accident not long ago, and was now the head of his house; Anna, though not quite of age, had no-one to say her nay. All that was required of her from her side was to marry for love. The wedding was in London from her sister's house and such of the Italian relatives who undertook the journey showed themselves enchanted with the arrangements made. They were highly pleased with what they saw and with all that was being done for them. Indeed, high pleasure all round appears to have been the first keynote of Anna's new life.

The house, noble, shuttered, peeling, stood in a back-street in the papal quarter between the Tiber and the Farnese Square. It was her home, it was everything she had ever imagined, and she loved it.

Anna succumbed to Rome at sight. It overwhelmed her as nothing had ever done before and this seemed to touch something in her nature; while her new relations, her husband's mother and the young sisters and their circle fell for her. They admired her looks, her ways, her dresses, her liveliness and initiative. They were as nice to her as they knew how, and very affectionate, and they shrieked with laughter and appreciation at everything she said the livelong day, and tried to do all she wished. It must have been very very different from what one has heard and read—gospel truth no doubt—of foreign brides subdued in the unheated houses of the Catholic European Aristocracy. No-one gambled away or tied up her dowry, no old lady told her that such was the Will of God, no-one attempted to tell her how she must behave. Rome is not Ravenna, nor Westphalia nor the Touraine, and in any case Anna was Anna. It was she who soon ruled the roost and everybody the merrier for it. Her husband's mother, the old principessa as they called her after her son's marriage, was a woman of simple heart and mind and of great good-nature. She saw Anna's entering their lives as a kind of blessed apparition, a fair paragon from a fabled land for whom nothing was too fine. Whenever she had the chance she would follow this precious creature about, hobbling after her swift passage through the flight of drawing-rooms. Anna responded graciously and was rewarded by the knowledge that she was filling the old lady's declining years with glamour and contentment.

Anna must have brought a goodish bit of money; but it, or a fair part of it, must have been hers to spend. And spend

she did, on hospitality, on the roof, the gardens, on her new
family, on herself, on charities. . . . Anna was always
generous. As to the religious question, that had hardly
stirred a ripple. It must have been obvious as soon as they
had thought of marriage that Anna would have to enter
the Roman Catholic Church. This she did. We know from
many curious and authenticated tales how christened savages
adapt in their practices and their minds the new religion to
their old beliefs. Saint Anthony can be seen sporting
Aztec feathers in many a village church in Central America.
In just such a way the principessa must have amalgamated
her conversion, if that is the right word. Inherited Puritanism,
her father's Agnosticism, misty private Transcendentalism
and formal adherence to the Catholic Creed appear to have
floated swimmingly one into the other and flowed on in a
harmonious stream of organ music, clever talk, enlighten-
ment, righteousness, tradition and the veiled vague imman-
ence of God. Those entrusted with her spiritual welfare may
have acted with the kind of discretion exercised by the
Missionary Fathers towards the Guatamalan Indians, what
is certain is that Anna got away with it. If anything, it was
she who was a little surprised by the lack of formality in the
observances of her entourage. If she had expected to be led
to High Mass in the Sistine Chapel leaning on her husband's
arm, she was disappointed. They all went, she found,
singly, more or less round the corner and at inconspicuous
hours. Soon she established her own custom, which was to
set out in mid-morning with her maid and a mantilla made
of the softest of black lace to some church that had caught her
fancy or her favour.

Rico, her husband, naturally had his part in the scheme
of things. If he was out a good deal, at his club, riding,
shooting, doing things with men, in Umbria looking after his
estate, Anna had been used at home to not having the men-
folk underfoot all day, and it suited her own habits. When

she saw him he was usually in fine good humour—at times he could brood a little—and he, too, laughed a lot at what she said and did, and would not interfere. When she said they ought to have someone in to catalogue the library, he said very well, although he did not see that there was much to catalogue; he teased her about her endless daily sight-seeing but arranged the introductions to museum people she had asked him for; and whenever she gave a dinner-party for a French archaeologist, an English poet or dear Lady Gwendolyn who was wintering in Rome, he would be there and do his best. It was only when she tried to organize a musical evening that he flung up his hands and broke into a little dance of horror. No, no, no, *cara*—there's better to be heard than that! She had been about to engage the wrong soprano. Anna caught on at once: her husband's ear was better than her own, and she was wise enough to act on that new knowledge.

She was aware that Rico was not clever—her word—but he was new to her and an exotic bird; and in some ways she was baffled. And of course he was absolutely devoted, she said, in fact he worshipped her.

Soon she had gathered a whole devoted circle, First Secretaries with a taste of letters, elder diplomatists with a taste for pretty women, American girls she was called to chaperone, some very polished clergy, visitors of every kind and of course a large number of charming and delightful Italians who flirted a little with her and she with them and to whom she did not give a thought next morning.

It was this circle which stood Anna in good stead at the time she decided that her girl was to have the advantages—educationally—that she had had herself. It was said in Rome that the way to the principessa's drawing-room lay through her daughter's school-room. Middle-aged scholars, eminent in their field, took Constanza on botanical outings and architectural promenades, collected insects for her, brought her books; painters let her squeeze their colours; bright young men just down from Harvard or Oxford introduced her to Euclid, Tales from Chaucer, Latin grammar and the English kings. The French Naval Attaché talked French to her for an hour twice a week (Anna saw to it that all was quite regular and systematic). A gentleman from the Bolivian Legation kindly proposed himself for South American geography, but Anna discovered him to be shaky in his subject and put a stop to it. American history and Constitution Anna chose to take herself, and Constanza quite literally learnt of the pursuit of happiness at her mother's knee.

Only in matters of religious instruction did the principessa relinquish all authority, feeling in honour bound that she must leave this sphere, as she had promised, to the child's paternal family. In consequence Constanza was visited, also twice a week, by their parish priest and made to learn a number of things by rote.

As she grew older, the range widened. Her mother's choices had proved wise or very lucky: Constanza all in all was taught extremely well. She was given a view of European history seen from many sides; literature was put into her hands in a way to fire her, she was helped to see and to connect art and told imaginatively of landscapes, cities, travel, ways of living; she learnt to grasp something of biology, economics, social history, the history of thought. . . . If the mentors came to please the mother, they stayed to educate Constanza. The girl had something that matched brilliance; she was as quick as a bird, and as live, and it all came easy to her, natural as life, as breathing, talking, reading, thinking, arguing, which indeed it was. She enjoyed being with people who knew things, she enjoyed logic and pulling questions apart and going to the heart of a matter and

looking at more than one side. Everything fascinated her,
to whatever they brought her there was resonance; teaching
Constanza was like training a strong young player at tennis.

The prince, when it became too evident, what with no
needlework and Stendhal and John Stuart Mill littering
up the drawing-room, that Constanza was not being led the
way of an Italian daughter, shrugged and said what did it
matter after all, she was only a girl. Let her mother have
her way, poor woman, all alone in a strange country, it was
the least they could do. Then he would laugh and add that
it didn't appear to be doing the *bambina* any harm, did it?
And his mother and his sisters laughed too and agreed, and
Constanza, who was growing more beautiful to look at every
day, slid out of her grandmother's embrace, exchanged one
volley of words with her aunts, flung herself into an
armchair—Anna's importations—and got on with her book.

She had done—for the time being—with her mother's
favourite authors before she was twelve. After that she
devoured Gibbon, Voltaire, Swift, Shelley, Racine, Tour-
genieff, Tocqueville and George Eliot. At fifteen it was
poetry: Catullus, Baudelaire, Byron, Pope. These and
La Chartreuse de Parme she constantly re-read; Pope and
Byron she loved equally.

If the prince by saying that education did not seem to be
doing the child much harm had meant that it did not take
up all her interests and time, he was quite right; Constanza
always had a good many things up her sleeve. When she
was little she played, and she played very hard. Seldom
with toys; there was a fountain with a dolphin in the court-
yard, she rode in the Campagna, and in the long summers in
Umbria on the estate she had the run of orchards and an
olive grove, but her personal belongings were scant and such
toys as came her way were more likely than not bought off
a booth at some fair. In Rome, her daily play-mates were
the Luigino children and the children of the other artisans

who rented holes and cellars in the palazzi of the quarter,
and there was also the resource of transient diplomatic children which usually provided a supply of spirited boys and girls.
Constanza formed them into gangs, organized escapes from
their attendants in the Borghese Gardens, and generally
taught them how to evade and terrorize their governesses.
Constanza herself did not have one. Her parents, though
they liked having her about, made little formal demands on
her time, they were much too busy themselves. She ran in
and out of rooms for a quick affectionate interchange,
reciprocal reassurance; her mother trusted her as she had
been trusted herself, her father was confident to leave it to
his wife; the rest—with complete mutual understanding—
was between Constanza and the servants.

Invitations to the houses of their relatives and connections
were rare; Italian parents of their own world who were
glad to accept Anna were bewildered by what Anna had
produced, and their children sniffled when pushed to play
with it; Constanza was considered " rough ".

Indeed her summer life was wild, and very much her own.
The house, low, long-shuttered, ochre-coloured, was frescoed
inside and not very comfortable; next to it stood the farm
with the vaults and presses, the stables and the houses of the
contadini; the hills were their land, producing oil, some wine,
vegetables, figs, a little maize. Lyre-horned oxen moved the
hand-ploughs along small patched fields; on the slopes goats
pegged to stumpy trees tore at harsh shrubs, there were
lizards on the walls and the days were strident with cicadas
and the nights loud with frogs. It was not a large place,
worked by some fifteen men and their families, but it had its
life. The old principessa went there every year from June
till October, the prince came often; Anna hardly ever.
Constanza knew every sight, every smell, every touch of it.

It was there that she knew solitude and the lucid wakefulness of the deep meridional noon, and the heady taste of a strenuous life. For days she was hardly seen; then she strolled on and turned her hand to the work of the farm, fell in with the cycle of broad bean, melon and quince. She knew the weight of the ripe gourds, the jar of the hoe against baked earth, the light tear made by the bark of stripped cork-oak, the sting of pulped fruit, the cutting harshness of sheaves and the wet ooze of grapes.

The people were kind to her and shared with her what they knew, and while she worked with them she gave herself to the work.

She liked milking a goat; she was fond of those creatures and did not pass one without stopping for some exchange. The farm children were as their parents: their days were their tasks. When Constanza sought companionship of a different nature, there was her grandmother, the indoor servants, often the prince; in yet another mood she turned to the tutor of the moment, some Englishman probably of a mellow turn of mind staying a few months to begin a book on Benvenuto di Gentile.

One thing Anna insisted on. Childhood summers to her had meant the sea, and so every year for a few weeks Constanza was sent down to an Adriatic beach. Constanza, though she never liked leaving Castelfonte, loved this well enough. The tutor came with her, and a maid, and they all stayed at a small inn. The coast south of Ravenna is lonely and flat, the beaches endless and wide. All day Constanza swam, floated, dreamt in the soft waters; at sunset she and her tutor rode. Sometimes the fishermen took her out in their boats. It was an existence of curiously isolated quality; to her those weeks were detached, a stretch of time passed as it were on a parallel, they were part of the seamless years of her youth.

Winter for her was Rome. The cherished slanting sun

leaving the tall houses too soon after mid-day; the animation at nightfall. She loved to go out into the evening streets, go with the cook on some errand, at the hour when the charcoal fires were being lit on the pavements in the quarter, and sniff the scents of wood-smoke, hot iron, decay and spilt young wine. The small braziers flickered with twigs and kindling, fanned and watched over by women: they would shout at her as she passed, raucous words in the dialect, half taunt, half caress, and hold out their pots, and Constanza would stop and shout back in kind and dip her hand in their *pasta*.

Chapter II

The first tremor came when the principessa got to know that her husband had been unfaithful to her. Anna behaved as if the heavens had fallen. The prince was more than ready to show himself contrite.

They had been married for about six years. How Anna learnt was not quite clear to anyone at first. The old principessa took her daughter-in-law's side; behind her back she scolded her son handsomely. " How could you—? " she said. " To *Anna*. So careless."

" *Già,*" said the prince and hung his head.

" It isn't . . . it isn't as if, as if——"

" she were one of us," said his sister Maria. The prince's sisters had themselves been off and married for some time by then. They had rallied at the signs of trouble.

" She's not used to it! " cried the old lady.

" Quite," said the prince, " quite."

" You should have thought of that before, my boy."

" Before when? "

" Mammina, he couldn't throw over Giulia," said Maria patiently, " just because he had met Anna, could he? "

" No, no, one doesn't want to upset the Monfalconi," said her mother.

" Before *being found out,*" said the prince's sister Carla, who was now given to voicing her opinions.

The prince groaned.

" Does Anna read your letters? "

" *Letters?* " said the prince.

" *Biglietti,*" said his sister, " notes."

" Carla," he said, " you talk too much."

" I saw three white peacocks this morning," said Maria.

" *Dio*," said the prince and touched something in his pocket.

" Three? " said Carla.

" Which way did the tail-feathers point? " asked the old principessa.

Her daughter told her.

" That's not nearly so bad," said the prince.

" It means misfortune postponed," said his mother; " but *misfortune*."

" *I* know who told her," said Maria, " Fabrizio—Fabrizio's been after Giulia for years."

The prince flashed at her, " Giulia isn't in the least interested in Fabrizio."

" Maybe."

" If you ask me, Fabrizio is after Anna."

" Who is not? " said her sister.

" Anna is *not* like that," said the prince stiffly.

" She is too good for you! " said the old principessa.

" So she is."

His mother turned on him. " She's a jewel—why can't you treat her properly? "

" But I do——"

" You don't realize who she is."

" Oh, come now, mammina, Anna isn't the only one, she isn't the first—Sciocco's wife is English, so is Boldo's mother, Uncle Teocrito married an Englishwoman, so did your own great-grandpapa—Anna isn't the first foreigner."

" Anna is *American*."

" There's not much difference," said the prince.

" Lady Cressida. I always thought so! "

" Oh shut up, Carla," said her brother.

" American husbands are different," said the old principessa in a reasonable tone.

The prince laughed for the first time. " Oh, no, no, mammina, you mustn't believe all they tell you." He added, " Cleverer perhaps—who can say? "

" And American wives? Are they cleverer, too? "

" No, Maria, not Anna," the prince shook his head; he was profoundly depressed. " Oh you know how it is. . . . No, you can't."

The old principessa had been thinking. " It's because she did not expect it," she said, " poor Anna."

" Really," said the prince, " first you tell me I was care-less. Should I have warned her? She reads so many books —novels—don't they tell her what people do? "

" That's why *we* weren't allowed to read them," said Carla.

" Oh, what *shall* I do? " said the prince.

" Go to her," the women said. " Go to her and make a fuss of her."

But Anna admitted nobody. For twenty-four hours their only link with her was her maid who reported on the silence, the pacing, the untouched trays. Then, once more, youth and native vitality prevailed and Anna began to express her need for action. Notes poured from her apartments: She must leave the house at once; she was going to leave Rome; *Rico* must leave the house at once; *she* was going abroad; she was returning to America.

The prince and his family, unused to this form of traffic, sat puzzling. The women felt for Anna but they did not understand her.

" To America? " the old principessa wailed.

" Don't worry, mammina," said the prince, " she won't go." He alone may have had intimations of what lay at the root of the trouble. If so, he chose not to pursue it, give it no shape—in exasperation, in self-protection, fastidiousness:

it was far too alien to his nature. Better not attempt to understand a woman well; better not attempt to understand at all: avoid complications, leading to nothing. If the prince chose to live on the surface it was not because he lacked all equipment for the other course, it was because his oldest, his most rooted instinct told him to remain where one was placed, to look no further, never to lift the lid—to skate.

The next note was brought in. Anna would leave the house as she was, taking nothing with her.

Nothing? A fear gripped them. Constanza? She is not thinking now, flashed through their minds. When she will. . . .

" She would not—she could not—she must not——"

" The three *pavoni*," breathed Carla.

" Great God," the prince cried in a frenzy.

They simply marched in on her. There was something in the dramatic quality of their entrance that appeased the part of Anna that longed to be appeased. One can be both deeply wounded and not wish to die.

They were shocked by what they saw. Anna's colour was waxen, her face fixed and drawn. Carla said later on, " I had no idea that Anna had a *grand passion* for my brother." The women threw themselves upon her. " Anna, dearest, do not leave us—what would we do without you—you must never leave us. . . ." Anna allowed, even returned, their embraces. " Rico is here to tell you how much he loves you." Anna shrank. " The poor boy's been wretched." The prince hovered; Anna turned her eyes from him. But slowly vehemence was begetting a response. " How could he? " she cried suddenly. " It is all so low! "

The prince stepped forward. " Anna," he said tenderly. " *Carissima*—forgive me."

42

" Don't touch me," she cried. He had made no move to
do so. She tried to look at him, found that she could, tried
to read his face.

" Anna," he said again.

" How could he? " She turned to his mother: " Why? "

The old principessa tried her best. " Dearest, it's nothing,
believe me. His father was *très courreurr*," she sounded every
r. " They all are, don't you see? "

Anna moaned. " But that low woman."

If they bristled, they did not show it.

" That low, common woman," said Anna, " how can he
even speak to such a creature——? "

Carla, stung, muttered, " The best blood in Italy——"
but a look from her sister quelled her.

The principessa said gently, " You see he has known her
for such a very long time, they grew up together practically——"

Anna, reeling with the sense that reality was slipping from
her grasp, said uncertainly, " Surely, she only turned up here
when she opened that shop——"

" *Shop!* " said the prince. " You must be out of your mind,
Anna! Of all the inconceivable things she would ever——"
but here his sister Carla gave him a savage nudge and he
stopped short. In time.

" The flower-shop, Rico," Anna said, now looking him
full in the face. " You paid for it. Mrs Waddington told
me."

They did not look at each other. The prince gulped; then
his face cleared and he looked like a man transformed. He
sprang forward: " My darling! You are right! You are
right! Fanette *is* a dreadful creature, it was nothing," relief
was making him eloquent, " less than nothing, I can't think
how it started, a thing of the moment, it's all over, I can
promise you, I promise you solemnly, I shall never see her
again."

And Anna, who had not expected anything else, was affected nevertheless by his sweeping sincerity.

Their lives did not settle down again at once, nor easily. It was Anna who lagged behind and appeared to find it difficult to effect a full return. At times it was she who outdid them all in her desire to pull down the lid and have things smoothed over and forgotten; at others she seemed to invite protestations, displays of feeling, scenes. It was as if she were in need of some gesture or event of weight to act as a full stop. The old principessa asked if it was not simply that Anna was *enceinte* again; Rico told them she was not. Then he hit upon the happy thought of suggesting that she should go round the world. It was not his own nor an entirely new idea, various English friends had been going in other years and Anna had debated whether she too should go; but it was an idea that tremendously appealed to her—she loved travelling, she wanted to see India—and now she took to it at once, treating it as something out of the blue and an offering from her husband, which in a sense it was. The prince was wondering very much what going round the world might cost. He did not know but feared that it must be a good deal (he was quite right in the event); the roof at Castelfonte leaked again but he decided not to mention it. Lord and Lady Chalmers and her bachelor brother and another couple were setting out in February; they had pressed Anna before and now it was decided that she should join their party. The prospect revived her.

In Rome, when the story came out, which of course it did, Anna was on the whole much criticized. She was ridiculous, she exaggerated, she was giving herself airs and Rico was a saint to put up with it. The men said to each other that they were not surprised. As to Mrs Waddington —a very transient lady who had dwelt in the relative

obscurity of a suite at the Grand Hotel (Anna had a tendency
to befriend such apparitions)—wrath was tempered by grate-
fulness. Mrs Waddington had not penetrated as far as
Giulia Monfalconi. Giulia, they all said, had had a narrow
escape. Or not? Anna was not born yesterday, *could* Anna
know so little of the ways of the world? Some people said that
of course Anna knew all about Giulia Monfalconi, Anna was
a deep one, and look what she got out of it.

" Would *you* want to go to China, *cara*? "

" Well of course not. But she could have asked for pearls."

They did not exactly keep it from Constanza, the whole
business simply by-passed her. Her mother was still far too
young then to be interested in making emotional demands
on children; Constanza was five. She realized that something was wrong, some grown-up disturbance. In the street
in which she lived the carpenter beat his wife on Sundays,
the *fruttivendola* across the road howled at her family for hours
at a time, in the drawing-room they talked freely of poor
Princess Ghirladaia who was shut up in a dungeon in Toscana
by her aged husband, while Anna's maid had been left by
hers after only a year—it was the way things went, it was
life, it washed over her.

When the time came for Anna to leave, the old principessa
was desolate. " Eight months," she said, " eight months.
Shall I ever see my darling again? " " It can be done in
Eighty Days, *nonna*," said Constanza. They all went down
with her on the train to Naples: Rico, the old principessa,
Carla and Maria and their husbands and Constanza. Anna
was taking a French maid, engaged at the last minute; her
own Italian maid, devoted though she was, had been so
very distressed at the prospect of going among the snakes that

Anna had not had the heart to persuade her. The French-woman did not like it much better, but was stoical about it and had asked for double wages. " Certainly, my dear," Anna had said, " but you know, you will find it a marvellous experience."

At the dock, Lord and Lady Chalmers and their party leaning against the rails saw Anna arrive, parasol in hand, looking very ravishing, followed by a line of trunks and surrounded by a family of weeping Italians and a rather grubby child, very foreign-looking. (Constanza had indeed managed to escape for some moments with a boy met on the quay and been taken to see some rats.) The old principessa was sobbing bitterly, the prince's face was bathed in tears. They kissed, kissed again. . . .

At last Anna was able to step on board. Their hand-kerchiefs fluttered. " Mama," Constanza shouted, " bring us back a tiger! "

" Yes, *carissima*," the prince called bravely, " bring us a tiger."

Anna's spirits were high.

Chapter III

Constanza managed her affairs more discreetly.

If ever there was a cradle Catholic, it was she. She had been taken to her first act of worship in her *bambinaia's* arms. She had been told that she would meet *Gesù*, the good Virgin, the Saints and everything that was holy, potent and miraculous. The *bambinaia's* own Saint had a shrine in that small, dark and rather mysterious church that stands behind the Trevi Fountain. It was there they went. It was evening and the waters were playing. Constanza saw gods, plunging horses, a glorious profusion of light and roar and spray and flung out her arms in ecstasy. She very nearly managed to tumble herself into the seething pool. The good woman carried her down the steps and held her while she put her hands and mouth to a spout and drank. If afterwards she was presented at another altar it held no separate memory for her.

When Constanza was old enough to have her lessons with the parish priest, what sank in first of all was the contrast between his teaching—authoritarian, uninspired—and that of her other masters; after a while it was the subject matter which gave her to think. Anna, keeping aloof from her daughter's religious education, made the mistake so natural to fundamentally not very religious people of believing religion to be capable of isolation. On the more practical and immediate level, it had not occurred to her that while Constanza was being taught—by a kindly and sincere old man to whom what he was putting before this child was no less than the most patent and most necessary of all truths and did not stand in need of explanations or expository refinements—about the Flood, Divine Omnipotence, Eternal Damnation, the Sacraments, the Virgin Birth, she was also taught and by men of very different abilities about everything else from geology to the Inquisition.

As Constanza grew up, her mind (at various stages) buzzed with questions. She did not put them to the priest, she suspected that it might be of little use and that it might give him pain. Constanza had tact, she was also very good-natured and did not like to cause offence where offence might be avoided.

She asked her mother. " Do many people go to Hell? People we know? "

Anna gave her full attention to this, but tried not to show it. She said lightly, " Oh, I don't think so, darling. Some say that hell exists, but it is empty."

Constanza looked at it. " With the Hell Fires going all the time? Through Eternity? Don't you think God would get to want to try the Fires out one day? I should, if they were all there and waiting. Of course *I* should order the Hell Fires to be put out at once."

" There is no hell fire," said her mother, " not really. It is only a kind of symbol."

" Hmm," said Constanza. " I don't think the *parroco* believes that."

" He may feel that you are too young; I suppose children are usually given the literal interpretation." Anna wondered if she ought not after all to rope in one of her friends among the Monsignori, but dismissed the thought. " God is all merciful," she said firmly, " there can be no hell—it is unthinkable."

" In pictures, there are always flames, *and* people. Is that symbols too? "

" In a sense."

" There is some *proof*," said her daughter, " there've been the ghosts, poor Souls in Purgatory, but nobody from Hell as far as one knows."

" Darling, *who* told you that? "

" Everybody," said Constanza. She thought. " It is common knowledge."

" I must get Dr Slater to tell you a little about Psychical Research," said her mother.

" I should like that," said Constanza.

" But really, my pet, people do not return." Anna quoted the appropriate passage from Hamlet. " At least not as individuals; we must take that as established now."

" What about the Resurrection of the Flesh, mama? "

" You must not take the Scriptures too literally, my dear."

" I don't do scriptures with the *parroco*; it's in the Creed." Constanza looked hard at her mother: " You are quite sure about Hell? Because if it *is* true, we have to be very careful."

" Of what, darling? "

" Not to die in a state of Mortal Sin."

" That's nothing *you* will have to worry about, my darling," said her mother. " What we must all hope for is to lead good lives according to our conscience."

" Constanza, tell me, do you . . . do R.C.'s ever have difficulties with their beliefs? "

" Difficulties, William? " They were doing geometry. Constanza (a few years older now) was quite good at it, but lazy.

" Do they find it difficult to believe what they are told to? "

" Oh, doubts? One does have doubts. That is accepted. You are supposed to pray to get rid of them."

" Do you? "

" It's bad luck to omit prayers on certain occasions," his pupil said lightly.

" How do you feel about Infallibility, for instance? " William was a very young man, just down from Oxford and an Anglo-Catholic.

" That's easy," said Constanza, " like the Immaculate Conception and all that. God is omnipotent, isn't he? "

" Yes."

" If he is omnipotent, he can do *anything*. If he can do anything, he can make the Pope infallible. Right? "

" Yes. . . . Wait a minute: the Pope is a man, and man is presumed to be left free to make his own choice between good and evil—God could not make a man his own mouthpiece? "

" Why not? " said Constanza. " If God chooses to, just *one* man. He may need someone to speak for him, although I do think that a direct voice from Heaven would be so much more effective. I often wish for one. Anyway, the Pope is only infallible as pope—like you in mathematics— he could be a sinner *himself*. And perhaps the Pope is not a man after all—who knows?—perhaps God makes us only think he is, perhaps the Pope is a Miracle."

" But why should God *want* to make the Pope infallible? "

" Because we are the One True Church," said Constanza.

" Do you *really* believe that? "

" I'm not at all certain," said Constanza. " It does seem odd that *everybody* else should be wrong, the Protestants and the Greeks and the people who think there isn't any God at all; the Buddhists, too. Mama says there are such wonderful religions in the East. It seems so like the lottery—think if one weren't born what one is."

" It's terribly important to know which is right," said William.

" Oh you know, *you* don't have to worry about your Salvation," she said, "even if you are a Heretic. You see, people aren't damned just because they haven't had the chance to be born Catholics—that would be dreadful—it's only if you have been given the chance to know better and reject it. . . . Oh *Dio*, this may *be* the chance! William dear, do be careful, perhaps it isn't at all wise for you to have come to Rome."

The young man blushed. "As a matter of fact . . . as a matter of fact——" Constanza turned her eyes on him. He said: "I may *take* the chance."

A few of Constanza's masters, particularly those who happened to be staunch Anglicans or Presbyterians, shared her mother's scruples and refrained from subjects liable to weaken their charge's allegiance to her own faith. Even they would not suppress the Marian Persecutions when the point was reached. Most of them, however, whether Darwinians, agnostics or believers, showed no concern other than to impart knowledge according to their lights. The origin of man was taken by their pupil in her stride; the interest to her was academic, what enthralled her was the way men behaved and not how they were made. Nomadic tribes and the Crusades were apt to bore her, the periods she had most feeling for were Republican Rome and the Italian Renaissance, while the history of the Reformation and the Counter-Reformation filled her with mounting indignation and dismay. Tolerance was bred into her very bones, and she abhorred cruelty.

"They did this?" she said, blazing, "to each other? Both sides? Burning each other, hacking each other to pieces?"

"Both sides."

"Because each thought they were right and the other wrong?"

"Yes."

" Each side thought that? "

" Convinced of it."

" How foolish! " said Constanza. " And then they had a
Thirty Years' War. I suppose they began by being a *little
right* each? Then everything got more and more wrong and
they couldn't stop it? The way it is when one quarrels."

" It is nearly impossible to stop anything, dear child, once
it involves a large number of interests and people."

" I see that," said Constanza. " But it couldn't happen
again now? Could it? "

Her master said: " No." And he added: " Not in that
form."

" That *is* certain? How does one know, I suppose people
nowadays mind less being wrong? "

" More and more people *are* being right."

" How do they know they are? " said Constanza.

" Mr James," said Constanza, " when I want to do something and don't, is it my conscience or the voice of my
guardian angel? "

" Does it happen, dear girl? "

" It was a hypothetical question. But it does."

" Then I should call it enlightened self-interest," said
Mr James.

Constanza laughed. " I *have* other promptings. Where
do you think they come from? "

" Your kind heart, possibly."

" That again might be my guardian angel? "

" Oh quite," said Mr James.

" Surely," said Constanza, " the guardian angel would be
something *outside* myself, a separate entity, whereas my
conscience is a part of myself."

" Which part? " said Mr James.

" It must be a part of my mind."

" Your mind. What is your mind. Will you describe it? "

" That does get us into deep waters," said Constanza, delighted. " I suppose the mind is brain and spirit——"

" How you do mix up things," said Mr James.

" Well, that's what they appear to be."

" What makes you certain you have a mind? "

" I'm not at all certain about my conscience, but I can't help being sure that I have a mind, I feel I know it's there."

" *Ergo?* " said Mr James.

" *Touché.*" But she added, " You are not telling me that my mind is no more real than my guardian angel? "

" More real! " said Mr James. " You'll never make a philosopher. And I am not telling you anything."

" *Dear* Mr James," said Constanza.

It was about this time that Constanza—who had nearly reached the age of thirteen—ceased to ask such questions of herself and others. She woke up one fine morning and found that she had (as she knew they called it) lost her religion—it was gone, she had sloughed it off. She realized that she believed in nothing whatsoever and she did not feel a sense of loss at all. In fact she shed interest in the subject altogether; her worries about people being damned appeared to her as childish things now put behind for ever.

This did not mean that she did not recognize that on a mundane plane it was a serious matter. If her family went about their observances and no questions asked, it was because these things and their acceptance were unquestionable. There had been foreign wives and therefore converts, there had been exiles, eloped daughters, a cousin who went to prison, but atheists (Constanza told herself that she was one now), never. No use inviting trouble, no use hurting loved people: Constanza merely kept quiet.

There were few real problems. First communion, and with it regular instruction, lay behind. She went on going to mass when it was required, or gave the impression of having been. Sometimes, standing in an aisle, hearing the priest's sibilant gabbling through the Latin words (she blamed them for not putting more fervour into what she did not believe), looking at the vacant, the rapt, the sheepish faces, the mumbling lips, she was moved to say to herself: I am the cleverest person here, I am the only one who has seen through it all, and I am younger than any of them. What filled her was not quite pride, but amazement and contempt—how easy everything was if one was clever. And she was glad she was: it was useful, it was fun.

The sacraments she shunned. She would have felt great dread kneeling at an altar rail—she might not be struck down there and then but it might follow her through life; the gods were powerful even if the Church was naught. This was confused, Constanza told herself, irrational (a favourite word), but there it was, stronger than her little chains of argument; she shrugged at it and lived accordingly.

She did not like deceit, but did not hesitate to practice it as the lesser evil. She was successful, her family assumed that she had adopted her mother's custom of choosing churches at the four corners of Rome. At confession she judged it politic to show herself occasionally, and so at Easter-time she went to their own man with a well-chosen catalogue of minor sins and nothing worse than an acute social malaise.

She also decided not to tell her mother. Constanza was perhaps the only one who had divined what a queer Catholic her mother made, and she wished to spare her unguessed complications. Besides, far better always to fend alone than with an uncertain ally.

The Story of a Marriage

§

At that time Anna herself was moving towards a crisis in her life. The years that lay behind her might be said to have been halcyon years. When she had returned to Italy from across the seas at the appointed time, her trunks multiplied, animated, serene, dispensing treasure, the then recent past was as if it had never been. Even the prince, himself past-master at leaving well alone, found himself outdone in gliding over what she did not seem to remember having been thin ice at all. Perhaps, he hoped, she really *had* forgotten. Anna had come back with the inevitable Oriental bric-à-brac, but to her husband she brought a clear ruby, a stone unset, though cut. It had been given to her by an Indian. Anna had intimated that she was unable to accept jewellery from a gentleman. The Indian had replied in a most pretty speech that he was no mortal gentleman but a ruler by divine right, that an unset jewel was not jewellery and he was sending this stone to the prince who had the honour to be her husband. They were all charmed. The prince was deeply pleased: rubies in the family, he said, meant luck. If he could not wear the stone, he would do better, he would carry it loose in his pocket and it should always be with him.

Anna's life resumed, the circle of admirers, art, the eminent visitors, dining-out, organizing fêtes, and travel. Constant travel, to Scotland in the summer, to London, to Swiss spas, a visit to St-Petersburg (where she would have loved to meet Count Tolstoi but did not), a visit to Madrid to see the Velasquez, travel in Italy, to Assisi, to Siena, to Milan, above all to Venice which she adored and Rico could not abide, he called it that damp hole. He seldom travelled with her; and Anna had not once gone back to her native country.

It could wait, she said. One day when Constanza was older she would take them all on a visit home. She told the prince he would be made to stay at Boston, and he allowed himself to be teased and flung up his hands in horror.

" Papa doesn't like crossing water," said Constanza; " *I* shall have nothing against it."

" I crossed the Channel, Anna," the prince said: " Once! To marry you. The ordeal. England! The other end of the world—America can't be much worse."

" Your sisters loved England."

" Oh women."

" In America," said Constanza, " everybody is equal, even women."

" More equal! " said her father.

" I can't see it," said Constanza. " People are not the same—it is unnatural to pretend they are."

" Darling, equality does not mean *being* the same," said Anna, " it means being *treated* the same."

" And that is just? " said Constanza.

Her mother gave her a quick look. " It is a long time since I heard that word. Yes, we do think it is *just*. It is our way of redressing, as far as we can, natural injustice. As you say, people are not the same, they are not born with the same advantages of mind and person, so we have a form of life where——"

" Yes, *cara*," said the prince, " but you do have rich and poor in your country."

" Oh we haven't come near to what we are going to be, this is not the end! And we have not your kind of poor."

" Nor we your kind of rich," said the prince.

" In the United States there is hope for everybody."

" For everybody? " said Constanza. " I see how one can hope to get rich. What if you are a fool, or ugly and nobody looks at you and your husband runs away, or you never find one? "

" You find one if you've got money," said her father.

" *Già*," said his daughter. " Still. . . . It wouldn't be so pleasant to be ugly—*una brutta*—even in America. Worse: if everybody is rich, nobody would *have* to marry her and she wouldn't get a husband. Of course one knows they haven't all got the *same* money, America hasn't adopted socialism."

" Socialism means all poor," said the prince.

" Socialism means all moderately well-off," said Constanza. " I've read the Fabians about it—you haven't heard of them—they have opened my eyes."

" Are you a socialist, *figlia?* "

" Well, I'm for it," said Constanza. " It needs working out; everybody would have to *agree*. But it's a generous thing to be."

" Little you know," said the prince.

" My darling," said Anna. " But you see in America, with our form of Government, we never do anything *unless* everybody agrees."

" Except the minority," said Constanza. " Mama, are many Americans like you? The ones in Rome are not."

" Your mother is unique," said the prince.

" But is she a *real* American? "

" I am no longer a citizen," said the principessa.

" And what am I ? "

" You are half American by blood," said her mother.

" American blood," said the prince, " what is that? Yours is Scotch and English, *cara*, the rest seems to be Sicilian or . . . German."

" What *is* blood? " said Anna. " I suppose it turns American at some point the way yours must have turned blue. All I meant was that she's part American through me."

" I'm not Scotch English," said Constanza.

" *Tu sei Romana*," said the prince.

Constanza turned to him. " And how not! What next? "

But Anna had the last word here. She looked at this alien

child, this girl, who stood before her, eyes flashing, talking with her hands. " There is a good deal of your grandfather in you," she said.

§

No Mrs Waddington or her kind turned up to disturb their peace. If for Anna the years were smooth, they were also much the same, one round like the other.

When she first arrived she had breathed some of her vigour into the local charities; she had done what she could, gone as far as she might without becoming strident. It was not a large field. There is a point up to which graceful femininity, determined, may gallop; beyond it, the femininity becomes a total liability. Anna, at least outside her family life, did not attempt to crash barriers. It might not have displeased her to have been able to see herself as the *éminence rose* behind some political movement or figure; the opportunity did not come her way. The prince and his friends, apart from complaining about the times, remained wholly aloof from public affairs. Her own cosmopolitan Rome was in some senses a backwater; she could hear the larger issues talked of by her eminent men; at the embassies she had gossip, the echoes of intrigue, she might get a glimpse of workings, but she never saw action, never tasted the illusion even of having her hand at some wheel, and she came to realize that in Rhode Island, in her first youth, hearing her father and uncles return at night, she had been nearer a helm.

She turned her mind to the family land, to some model reform that might one day point the way in rural Italy. The prince gave his nonchalant consent and said how would she find the money? Obstacles appeared. She made a plan for the figs to be dried in a more scientific way, packed in pretty boxes and shipped to foreign countries. She was told that the crop had always been sold to a man at Gubbio who very likely did export it in the end. Precisely, she said, they must cut out the middle-men. She got as far as having a young protégé design a label which showed their house but not their name; then the whole scheme petered out. The principessa turned to cows, cows to replace the goats. The prince told her there was no pasture. She had no first-hand knowledge of such things, and agriculture did not really interest her. She decided to do something for the peasants. She loved the people. When she said people, she saw sales-girls, dressmakers, waiters, clerks, her servants. Italian servants had been one of the joyful discoveries of her new life; she charmed and spoilt them and they gave her their sincerest flattery. Now she proposed to install up-to-date coal-ranges in the *contadini* kitchens. Everybody raised their hands to heaven and talked about the price of coal in the peninsula. Anna, relieved perhaps, returned to Rome.

§

The old principessa had survived her daughter-in-law's return for nearly seven years. Now she died. The family was united in gentle and copious grief. Constanza ceased her roamings and joined the circle in which they all sat together, hugging each other, shedding open tears. When life claimed them again, it was Anna who appeared to remain the most bereft; she was restless, nothing pleased her, she seemed to find it difficult to take up things. She began to find fault with Constanza (then in her first flush of atheism), but at crucial moments Constanza simply was not there. She tried to provoke the prince, drive him into some kind of duel or storm, telling him he was idle, that his life was useless, that he lacked convictions. The prince, still a very sad man him-self, became more transparent or withdrew a little further—

it was never possible to say which—and would not let himself
be provoked. " Anna, poor woman, is missing mammina,"
he told his sisters. He found it natural.

In her time the old principessa had been passionately
devoted to her husband, whom she seldom saw but who was
handsome and kind; her old age had been animated by her
disinterested romantic attachment to Anna. While she was
able to move she had never relinquished her habit of following
Anna about the palazzo with a fragile nimbleness; whenever
Anna returned from a party or a journey, there had been
the old lady, benignly waiting, giving welcome. She hardly
went out herself, but had wanted to hear every detail, not
about the world, but Anna in the world; there was nothing
Anna did that was not of exciting interest to her, nothing
Anna had to tell that she did not long to hear; she admired
everything. The emotion which she poured upon her idol
was of a quality other than that which Anna received from
her husband and her daughter, self-contained creatures whose
affection was an almost indiscriminate overflow of their own
natures.

" She was like a mother to me," Anna told her maid,
" the only mother I knew."

Mena who had been watching them for on to fourteen
years, said nothing.

Chapter IV

It was in the autumn following the old principessa's death that Anna became involved in the rather mysterious episode that is said to have affected her so much. What exactly happened nobody does know as Anna never told the whole truth to anyone.

Among Anna's admirers there was one Sir Charles, a widower, well-off, who had been a soldier and in the diplomatic service and was now something of a dilettante. He was a tall, blue-eyed man, always perfectly turned out. Constanza later said of him that even in those days, when people did not exactly go about in flannel trousers, he was a wonder to behold. She and her young cronies used to call him The Portrait of a Gentleman. He did water-colours, was a bibliophile and had a flat in the Theatre of Marcello. He and Anna went to every symphony concert together, saying how much they preferred these to the opera.

He and Anna had been going everywhere for years. At home she was teased about Sir Charles. Anna has become acclimatized, the prince would say, she has taken a *cicisbeo*, *meno male*.

But even Roman gossip had ceased to doubt Anna's virtue. Nobody bothered any longer to call her deep. They had marvelled long enough at her capacity for resistance, her capacity rather for ignoring that there was anything to resist; now it had become a fact of local life.

What was not known was that Anna and Sir Charles moved in an exquisite cloud of renunciation. Sir Charles had not attempted to conquer. One day across the tea-table he had declared his hopeless passion, making it quite clear that for people such as they it could be nothing else but that. Anna found it beautiful. Sir Charles told her that she was the love of his life; she was able to tell him that if only the fates had willed it otherwise. . . . This, they told each other, was all they would ever have, the knowledge of each other's feelings. For a time they were very happy. They continued to address each other as Sir Charles and Principessa even in private and they were proud of this. Anna became convinced that she had missed her life, that in her youth and ignorance she had made a grave mistake, at last and too late she knew the man she should have married. This, then, was her secret, the key to herself. She bore it nobly. It gave extra point to her whole situation, focussed discontents that might have stirred, and she was able to pursue the serene bustle of her existence with an added glow.

Liaisons such as these, if more long-lived than consummated love, do not last for ever. The magic either becomes too potent or it fades. In Anna's case, Sir Charles in due course became a fixture, a shadow. Then he provided a new stimulus by saying that he must go away.

" Leave our beloved Italy——? "

Sir Charles told her that it had become too much, it would be best for him if he did not see her again, Sorceress Principessa, at least not for some years.

It was the spring after her mother-in-law had died. Anna was getting on for thirty-five. She always told her age; but she also thought about it.

He would go to the East, he said, a good place for a man with a broken heart.

" But you *have* my heart," said Anna.

He never saw her, he complained, at least only among strangers, in public places. . . .

" This is not a public place." Anna smiled. They were sitting once more at his tea-table—laid with collector's china, in the flat in the Teatro di Marcello, one of the most coveted flats in Rome.

For an hour! he said. Less as a matter of fact, said Anna, she would have to go, she had to change early.

" Can't you *see*? " he said.

Presently his man-servant came in to remove some things. Anna did not become aware of an intrusion.

" Shall I never have you to myself, then? " he asked.

All summer they sparred. At last she agreed to meet him somewhere. I promised to give him two days, she put it later on.

They arranged to meet at an hotel in the Dolomites in October. She would be on her way to stay with a relative in Vienna who had been Godmother to Constanza. She was to break the journey at Cortina d'Ampezzo for forty-eight hours; Sir Charles would be already there. It would be the last of the season, the hotel still open, but empty of people they knew. Whatever Anna envisaged when she agreed to this plan, she did know that it had to remain clandestine and involve at least a minimum of subterfuge and management. Whatever the facts, in the society in which she lived, the appearances for a married woman such as she were sacrosanct. Did Anna know the whole of the risk she ran? Did she, possibly, court it? More likely she was ignorant of the extent of it, for whatever the look of things she expected the world to have the faith in her that she had in herself. Anna's innocence may have been monstrous; it was genuine.

In the event she never got to Vienna. She came home less

than two days after she had left, in a hired cab from the station. No-one saw her return. Her maid, Mena, who one must realize had been with her all the time, helped her upstairs, to her bed, shuttered the room.

Mena was a tiny, wiry woman with a screwed-up face, she might have been any age; actually her age was that of Anna. She went off to assure her mistress's peace.

" What's the matter? " said the prince.

" It is nothing," said Mena, " the Signora Principessa has had a kind of fright."

" On the train, *poverina*? "

" More at the hotel, *Eccellenza*. It was nothing. But it has given her a headache, she had better be left quiet for a few days."

" A fright at the hotel? Perhaps some fellow in his cups tried to rape her! " The prince found this a beautifully fantastic joke and enlarged on it. " Fellow must have been pretty tipsy. . . . Did he kick her door down? "

Mena, who was really devoted to Anna, laughed duly.

But the prince must have come very near the truth.

Anna lay on her bed, her eyes wide open.

Mena came in with a cup; hovered; Anna did not respond. " I told them downstairs it was migraine."

Anna moved her lips: " Men are . . . vile."

" Men are men, Signora Principessa."

" That is dreadful," said Anna.

When Anna moved once more amongst them, they found that she was no longer at all easy to get on with.

There lived in Rome at that time a Protestant lady of vast rectitude who disliked most things that went on in Italy, her name was Mrs Throgmore-Wylie. With this woman, who was English, rich, a widow, a good deal older and quite plain, Anna now closely allied herself, in fact made her a confidante. As neither of them was given to call a spade a spade, it is not easy to make out what was divulged. They worked themselves up to a big scene during which Anna gave a profusion of hints which Mrs Throgmore-Wylie spread, thinned and considerably darkened, in other carefully managed *tête-à-têtes*. Those hints did not refer to Anna's recent escapade but to her past life with the prince. Apparently Anna had another secret. Perhaps she did not find it possible to live without one.

Sir Charles did not return to Rome. His man and some very expert packers came to shut the establishment in the Teatro di Marcello. He did not go to the East but to Paris where he found and furnished for himself a flat on the Île Saint-Louis.

§

A year, a full year later, Anna showed once more acute signs of distress. In turn she remained locked upstairs or dragged herself about. She talked about taking her own life. She refused to see her doctor; then went to see one furtively. She took against the prince and more than anyone she shunned her friend, Mrs Throgmore-Wylie. When at length the cause of all this could not longer be concealed, the family were very much relieved.

" It takes some of them that way," said the prince; " Giulia's husband tells me they had quite a time over her fourth."

" It wasn't like this when Anna was expecting Constanza,"
said Maria.

" Fourteen years ago! We are all a bit tired of it now."
The sisters had had nine between them.

" Anna's out of training," said Carla.

" Anna cannot have it both ways," said the prince. And
he said it in a tone they were not used to hear from
him.

When Anna's pregnancy became generally known the men
in Rome said *meno male*, better late than never. Then they
made a joke which was mildly blasphemous.

" Good old Rico."

" Rico's a hero."

" He took his time about it, didn't he *want* a son? "

" Rico's forgotten all about it, he's so wrapped up in that
devil of a girl of his."

" They say she was out with the Simonetti boy in a boat
this summer, all alone they were, till past midnight. When
they came in she said they'd run into rough sea and had to
put by. Not a cloud in the night. Rough sea in the next bay,
she said."

" She is *furba*."

" Do you believe it? "

" The rough sea? No. But I heard it was the notary's
son."

" That was another time. They were lost in the hills. Do
you believe any of it? "

" Of her? Of young Constanza? How not? Well, *meno
male*."

" *Meno male*."

Giulia Monfalconi said: " I am so very glad. They ought to

have a boy. Rico hasn't missed one so far, but it will be comfortable for him later on."

" Later on, boys spend money. There can't be so much left now."

" You would think so, the way Anna's been carrying on. As a matter of fact there's still quite a bit, something Anna's got and can't touch and that will go to her children."

" Well, as long as Anna doesn't get her hands on it. I suppose it would go to a boy now? "

" Well no, actually. The way they arranged things over there, Anna can leave it anyway she likes."

" Since you know everything—whom would it go to now? I mean if anything happened? "

Giulia said, " I haven't the faintest idea. Nor, I'm sure, has Anna. Anna never thinks about her money."

" She doesn't have to! "

" It's never only that."

" She will one day. We all come to it."

Giulia said, " Rico is being very gloomy."

" Isn't he at all pleased? "

" Not really. He's too worried about Anna. All those tantrums. The women he knows have never had a day's illness. Not that she *is* ill that I know of. And he says it's too late anyhow, there's no more point in having sons nowadays, he doesn't like the new Italy."

" Who ever did? "

" Men mind more when they get older," Giulia said. " Now he thinks it's here to stay. Rico is getting on for forty."

" Rico! Not that one would say so."

" No," said Giulia smugly.

Her friend said, " What if it *is* a girl? It's not beyond the bounds of possibility."

" Heaven help her. No second girl could hold up her head in that house."

" It *would* have to be something pretty special."

" Do you know, I have a feeling that this time it won't," said Giulia.

" Rico adores Constanza, doesn't he? "

" She's the one human being in the world he really cares for."

" Mama," Constanza said, " I just thought of something. Weren't you late-born yourself? "

" I suppose I was."

" Well, how old was your youngest sister when your mama had you? "

" About your age."

" You see? The same."

" Not at all the same," said Anna crossly.

" It's a curious coincidence though," said Constanza, " I wonder what it means? "

" *Eccellenza*—La Signora Trommo-Vailé."

" I am not seeing anyone, Socrate."

" Very good, *Eccellenza*."

But Mrs Throgmore-Wylie had been following on the butler's heels. It was the kind of thing she did. Anna rose; her visitor thrust herself upon her. " Just a glimpse, dearest Principessa . . . just a minute. . . . My entire understanding . . . your great fortitude. . . . These lapses. . . . We are so helpless . . . your magnificent courage. . . ."

When the prince came home ten minutes later, he said, " I saw la Throgmore flapping down the stairs, when she saw me she bolted. She looked as if she would have crossed herself if she knew how."

" Oh leave her alone," said Anna in a mellow tone: " she's a person of very fine perceptions."

The prince made a face. "She gives me the creeps. Perhaps *I*'d better cross myself." He turned the ruby in his pocket. "Well, *cara*, as long as her visit has given *you* pleasure. . . ."

Giorgio, at Anna's insistence, was born in a nursing home. He was not easy. Presently Anna came to feel herself as the mother of the Gracchi and began to speak of her son, though she did not take much interest in the actual creature who was a perfectly healthy and well-formed baby with the dark eyes of his father and his sister. When the wet-nurse from Castelfonte came for him, Anna was displeased to see a new face. "Why can't we have the woman we had for Constanza?" she complained, "she was satisfactory."

"I don't think mama *is* very maternal," Constanza said to the young man she was doing Latin with. "What a good thing I never noticed at the time." She added, "Not that I blame her."

The young man, who was an American, said, "Your mother has a good deal to put up with!" His voice was rather adenoidal.

"I don't know what you are talking about," said Constanza. And then she realized that this was the first time she had ever put anyone in his place. She did not like it, nor the self that spoke the words: it was as if something new and perfectly ready-made had slipped into her. It was ugly and easy and fascinating, and she knew she would do it again. She also knew that in the eyes of the world she had done exactly as required. It flashed through her: this is growing-up. With her old self she softened it by saying lightly, and smiling, "Well, you know, Milly, it isn't your business, whatever it is."

"I shouldn't have spoken to you," the young man said,

" it's all the immorality in this place that gets me down. And I ask myself how a fine woman like your mother——"

" Whatever it is," said Constanza, coolly again, " my mother knows *nothing* about it."

The young man, who was half in love with Anna, took it in.

Chapter V

They had two more years. Anna never quite settled down
again. She tried this and she tried that; she thought of
reviving the fig scheme; she made plans for building a
hospital or at least a first-aid station at Castelfonte; she
turned her mind to starting something about women, but
what was going on in England then was neither encouraging
nor really to her taste, and when the prince said: *cara,
carissima*, you haven't got the vote even in America, have
you? that was really that. She turned to schools.

" Rico, do pay attention—these people cannot read or
write."

" *Già.*"

" Not *read* nor *write*. One must do something about it! "

" Why? "

" Really, Rico. Why, it's the beginning of everything."

" Oh *everything*. . . . Dear Anna."

" You are evading the issue."

" What issue? "

" Illiteracy is bad."

" Come to that, we haven't all of us been reading and
writing for such a long time in our part of the world. Our
ancestors left it to the professionals."

" And theirs to the slaves. Thank God, things are
different now."

" They *are* different," said the prince. " But does it make
a difference? Look at our Pina, she had six years at school,
I daresay she didn't mind, sitting still all day and no work,

but look at her now, and look at Cosima who can't even write figures."

" I admit that Cosima is three times more intelligent," said Anna, " but that's an accident. All the more pity that *she* did not have the schooling."

" And what would she do with it in her kitchen? Do you want people to read Leopardi in the evening after fourteen hours in the fields, and buy the newspaper? They haven't got the time or the money, they haven't got the *soldi* to buy lamp-oil. They wouldn't enjoy Leopardi and they'd believe the newspaper. Most people are stupid and many things that are printed are stupid and stupid people always read the stupid things, so what you get is a more stupid world. When the stupid peasant has read the stupid newspaper, he feels he is a clever man and knows everything."

" We must raise the standard of newspapers and see that the people are less poor and tired. Nobody should work fourteen hours a day."

" Quite," said the prince. " Only in Italy they would be even poorer if they didn't."

" All that has to be changed."

" How? how? how? " said the prince. " How do you change things without making them worse? Where is it going to come from? Who is going to do it? Who is not out for himself? "

" Changes are perfectly workable in a democracy."

" And how do you get that democracy, how do you change to that? It seems more unlikely than Constanza's socialism."

" *Fabian* socialism," said Constanza, who had been reading on the floor.

" *Ciao*," said the prince, " and how is my nihilist today? "

" Very well indeed, papa. I never really had that phase, though it *is* attractive; but not so reasonable."

" If you've been listening," said Anna, " do tell your

father that we've got to do something about these disgraceful conditions."

" But you see, mama, I'm only for socialism with *consent*. Do you think people would consent to it in Italy? "

" Oh, we would be asked, would we? " said the prince.

" That's my *point*, papa. I am not considering Revolution. The peasants might say yes, but they wouldn't grasp what it's about, and anyway it is known that it should be tried only in highly industrialized countries——"

" *Cristo*," said her father.

" Education," said Anna, " that's what I've been saying, economic progress is inseparable——"

"—and people like papa wouldn't consent at all—I don't think *I* could persuade papa, he is really quite obstinate— the rich won't consent, it wouldn't be like England and the Reform Bill when some of the rich were for it."

Anna, with automatic distaste, said: " Darling, you know that we are not what is called rich, besides it is not nice to refer to oneself as that."

" Mama," Constanza said with firmness, " in Rome there are the rich and there are the poor. To say that we don't belong to the rich is an insult to the poor. Even if papa does tell us we shall be ruined before Giorgio is a man."

" What are you going to do about it all? "

" *Do, do, do*," said the prince.

" I'd get rid of the Salt Tax straight away," said Constanza, " and I'd try stopping people from having so many *bambini*."

" Yes, that *is* shocking," said Anna. " But one must begin with government. Why does nobody try to learn from us? The United States——"

" Did they bring it off? " said Constanza. " Something went wrong." She looked at her mother with personal reproach. " You had a civil war."

" Yes," said Anna. " Something went wrong."

" And you didn't always do right by the Indians."

" Nobody's done right by *us* for centuries," said the prince; " we're Indians. Sack and invasions, sack and invasions—nothing's gone right with Italy since . . . since, oh well. . . ."

" The Fall of Rome? " suggested his daughter.

" Quite," said the prince.

" The Empire was a most corrupt society," said Anna.

" So unlike the present Court," said Constanza and giggled.

Her father joined her. " *Sono piemontesi.*" It was a family joke of long standing.

" Do leave the Royal Family alone," said Anna.

Bent on teasing her mother, Constanza went on, " Ought you really to interfere with your *illiterati,* mama? and the poor? Isn't that flying in the face of providence? When it's all going to turn out for the best in paradise—the last shall be the first? Do you pay attention to the teachings of our Church, mama? "

" It's in the Bible," snapped Anna, " and it's never been an excuse for twirling your thumbs. Heaven helps those who help themselves."

" But it is *you* helping the illiterate."

" Helping them to help themselves," said Anna.

" Are you really going ahead with the League? " said Constanza.

" League? " said the prince.

" *Contro l'Analfabetismo.*"

" *Misericordia!* And where——"

" —is the money coming from? " said Constanza.

" Mrs Throgmore-Wylie has promised us substantial——"

" Heaven help us *all*," said the prince.

But nothing came of it. Nothing. Nor of the plan for a hospital; even the more modest first-aid station had to be abandoned. Here circumstances had seemed to be playing into Anna's hands. One of the men at Castelfonte had his hip hurt by a falling tree. They sent for the nearest doctor and the prince. Both arrived at night-fall. The hip was found to be badly injured and a kitchen-table operation out of the question. The prince rode fifteen miles to a neighbour who owned a motor car. They got the thing out and there and up the hill, they threw out the back-seats and put in a mattress, and they managed to get the injured man to the hospital by dawn. It was a near thing, but they were in time. After a lengthy convalescence and a complicated treatment at Milan, the man came home without limp or pain. But when Anna said, " Well, now you see," the prince said: " *You* see, if we had built that first-aid place there wouldn't be any money left for this kind of thing."

" Did it cost a great deal then? " she asked.

"A great deal. And that damned thing lost an axle or something after that night. Poor Archimede hasn't been the same again either." Archimede was the prince's horse.

Anna's sister and her husband came to stay; an elderly couple, their children married. In a sense it was a farewell visit; he was retiring from the Diplomatic Service, after a not undistinguished career, leaving friends in many places; they were planning to settle in the American South-West for their old age.

" Already," said Anna. " Oh, Harriet, how time has flown."

" Not for you, Noushka. With your darling baby boy. . . . But it does seem like yesterday when you were a little girl and Jack taught you to skate. . . . Remember the time you came home from Florence and insisted on talking Italian to us all, and only papa was able to answer you back? Now and here you are. I just look at you. . . . *You* ought to have had my job really, you would have been able to help Jack ever so much more than I was able to. If only papa could see you! I wonder what he would say—you a Roman Catholic, and become so very foreign: you're like an Italian woman to me, our little Anna!"

Anna put herself en fête. She arranged dinner-parties— she had become rather slack over these in the last years—and tightened her hold on the happy-go-lucky ways of the house. The house played up; when stimulated they could put up quite a show, and now they did.

Anna's sisters had always been kind to her, more than that. Now it was like having mammina in the house again, only the standards were higher.

She saw to it that they met everybody, saw that her sister —half shame-faced, half excited—had the right kind of audience with the Pope. The prince took them to the Opera, and their box overflowed with people who came to talk and be introduced.

" My, what a handsome couple."

" The Monfalconi," said Anna, " very dear neighbours of ours."

" Isn't she gorgeous? I bet your girl is going to look like her when she's more grown-up, they're the same type of beauty."

Morning after morning and often again at sunset, Anna took her brother-in-law to see the sights of the City. She had done it so often; to her it never palled. He responded, Anna was pleased, she had always got on with Jack. They were standing on the Capitoline.

" Do you know, I was once offered Rome? I took Berlin. Nearer the hub of things, I thought. Look what I have missed!"

Anna said, " It is my home."

" Perhaps I was a fool," he said, " I went after what I

wanted, wanted most. Then. Now is another story. It won't matter a darn in Arizona."

" It was Rico who taught me Rome. Rico never goes and looks at anything, he doesn't have to; one gets Rome by being here."

" That house of yours," he said, " the palazzo, it's got something."

Anna was immensely pleased. She never praised or showed off the house, she could not bear to. She had feared that her relations, used to larger places, to more luxury, impersonal comforts, might not see what she saw.

" That's what I used to admire about you," he said, "*you* always went after what you wanted."

" Did I? " said Anna.

" Oh my good girl! For a clever woman you know precious little about yourself. And when you got it, you didn't look back at the price."

" Price? " said Anna.

He turned to her. " Well, maybe there isn't a price, maybe you got it all free."

Anna, who had rarely an intuition but who had slipped back into more open ways with this companion of her youth, said, " You don't like Rico, is that what you mean? "

" Oh I," he said, " I like Rico very much. I've learnt to like the likes of him." He considered her. " I shouldn't have thought he was the sort of man you would have picked. You are a romantic, Anna, always were; people didn't see it because you were so clever and gay; but that's what you are, my dear."

Anna, still in her open strain, said, " Haven't I made a romantic marriage? " She offered him a smile.

" Oh, if you are thinking of the trappings. . . . It's supposed to take two to make that kind of a marriage. Rico is not a romantic figure."

Her brother-in-law looked straight ahead, down at the Forum. He was far from being a fool and he had lived in Europe for twenty years; he had heard things. Had not Anna? Anna must have changed a good deal if she could take all that in her stride; but then she *had* changed. Jack was very fond of Anna, wrong-headed though she appeared to him, and he did not think much of her entourage: flatterers, all of them. Anna had always drawn these, but he thought he knew Anna better, what she wanted was firmness, firmness from a source she could accept. Poor thing, she will not get it here; ah, and then she is spoilt, so very spoilt. And alone. He thought he saw a duty. " My dear girl," he began, " no woman ever *is* everything to a man." He did not say, any *one* woman.

" Oh, if you are thinking of men like my father," Anna said readily. " No woman would have minded playing second fiddle to a man like him. Not that he didn't worship my mother. But Rico has no ambitions, no ideals. . . ."

" My poor Anna, it isn't only those——"

" It is I," she cut in, " I, if the truth were known, who have given up a great deal for Rico! "

Her tone was fatuous, insulating. He decided to keep his mouth shut. They were still looking at the Forum.

" I could stand here for ever," said Anna.

All he allowed himself to say was, " My dear, romantics are dangerous animals. To themselves, and to others."

It was decided to mark the visit by a family photograph. When it came to the posing, the men balked. " We'll leave it to Giorgio," said the prince, " he'll represent us, he's dressed the part." Giorgio was wearing a lace frock and kid boots. Anna's sister also backed out, so what remained of the group—*remains*, on a gilt-edged rectangle of thick pasteboard above the photographer's florid engraved signature,

is Anna, seated, hands in lap, flawlessly pretty, smiling,
flanked by Constanza brushed and tidied up for the occasion
yet with a look as if butter would not be entirely safe in her
mouth, and Giorgio in his finery, perched on what must have
been a stool concealed behind a papier-mâché column.

In Early June, a few days before they were due to leave,
they went to watch the *Girandola*, the great fireworks in the
Piazza del Popolo. It was splendid and breathless and loud,
and the crowd was in ecstasy.

Anna, exalted, said to her sister, " We ought to have had
a ball for you—if we'd had someone to give it for." In two
years from now, said the prince, they would be giving one for
Constanza. " Oh," said Anna, " you must come back for
that, you must promise to come back."

They promised to come back.

Another great burst of racing crackling light, another soft
fall, another great sigh from the crowd. *Bravo—! Bravo—!*
Constanza and the prince were clapping their hands like
demons. Overcome, Harriet pressed her sister's arm: "What
a lovely, lovely life you have! " Anna turned to her and her
own face, too, was alight.

When at last they had to go, Anna decided to see them on
their way and went with them as far as the Italian Lakes.
She would have liked Rico to come too and do the honours of
his country, but the prince said he had business.

Meanwhile Constanza was lying at Castelfonte in the shade.
Her lazy hand was tracing tangles in the boy's dark hair, as

dark and curly as her own. They were in the mulberry grove; outside the heat was shimmering, here the air was light and flowing like brook water.

The boy raised his head. " Listen."

Constanza did not stir.

" Did you hear foot-steps? " he said.

" Nothing human. It's too hot; they're all asleep."

" Asleep—or doing as we do."

" Doing as we do," said Constanza fondly. " Half the world doing as we do: the others are too old."

The boy laughed. He, like her, had beautifully perfect teeth, delicately shaped, white: animal teeth, effective, workmanlike. " Fools sleep," he said.

" A good hour," Constanza said, " we are awake and they are asleep."

" The night is good too," the boy said, " the night is best."

" More difficult," she said. " The night is fraught with dangers."

He gave her a quick suspicious look. " You promised," he said.

" Yes yes, *caro*," Constanza said, " I'll manage."

" When? "

" Soon."

" Truly? "

" Yes."

" You will give our signal? "

" I'll give the signal."

" Oh, Constanza."

" Now is now," she said.

Presently he said, " Do you love me? "

She moved so that she could look at him. " *Sei bello*," she said.

Exultant, he said: " *E tu!* "

Later he said, " Shall I see you tomorrow? "

" How not."

" And Thursday? "

" Thursday."

" And next week? "

" *Dio volente.*"

" And the week after that? "

" You look too far ahead," said Constanza.

" You don't love me," said the boy.

Constanza touched his cheek with her finger-tip. " Today I love you very much," she said.

" Two months from now I shall be at the *collegio.*"

" *Già.* And tomorrow there may be an earthquake. Two months are a fine piece of time."

" What about the *inglese*? " he said.

" What about him? "

" You like him? "

" I did," said Constanza.

" You don't like him any more? "

" Not that one," she said, half teasing.

He scowled. " I'd like to wring their necks," he said. " You and your *inglesi.*"

" *Inglesi* are not stupidly jealous."

" Why not? " asked the boy.

" It doesn't occur to them so quickly. You think of nothing else."

" Constanza," he said, " *mi amore. . . .*"

" A conditioned reflex."

Again he gave her that suspicious look. It did sound rum in Italian, and to her too.

" Promise you will never make love with an *inglese.*"

" You're mad," she said. " How can I promise such a thing when it's probable that I shall. We know so many."

" You'll be disappointed," he said, relaxing.

" Oh, I don't know," she said, " I'm not at all sure."

They both laughed.

" Oh *tesoro*," he cried, " will you love me next year? "

" Who can tell? " she said.

" If only this summer would last. . . ."

" It's here now," she said; " if you don't spoil it with worrying about the *collegio* and worrying about *inglesi* yesterday and *inglesi* tomorrow."

He said, " If only it would all last for ever! "

" It will not," said Constanza. " And don't think that *my* future isn't too hideous to contemplate. You realize, I shall be seventeen and a half next summer? They'll be bound to notice sometime, and then everything will be different. Not too different," she stopped and kissed him on the mouth, " not *too* different. Mama will be very good about it, and I suppose papa will be quite easy, but it isn't them I am thinking about—it's out of their hands, really. I shall have to be launched in society, it's the only way there is, they can't help it. I don't think mama quite sees how it will be. I am not looking forward to a Roman début; I dread it. I shall have to be an unmarried girl—the dullness, the constriction. I know the kind of life my aunts had before they were married. *I* haven't even been trained for it."

" You are *furba*," he said, " you know your ways and means; you will manage."

" There's always fun to be had," she said; " but I shall not like the part and I shan't do well in it and I must be careful not to cause some stupid scandal that won't do anyone any good. I shall see to it that I'm not going to play the *jeune fille* for long. Ah, but again, one can't marry quite at once—I shall need time to look round. It's a mistake to marry too too quickly, one is bound to make a bad choice. So I'm just in for it. It'll pass. But for the next few years, the future looks far from rosy. A waste."

" You could marry me," he said.

" Madman."

" Who *will* you marry? "

" That's the trouble," she said. " I don't know. I shall
have to find out. I know that I want to travel. I think I
want to get out of Italy. You know, mama has never taken
me anywhere—not that I really wanted to go up to now—it's
one of her ideas. One ought to stay put as a child, she says,
in the same place, make roots, and start travelling all at once
later on. That's the way it was with her. Only, once *she*
started travelling, she never went back. One wonders about
the roots."

" If you married a diplomat, you'd be able to travel," he
said.

" I don't want to marry a diplomat. I don't want that
sort of life, and they are not statesmen. It's all surface stuff
and I daresay other people's secrets. I might like to marry
an explorer, and go with him of course, or perhaps an English
Cabinet Minister, if he'll have me, somebody like Lord
Melbourne. Oh, be quiet, the man's been dead and buried
these sixty years. The more's the pity, I may never find
another like him."

" Why not marry an Italian and have me as your lover? "

Constanza looked fierce and also nearly sad. " I want
more than *that*," she said.

They were both silent. After a minute or so, she said,
" I did not mean you."

" I know," he said.

" Look at my Aunt Carla. . . . Even at Giulia. Though
I rather admire *her*. And then—all those brats."

" Don't you *want* any? "

" There you go," she said. " It's another Italian reflex,
like the jealousy. *Bambini.* No, I don't. I expect I shall have
one—*one*, mind you—it seems more natural. So you won't
be saying, ' *No bambini?* poor woman.' Poor women indeed.
Their lives; and what it makes them be. They feel they
have to have a temper to be interesting. Everybody
here is playing their men; they boast of being capricious,

difficult. Even mama has caught it. Heaven preserve me."

" *You* are not that," he said.

" No," she said tenderly. " I am not that."

" Listen! " he said.

" It's nothing. It's all right—they're taking out the donkeys—they are going away—they're going up the hill—they're all going into the other valley to pick figs. They won't be back till evening."

" We shall have till evening," he said.

" Yes, my sweet," she said, " we shall."

Chapter VI

When disaster came, they were unready and did nothing to divert it. When Anna broke into his room like a creature pursued by furies, the prince had just come in from an interrupted ride. Nobody had warned him that the horse was going lame and he had had to turn home halfway. Earlier that morning the steward from Castelfonte had been to see him with the accounts and a mass of pressing requests. It was a September day and the sirocco was blowing. The prince felt dejected and he was, for him, in an irritable mood.

He said, " Oh Anna, what is it *now*? "

This did not matter as she had not heard him.

The tale burst from her in smouldering fragments. Now she was eloquent, now choked by outrage, pain. Giulia— He—They—For Twenty Years! For twenty years Giulia had been his Mistress. She found it hard to speak the word.

She was standing, ready for a storm to match her own. The prince was seated.

He said wearily, " I thought you knew that by now." And added, " Like everybody else."

" *It is true then?* " she cried. " Don't *tell* me it is true."

But at that moment he was past wishing to restrain her. The whole scene bored and repelled him. If Anna's cry for help, her need for a denial, was plain, he did not hear it.

Suddenly she was near collapse; the prince sprang up, helped her to a chair. Then he went back to his original position.

" The whole of our marriage then——" she tried to say,
" My life——"

The prince not only refused her denial, he refused her
drama. He was getting frightened himself by now and he
took refuge in anger. He said: " Oh, Anna, *be* your age."
It was his second fatal mistake.

§

Of what followed, my childish mind had formed a simple
image. Anna's discovery was the immediate turning-point
in all their lives: the great door of the palazzo slammed, the
principessa with Constanza by the hand stood outside, they
were gone, it was over. It was only many many years later
when we were in France and it had become necessary to go
into it that I was able to shape a picture nearer the reality.
It had neither been as simple nor as quick nor even as
inevitable as I had imagined. Between discovery and flight,
there had been a row of days during which everything hung
in suspense, days of negotiation, entrenchment, influences,
fear and hope, like the days before a war.

The prince was no longer a resilient young man. Mammina was dead. Anna's demanding nature largely ignored
itself. Hindsight is struck by how alone they stood, at that
hour when the demons were upon them, their selves and
what they had become, how bereft they were of help, of any
effective benign or moderating influence, any source of
reason, charity or humour that might have turned into a
healing force.

§

They fell back, as people—and nations—in a crisis do, upon ready-made standards and emotions. Anna, hurt, denied herself any original response, she did not choose or was not able to link her experience with her own immediate reality, her actual self; instead, she dealt with it in the terms of a set past: she judged and felt about the prince's conduct as once it might have been judged and felt about by her New England family. Between her—real—pain and the handed-down reaction, the living experience of half a lifetime lay blacked-out and fallow.

The prince, within his own terms, did the same. He fell back upon a concept of his forebears. Like Anna's, it was one that suited and had shaped his nature. It was a concept of the family tie: the world was hopeless, all strife doomed to failure, the sole aim to get by, to be left in peace, and peace, safety, was only to be found within the family. Anna—after so many frittering attempts—had made a frontal attack against the sacrosanct.

They had their scene. Anna said most things a woman can say in that situation. The prince, though furious, tried to stay aloof. When he spoke it was to relieve himself; he attempted neither to appease nor to explain. Too angry, he refused to appeal to her emotions; even angry, he did not present a case for himself. There were too many things a man did not say to a woman, did not say to his wife, to Anna. For seventeen years he had tried to ignore Anna's prudishness, now it paralyzed him, and whatever he did say was too little and too much.

"A lie," Anna had cried once more. "That was all it was—*one long lie*. Oh, what have I done to deserve *this*!"

The prince did not tell her.

" The laughing-stock of Rome! "

" Not at all. Everybody presumed you knew."

" And condoned your vile deceptions——? "

" Oh deceptions, *cara*? " he said. " Politeness. *Gentilezza.* You, too, were polite. I could have sworn you knew: I can still tell you the day, the hour I knew you knew."

She swept over this. " Your vile life, your vile immoral unspeakable life."

He shrugged.

Her voice rose. " I have spent my life among vipers! Dear mammina—for the first time I am glad that she is dead."

" *Anna,*" he said on a warning note.

" At least *she*'s been spared this day."

The prince said in an icy tone: " My mother was a real woman."

" I want to go home," said Anna.

The prince's anger went flat. He was a compassionate man. " I wish mammina were with us," he said.

" *You* have ruined everything," said Anna.

The prince said, " Who the devil told you? "

" According to you, the roof-tops."

The prince flared: " There isn't a man, or a woman, in Italy who would bear such a tale."

" *Such a tale.* You are all depraved."

" Who was it? "

" A better man than you. A man from my own country."

" *Già,*" said the prince. " One of your aspirants. Tired no doubt of being kept at arm's length. Getting his own back. I should have known this would happen."

" Mr Miller told me because he could no longer bear to see me in my position."

" Have I had the advantage——? " said the prince.

" He used to come to the house a year or two ago, he did Constanza's Latin."

" The Latin tutor. An unmarried man, I presume? "

" He loves me," Anna said, " inconceivable as that may seem to you."

The prince, exasperated again, said, " Why don't you go to bed with him? Why don't you go to bed with one of them? "

" You are *unspeakable*," said Anna.

" The trouble with you," said the prince, " you've never been in love with anyone."

" How dare you speak of love? "

They got nowhere. They were not trying to get anywhere. Neither of them at that hour was looking beyond it. The prince being the cooler might have seen further, might have established some initiative : Anna was shaken enough to be malleable. He did nothing. There was no catharsis. When they had done with each other they parted. Anna did one of the few things women—women without a job in front of them—can do, she went to her room. She went upstairs, locked the door and went to bed. The prince went to the club.

In the afternoon a messenger came for his things and to say that the prince was off on a duck-shooting trip. Constanza was still at Castelfonte with her Aunt Maria. Carla was taking the cure at Montecatini. Thus, Anna was left to herself for forty-eight hours.

When two days later the prince came home, Anna was waiting for him. " I wish to dissolve our marriage." Her tone was composed.

The prince, having meanwhile breathed other air, found this so preposterously unreal that he allowed himself to laugh. Whatever next? he said. Did she think they would give her an annulment? Even she would find that hard.

If Anna's announcement had been a *ballon d'essai*, her

resolution hardened. She had not meant annulment, she said.

Still humouring her the prince asked if she had forgotten that there was no such thing as a divorce in Italy?

She lashed out at him. Divorce? There had never been divorce among *her* people—she had not been thinking of the laws of his immoral country, but of her father and mother turning in their graves. " I have decided," he said, " on a legal separation."

She must be mad, said the prince. *Paziènza*. Again both withdrew.

Later on that day Anna's maid waylaid him. Her mistress was in a very sad mood, she said, a very sad mood. Would he not go to see her?

" Does she want me? " asked the prince. " No—Mena, I can see she does not. She is out of her mind, she is talking of a Legal Separation. Did she tell you? "

" I *wish Eccellenza would come.*"

" What's the use? " he said. " Not until she's more reasonable. She's making us all ridiculous—can't she see? "

" She needs someone to talk to."

" Let her talk to you."

" The Signora Principessa is not enraged with *me*," said Mena.

" All the better," said the prince. " You must try to calm her, Mena *cara*. Tell her to see reason, tell her I'm dining out, tell her what you like."

The prince went out to dinner and Anna saw Mrs Throg-more-Wylie.

Mrs Throg had been in a state of agitation for the last two days. Young Miller, scared out of his wits by Anna's face after his revelation, had rushed to her in distress.

" Oh, Mrs Throgmore-Wylie—something terrible. I told the principessa *everything*."

Now as it happened, Mrs Throg, though all too ready to believe the worst, was one of the few people in Rome who did *not* know everything. A foreign male or an Italian woman would not have been excluded from such general knowledge, it was the combination of being alien, female and herself that had defeated Mrs Throg.

When Miller realized this, his face grew very red. " Oh, my God," he said.

Mrs Throg ruminated. " The Marchesa Monfalconi, did you say? "

There was no turning back. Reluctantly this time, in subdued terms, Miller repeated his performance.

Mrs Throgmore-Wylie's reception of it revived his sense of mission. " You think I did right? " he said. What he had seen was still with him. " I'm not so sure now. I didn't mean to hurt the principessa that much."

" You did absolutely right to tell her," said Mrs Throgmore-Wylie.

Promptly Mrs Throg went on a round of calls to glean more ample information. Possessed now of the pass-words, there was no more difficulty. It was an old, old story, some of her contemporaries remembered how it all began: At Castelfonte. Rico was a boy, Giulia had been married for some years to a man who was rich and himself devoted to the eldest of the Baldovici sisters, who was married to a Neapolitan engaged with an opera singer. Rico did not go wholly without censure. Giulia had a good deal to put up with, Rico was so flagrantly unfaithful, dancers, English women, *contadine*. . . . All the same, the older people said, it had lasted, it was nice to see the way it had done that.

It was a bursting Mrs Throgmore-Wylie who arrived at Anna's. At the end of her visit, Anna's mind reeled. But it had been made quite clear to her that she was the heroine of a tragedy, the victim of moral outrage and one hundred percent in the right.

Leaving, Mrs Throgmore-Wylie stood still on the threshold. " You must punish him," she cried, " Do you hear me? You must punish him! "

The next step was a lawyer. Anna shrank from laying bare her life. Mrs Throg, who came to the palazzo daily, offered to do it for her. The man she chose was an American lawyer who though sympathetic thought it wise to get the opinion of an Italian colleague. After some little delay Mrs Throg brought the gist. Given the circumstances, Anna would be able to get a Legal Separation for the asking. There was, however, one difficult point: the custody of the children.

" Difficult? " said Anna. " He is the guilty party."

Mrs Throg was obliged to explain what had been explained to her. The Italian Court might hesitate to take the boy entirely from the father, particularly if the mother, however innocent, was a foreigner and likely to bring him up in America. " I don't believe it," she added; " I've arranged a consultation with another man tomorrow."

Anna said she could believe it only too well.

" You must fight them," said Mrs Throg.

Anna said she would.

" How is she? " The prince was asking on the staircase. He was leading his habitual life, only more so. " Is she eating? "

" A little," said Mena.

" Good. We must give her time."

" I don't like it," said Mena. " *Things are going on.*"

" What things? "

Mena shut up. " The Signora Principessa trusts me."

" Naturally," said the prince.

" If only *Eccellenza* would try to see her."

" Try—did you say *try*? "

Mena hung her head.

" You mean she wouldn't let me in? "

" I beg *Eccellenza* to try."

" To get into my own wife's room? You are all mad, it's all women's talk. *You* look after her, she'll come round— I know her." And he was off.

Anna decided that as the facts were out now, she might as well see the lawyer herself. He was sent for, came, and was received in Mrs Throgmore-Wylie's presence. He began by complimenting Anna on her beautiful Italian.

" But then you see, I *am* Italian," Anna began graciously and was about to complete what she always offered on these occasions: " Italy is my adopted country," when for the first time she had an intimation of what she was to bring about. It was to her a truly ghastly moment and she wished to cry out to put a stop. She saw Mrs Throgmore-Wylie in her voluminous dark silks and the neat and handsome lawyer carrying on, rapidly. She felt unsteady, there was a swish of noise inside her ears and she was seized by total fear: it was like being in a bolting carriage in a dream—then came a rush of giddy wicked daring. When she regained composure, there was left something like a sense of triumph; it was the heady draught of self-destruction.

She cut in: " Please explain to me exactly the position."

Well, said Signor Giglio, were they to presume that their client wished to leave the country?

Mrs Throgmore nodded.

Taking her children with her?

" It is her right."

This was a cardinal point. Would the father wish to oppose this move?

He would.

" He would," said Anna.

That was what he had presumed. The father would wish to keep the children. So—naturally—would the mother. He said, *la mamma.*

" They belong to her," said Mrs Throg.

In fact both parties wished to keep the children. One could not expect this to be otherwise, one could not expect the father to step back, it would not be natural, not human. There would be a general outcry. They must see that the prince would not be able to hold up his head if he allowed his son to go.

" You are taking the prince's interests to heart," snapped Mrs Throgmore-Wylie.

But Anna, because her manners were better or because she held a higher opinion of the legal profession, apologized. " I know you are bound to tell us where we stand. Please go on."

" If maternal custody is opposed," said Signor Giglio, " as undoubtedly it will be, the ultimate decision lies with the court."

" The prince is guilty."

" There is an allegation, one might call it a strong presumption of adultery. But is it proved? "

Mrs Throgmore wrung her hands.

Proved as it would have to be in a court of law—with all the attendant publicity—if the case were fought?

" He can't deny it."

" Rank perjury," said Mrs Throg.

" Ladies," said Signor Giglio, " we cannot even bring it into court unless we have evidence."

" But his guilt is as plain as night ! "

Signor Giglio said he had no wish to go into detail as to what constituted valid evidence of adultery. They must take it from him that it had to be quite specific within certain rules. The parties involved were popular in Rome, very popular indeed. . . . It might not be at all easy to find a witness to testify against them.

Surely these things could be *arranged*? In this country, said Mrs Throg.

" I was speaking of a creditable witness," said Signor Giglio. Even so, they would be far from having clinched the matter. Adultery was indeed a serious matter, a grave matter, but was it not here a case of adultery of long-standing, established adultery as it were? There was the question of time. The Court might consider the offence already long condoned by the injured wife.

" Tell him about the dancing girls and the farmer's wives," said Anna.

Cases of casual adultery, said Signor Giglio, reprehensible no doubt, but the Court might hold the view that they were not of a gravity sufficient to take away the father's custody of the son, his only son, the heir to his name. "And that is the very heart of the issue: we would have to have conclusive proof of a profligate life, of actual moral depravity, to induce them to deprive this father of this son."

Mrs Throgmore made an exclamation of disgust.

Anna said, " I see."

" We should have to fight very hard, and it would be an ugly fight. It sounds far-fetched, but the defendant may even bring in counter-allegations."

" *Let them try!* " said Mrs Throgmore-Wylie.

" As you are aware, Signora, there is such a thing as

bought evidence," said Signor Giglio who was not as invulnerable as he had had to let himself appear. " Altogether we have a chance to win, but I should not put it too high."

" Then do you wish to see the mother deprived of her children? "

" Most certainly not. It was my duty to point out the elements of this particular situation. It contains an insoluble element, we are faced with a veritable Solomonic tangle."

" And what course can you suggest? "

" The expected one would be for the principessa to forgive her husband and continue life with him for the children's sake."

" You will find her adamant," said Mrs Throgmore-Wylie.

" There is another way," said Signor Giglio. " If the principessa were to give an undertaking to remain in Italy, so as not to bring up the children abroad, it would change the complexion of the matter considerably. If she consented to stay, set up her residence anywhere she chose within the Kingdom, and allowed some arrangement for access to the children by the prince, there could in my opinion be few difficulties."

" Would the prince have access to *her*? "

" Not at all. The principessa would be entirely free of any former obligations."

" Ah," said Mrs Throgmore-Wylie. " And you might live in Florence, dearest."

" Signor Giglio," Anna said in a clear voice. " Do I understand you to say that the main difficulty arises from what is regarded as my son's position in his father's family? " He inclined his head. " Very well then, I have decided. I shall leave the custody of the boy to the prince. I reserve access, of course, the boy can come to me from time to time. I shall

not remain in Italy. My daughter and I will live abroad.
I shall keep her custody; naturally."

" Naturally."

" And I shall not grant access to her father. I consider his
influence noxious in the highest degree to a girl her age. Will
this meet your difficulty, Signore? "

" Admirably." Signor Giglio all but applauded. " A
most ingenious, a most lawyer-like solution and, if I may
say so, a most generous one."

" Much *too* generous," said Mrs Throgmore. " She is an
angel upon earth."

" With the true heart of a mother. Principessa—I stand
here as your legal advisor, and in that role I must ask you to
re-consider carefully the sacrifice you are about to make;
but as a man of feeling, a lover of human nature, on behalf
of one of our Roman families, on behalf of Italy—I must also
thank you."

Anna smiled. " I think this will be all for today," she
said and began to rise.

Mrs Throgmore-Wylie bustled to offer her arm.

" Thank you. I require no assistance," said Anna.

§

When Carla was back in Rome, she found a pretty kettle of
fish and told her brother so. After she had been to Anna's,
she changed her tone. " My God, I had no idea things had
gone so far. You must do something, Rico. At once."

" What can I do? " said the prince. " It's she who got us
into this absurd mess. Let her get out of it."

To Carla, Anna had behaved as if she were a visitor
from a distant past. She refused to discuss matters; all

she said was, " I have made up my mind. I can see my way."

Carla was not without boldness. She was able to say with warmth, " Anna, look at me—have *you* never been tempted to take a lover? "

Anna pursed her lips and stared at her with distaste.

" Then believe me, it is you who are not like the rest of us—can't you see it as what it is? Our mother *loved* our father and she did." She tried her last shot. " Anna, I . . . I have had lovers."

" *You, too.*"

The next day the prince received a letter from the lawyers. It set forth what was being done in no uncertain terms. It ended by informing him that the ladies would be leaving the country at an early date, as soon in fact as certain preparations had been made; until then the prince should leave the common roof and was requested to do so at once. He was thunderstruck.

He ran upstairs. Outside Anna's door, a woman he had not seen before sat knitting. The door itself was locked from the inside. After a few moments the key turned and Mena came out to him; she was weeping. Behind her stood Mrs Throgmore-Wylie.

" Good morning," said the prince.

Mrs Throgmore-Wylie looked through him.

Mena wept more loudly.

" What is it? " said the prince.

" I cannot say it."

" Will you not give your mistress's message? " said Mrs Throgmore-Wylie.

" Please, Mena," said the prince.

" It should not be spoken."

He stood, waiting to hear.

Mena said very low: " ' Tell the prince I will never see him again as long as I live.' "

Carla turned over the lawyers' letter. " It cannot mean what it says. *We* must have legal advice." The prince said it was too dangerous; once you let the lawyers in, it was out of your hands, you found yourself doing things you had never meant to do. He went off to the club to ask friends.

The first man he ran into was Monfalconi. Monfalconi gave him a slap on the back and said, " *Coraggio*." The prince gave him a wan but grateful smile. In the billiard-room he found one of his brothers-in-law, Carla's husband, who blustered a bit at first. Couldn't Rico manage her? Never could, said the prince. Then the brother-in-law, also, spoke of legal advice.

Together they went off to see their family man, who was called Rossi. He sent out across the street for three little cups of coffee, and they settled down to talk. Much of it Rossi knew already by the grape-vine; the prince had the other lawyers' letter on him and laid it on the table. Rossi pulled a very long face. They lit cigars and they thrashed it out in one way and another but it all boiled down again to the same thing at the end: the prince did not have a leg to stand on. It was all too well sewn up. There must have been a master-mind behind it, Rossi said. Ah, if she had claimed the boy, if she had not turned herself into Niobe by that gesture, it would be a very different story. As it stood there was not much the prince could do, nothing to stop her from carrying out exactly her intentions; unless, that was, he succeeded in persuading her to stay——

He'd be damned, said Rico.

" Now, now," said his brother-in-law.

" She can do as she pleases—she can stay or she can go, or she can go and come back——"

" He's upset, poor fellow," the brother-in-law said to Rossi.

Rossi said, in a long practice he had yet to see a wife who actually left her husband. It was all the other way. " You don't want to push her? You do want to get your wife back? "

The prince said, " *Gran Dio*, she's impossible! But I'm fond of her."

As for the girl, Rossi said, that was quite plain: if the mother went, the girl went with her, the girl belonged to the mother.

" What does no access mean? That he cannot have her on a visit? " asked the brother-in-law.

" It means more than that, it means that the prince will not be able to see her at all. But well, how old is the girl? She'll be of age in a few years. Now, as to the financial questions——"

To hell with them, said the prince.

" That's all very well," said Rossi, " but I'm here to protect your interests. I've got to know how matters stand."

" You ought to know. Your father was in on the whole thing."

" And well do I remember him telling us how stubborn you had been. Your wife brought you a fortune—yes, yes, it was quite a fortune—but there was no settlement. It was all left in her name."

" She's welcome to it. To what's left of it," said Rico.

" They've had her income," said the brother-in-law. " What she gets from America. It comes every year. How can he do without that? "

" We'll survive," said Rico.

" She must be asked to contribute to the boy's education," said Rossi. " She must be aware that you cannot pay for that and keep up the house in Rome."

" We can carry on at Castelfonte."

" Don't be stubborn again. You remember how you fretted when your father died and you saw how things were and felt afraid you wouldn't be able to keep the palazzo open for your mother and the girls? "

" Rossi," said the brother-in-law, " we don't want to lose Constanza."

" Is that it? I'm afraid you may have to, unless you manage to persuade the mother to change her mind and stay. Or hide the girl. . . ."

When they stood in the street, the brother-in-law said, " Where do you want to go, Rico? "

" I don't know," said the prince.

" Don't worry too much. We'll think of something."

They started walking. When they were crossing the Piazza Navona, the prince stood still. " When we had that first trouble with Anna, Maria saw three white peacocks. It must have been round here. I haven't thought of them since. Now I wish I had paid more attention to them then."

" And what would you have done? "

" Quite," said the prince. " You are right."

" Warnings that come too early are of precious little use," said the brother-in-law.

They had Rossi try to call on Anna. He was not admitted and told to get in touch with Signor Giglio instead. When it was Carla's husband's turn, he learned that Anna was no longer at home to any member of the prince's family.

" You could kick down that door," said Carla who had come with him that far. Her husband pulled her away.

A priest offered to remind Anna of her obvious duty. He

was received and she rather touched his heart. She told him, he revealed, that she was leaving for the good of the prince's soul, she was doing it for his sake, not her own. As for that, she was renouncing all further happiness in this life. " I believe her, poor woman. I had to tell her that she is taking a great deal on herself. Her ears are closed. She would not accept that such things are not for her to decide. Whatever may be sinful in her conduct, she is atoning for it by great suffering."

" What is it, Socrate? "

" A signature."

" You seem to know all about it? "

" How can I help it, *Eccellenza*? "

The prince signed receipt, broke the seal and read. " It's only about my leaving the house—the common roof. It went out of my head."

" There can be no question of it," said Carla. " Your own house."

" Well, have you packed, Socrate? "

" Certainly not, *Eccellenza*."

" All right. I shall stay where I am. There's no sense in moving. I haven't set eyes on her for ten days—the house is large enough for the two of us."

When Mrs Throgmore-Wylie heard about this, she said to her circle, " Those people are all cads."

That evening Mena asked to have a word.

" She has sent for the principina."

" It has come," said the prince.

" I am delaying the message for as long as I dare."

" *Grazie.* "

" I am doing it to save her from herself," said Mena.

By night Maria's husband had a plan. The two brothers-in-law with Carla stayed late to settle it. It had at least the virtue of simplicity. Maria's husband had a *terra*, a bit of land in the Basilicata. Anna had never heard of it, the land had come to him only recently at the end of a law-suit. There was a house of sorts; it was a remote place in a region itself remote from the sight-seer's Italy; the country people were loyal. If Constanza were to go there and lie low, it would take weeks, months more likely, for her to be found.

" Years," said Carla's husband. " Anna would want to go about it quietly."

" A fine figure she'd cut, scouring the countryside for her own child."

The prince kept his hand in his pocket and said nothing. Meanwhile . . . well meanwhile time was gained. Time worked wonders. While there was time there was hope.

They became quite happy working out the details. Socrate was to go to Castelfonte by the early train and prepare the ladies. Maria's husband was to set out South and prepare the ground. Maria was to accompany her niece. They discussed the route. Carla wanted to avoid their passing through Rome, or at least have Constanza veiled. The prince talked of borrowing once more his neighbour's motor car, but was told it would never get beyond Potenza. They envisaged a boat steaming down the East Coast to Taranto. Carla said, Maria would sooner die. They settled for the railway followed by a team of mules. At midnight they parted. *Auguri*, they said to one another. *Auguri.* . . .

Carla's husband stopped by at Rossi's house. They had promised to do nothing without his consent. Rossi killed it flat. People might laugh but the authorities would assist the principessa, and the prince would have put himself irretrievably in the wrong.

So Carla's husband had to go back and ring the bell at the palazzo to say it was all off. The prince if anything seemed relieved.

When they met again the next morning it was with a sense of urgency. They knew that Anna's message had gone through to Castelfonte; they had seen trunks going down the stairs. At noon Rossi joined them.

He looked young and strong and well-slept, and he was freshly shaved. He might have something, he said, he had not been idle. He did not know how much it might amount to. Did Cortina d'Ampezzo mean anything to them?

They looked blank.

" I have an Austrian waiter who will swear that three years ago the principessa spent a night at an hotel there with a man."

" It can't be possible," said Carla.

" *Per Bacco!* " said her husband.

" It *is* not possible," said the prince.

Rossi continued. " The man is neither more nor less trustworthy than you would expect. But he gave me an extract from the hotel register with the principessa's name and the man's name. He described her and when I showed him some photographs he picked out hers without hesitation."

" She would hardly have put her own name," said Carla.

" Her name and address, and the date; the destination given was Vienna."

" Vienna? " said the prince. " Three years ago? But that was the time she had that fright and came home. Mena never said they stopped over at Cortina, though I daresay they did. It must all be a mistake," he shook his head. " Mena was with her all that time, there's nothing in it."

" Could we have Mena? "

Mena came, directed her words only to the prince, and swore there was nothing in it. They *had* stayed at Cortina, the gentleman *had* been there, but there was nothing in it, nothing at all. " Could you tell us what *did* happen? " Rossi said.

Mena looked at the floor.

Rossi knew better than to insist. He only asked if she could swear to what she had told them in a court of law.

Mena said she could swear. Then she said scornfully, " *Eccellenza*: there was a commotion in the corridor—the Signora Principessa had to ring for help—many people heard! "

When she was gone, Rossi said, " I saw that you believed her."

Of course, they said, they believed her. They knew her and they knew Anna.

" Oh, knowing Anna . . ." said Carla.

" I told you it was no use," said the prince.

" The appearances are very damaging," said Rossi, " not to say scandalous. It could be put to use."

" Not so long ago a wife would have been locked up in a convent for a good deal less," said Carla. " Of course we can use it."

" This business won't help her," said Maria's husband, " once it gets out."

" Anna is a strange creature," said the prince.

" Does that waiter want money? "

" Let's give him some to shut up again," said the prince. " Getting herself mixed up in hotel corridors with that nincompoop. . . . Poor woman—she's no idea what appearances are. Of course we can't use it. *E che figura fa?* She's made me look silly enough as it is, we've got to think of Giulia."

There were protests, but Rossi finally backed up the prince. Given the maid's testimony, it was risky, he said; better not touch it when all was said and done, it might boomerang.

Very well, what then?

" You will stay for *colazione*, Rossi? " said the prince.

It was a wretched luncheon. They were mostly weeping in the kitchen and the *pasta* was badly drained and stuck together, and the fish was poorly chosen. It was only after Socrate had told them of the face they were losing before the *avvocato* that they pulled themselves together and sent out for fresh salad greens and decent fruit. There was very little talk at table. At one point they all heard a great bumping noise outside.

" Another trunk," said Socrate.

Rossi, who was normally a cheerful man and used to better things, felt depressed.

It was only when at last they left the dining-room that he felt buoyant enough again to take an initiative.

" The principina is expected tonight? "

They all turned to him. " She is."

" And her mother has the railway tickets."

" We were told so."

" They say that your daughter is a girl with a will of her own? Now tell me, if she were told the whole truth, if she were told that her mother was leaving her father for good and was taking her away to a foreign country where she would not see her father or her home again for many years, what would she do? "

" She'd say we'd all gone out of our minds."

" Would she refuse to go? "

" *Could* she refuse to go? "

" She could make it very awkward for her mother. She

might make it impossible. And if the daughter will not go, the mother *cannot* go—imagine it, leaving both her children and after that Cortina story. It's in the girl's hands. All she has to do is to tell her own mind to her mother and put her foot down, quite literally put her foot down. If they have to *drag* her to the carriage, into the station, on to the train, they won't."

" It sounds like those suffragettes."

" It will require a great deal of resolution from a girl her age. But it need hardly come to that. One moment of initial firmness may turn the tide: Telling the mother that she will not go. Do you think she is capable of doing this? "

" Yes! " they said.

" Would she choose to do it? "

" She might," said the prince. " It depends on how she sees it. Yes—she would choose not to go."

" *Già*," said the others.

" It is not something I would like to have to tell my own daughter, but there it is. If you want to keep either of them, this is your only chance."

Rossi allowed it to sink in.

" And once the principessa has been faced with this defeat," he went on, " we follow it up with a peace offensive. First you do exactly what she is asking you to do, you move out of the house, then you send an offer of reconciliation, promise anything, ask for her conditions, say you're ready to turn over a new leaf—say yes to anything she may propose."

" Rossi's right," said Carla's husband.

" Match her against Constanza. It's brilliant. Checkmate to Anna."

" We use her own pawn."

The prince said, " Constanza is very much attached to her mother."

" If *you* were asking her to stay, would there be much doubt as to her choice? "

" None," said Carla.

" You needn't even do that, Rico," said her husband. " All you have to do is make it clear to her that by not going she will keep the family together."

" Remember: it is your one chance."

Carla said, " Rico, *I* could talk to her."

" Or I," said Rossi, " if you prefer that. It is quite true: it's simply a matter of keeping the family together."

The prince said he would think it over. To their consternation he got up and left them. They were unused to any of them wishing to be by himself.

The prince's answer was no. Just no. You could not do this thing to the *bambina*, you could not mix her up in it, you could not put it on her. Imagine putting her before this choice, in this position against her own mother. She was too young. And too old to be handled like a child. Whatever the *bambina* might do now, how would she feel about it in a few years' time? No. Simply no.

There was an uproar. They implored him. But the prince would not be budged.

One more thing, he said, he might as well move out. He had been told that Anna was made frantic by his presence, she was as unreasonable as a shying horse. He might as well go with them now, Socrate would send on a few things.

Poor Rossi cried, " That was the move that was to have been saved for after the defeat! "

" There's enough defeat," said the prince. Together, in a straggle, they left the palazzo.

§

The rest was swift.

Constanza arrived that evening. When she entered the main drawing-room she found her father there. " *Papa!* They told me you were gone. They told me you had left the house."

" And here I am, *figlia*," he said comfortably. " You mustn't believe all you hear." He was lying. He had let himself in by the back-door not five minutes ago.

" I've heard plenty. Darling papa—now that I see you're not gone, it can't be half as bad? What's up? "

He laughed at her. " Everything, *tesoro*. Your mother is furious with me. Let her tell you about it. She is going on a journey to change her ideas, and she is going to take you with her."

" I know," said Constanza. " Like the time she went round the world. Will it be a long journey? "

" We don't know," said the prince lightly. " You know the way she talks. You must calm her and see that you're all back soon."

Constanza said, " I've just been with her. I don't like it."

" What did she say? "

" If I loved her not to ask her any questions now—we are going away tomorrow—she would explain as much as she could later on."

" She is very very upset."

" I am upset, too," said Constanza. " Papa, where are we going? Are we going to America? "

" Your mother has taken tickets as far as London."

" Hmmm. Papa—she said something else, she said she needed me."

" Be good to her," said the prince. " Go with her, and talk to her. Don't stay away too long—or I'll come to fetch you. Meanwhile enjoy yourself, it's your first real journey."

" Giorgio is not going? " she said.

" He's not going."

" He's too little to be of use to mama."

" Much too little," said the prince.

" Papa, I love you."

" Don't cry," he said.

" But papa, we always cry before journeys, we always cry when mama leaves."

" This time is different," said the prince.

" We don't cry."

" We don't cry."

" Good."

" *Ciao, figlia*—mind you enjoy yourself—and if you need anything let me know." He was gone.

The coachman, as had always been their custom, made the detour before heading for the station. Before Anna realized it, they had stopped in the Piazza Trevi. Mena and Constanza leapt down to fling into the fountain their bits of money, the tribute that is said to grant the traveller's return. Anna did not move.

" Mama, you must."

" Signora Principessa! "

" Can we not drive on? " said Anna.

Quickly the two took matters into their own hands. It could be done, they knew, for those who were unable. Constanza had a piece of gold; this, together, they gave up to the waters, thinking Anna's name. Their unspoken incantations mingled; but Anna's face was turned away.

PART TWO

In Another Country

Chapter I

They arrived at Victoria Station the next day, late in the afternoon. In the streets the gas-lights were on and it was drizzling.

" Look," Constanza said, " look—all the tall hats. Oh, it *is* like Sherlock Holmes. And so many people have rain-coats, how convenient for them, and walking so fast, where can they all be going? And look, do look! " This time it was a hansom cab.

Mena, who had seen it many times before, nodded smugly.

" And here is the King's Palazzo."

Constanza craned. " The guardsmen—so it is true. And is that Hyde Park? "

Mena exhibited superior knowledge.

Anna, silent in the back of the closed carriage ordered for her by Brown's Hotel, emanated aloof benevolence. She was capable of her own disciplines, and with her the claims of servants and the young stood very high. They felt free to chatter.

" You will find things here quite nicely done," Mena said. " Once you get used to the food. And the wine is exquisite."

" No vines have been grown in the British Isles for three hundred years," Constanza said, fresh with her school-room knowledge.

" *Proprio squisito*," said Mena.

At the hotel Anna retired at once into a suite. In her room, Constanza found a live fire burning in the grate.

" And what did I tell you? " Mena said, " carpets everywhere."

Immediately they wheeled in an exotic and delicious tea. Constanza tried the Gentleman's Relish and all the jams and devoured half a dozen thin brown bread-and-butter sandwiches and four scones. Next came a knock followed by a mass of flowers. One of the baskets bore the card of the management. " It must be the charming man in the frock-coat who saw us upstairs," said Constanza. " How sweet of him." She examined the other flowers. From the Italian Ambassador. " How extraordinary."

" We always have flowers on arrival," said Mena.

" How do they know? "

" It is like that when you travel with the Signora Principessa."

Later on they both set out for a stroll in Piccadilly.

Constanza slept, and she slept late. She had hardly been confronted by more tea, when a message came saying she was wanted on the telephone. Much intrigued (of course they did not have a telephone at home), she complied.

" Dear Constanza, what splendid news! "

It was one of her tutors, now a fellow of his college.

" You must come down to see us, I am arranging a luncheon. Everybody wants to see you."

Constanza said she would love to be shown it all.

" Let's settle it now, shall we, before you're all booked up. Good. Have I beaten Balliol? "

A few minutes later there was another summons.

" Connie! "

" Kit! "

He was a boy whose parents had been *en poste* some years

ago. He and Constanza had ridden together in the Campagna and he used to be one of her staunchest A.D.C.'s in the rout of governesses.

" What fun you've come at last. It's a rotten time of year, though, we're just down from Scotland. Tell you what—we can go racing. What about this afternoon? Tomorrow? "

" How on earth did you know? "

" I heard father getting up a do for your mama—and he wants to fix it up for you to go to the House of Commons. How long are you going to stay? "

" I don't know myself. We had rather a rumpus."

" Does it mean a long visit? Will you be here for Christmas? "

" We may."

" Oh, *good*. We'll get some hunting. You will hunt, won't you? "

" And how not? " said Constanza.

All morning people came leaving cards on her mother and messages for her. At noon a string of girls appeared, playmates from the Borghese Gardens, to bear her off to a parent's house for luncheon. But Constanza was already engaged with Mr James, another apparition from her school-days and her favourite; he had come to call on the principessa, who was at home to no-one, and had stayed. He took her out and gave her oysters; she tasted her first glass of stout, and he teased her about what he called her pragmatic view of metaphysics. Mr James was a bachelor, fairly elderly, who came originally from Massachusetts and had elected to make London his home. She asked him what it was like to know H. G. Wells and Arnold Bennett in the flesh. He told her about his namesake—Henry—abysmally underrated to his mind, and about some young ones, Forster, one or two Irish chaps and a magic girl, Virginia Stephen.

Of the stout, she said, " Not half bad, after you get used to it. But *can* it be Mena's exquisite wine? "

Mr James was delighted. So the wine had been a success? he said. He must tell her the whole story some day, it was wonderfully typical of her mama.

Just as Constanza was trying to make up her mind whether she should talk to him about it, Mr James approached the subject.

" And now tell me what you're up to? "

" I? "

" What are you doing here all of a sudden? You know your mother's ideas, she's often told me how she planned to take you to London for the season when you are nineteen. Now here you are, sixteen, if memory serves, and the date is the third of October."

To her own surprise, Constanza's answer was evasive.

" You aren't under any cloud? "

" I? "

" You haven't by any chance decided that you want to go to school? "

" Good heavens," said Constanza. " Isn't it much too late for that? "

" That is what I should have thought," he said. " Though I'm told the schools are full of girls of sixteen. You know you could get into Oxford tomorrow and standing on your head."

" Mr James! "

" Cambridge, if you prefer."

" A *woman's* college? "

" Dear child, it might do them a world of good. But you haven't told me yet *what* you are doing? "

Constanza felt sure now that it was not possible to talk until she had heard her mother. " Oh, I think mama just thought she might get lonely here without me."

Mr James did not appear to find this plausible, but he forbore to probe. They parted on his promising to take Constanza to meet writers.

" Which ones? " she said, " the old ones, or your new? "
" Which do you want to see the most? "
" Oh, the real ones."
" They will be the most easy," he said.

That afternoon Anna braced herself for talking to her
daughter. Unable herself to cope well with suspense, she
felt she must not leave the girl in it much longer. The task
was not made easier by her not knowing what she had to say.
She had planned thus far, but no further. She had got away,
had made an end, arrived. Now it was the end: there was
nothing. She had not felt such desolation, had not been so
unhappy in all her life, not when she was in the grip of that
queer panic before Giorgio's birth, not when Rico's first
perfidy had been discovered; not when her father died. She
did not know why she had come to England. The familiar
comforts of London to her were stale, unbearable. She had
got through twenty-four hours by saying No. No to callers,
invitations, No to friends. Her own attitudes, her views of
the situation, which were to be so very determined in the
future, had not yet crystallized. Some of them took an
early shape in the course of her talk with Constanza, the
first of many.

Constanza had hardly seen her mother in broad daylight,
unhatted or alone since the time she had been snatched away
from Castelfonte. Now she found her neither aged nor ill,
only rigid; so very rigid. It struck into Constanza's heart.

" Does *Eccellenza* require me? "

" Oh Mena. Perhaps you had better go, Mena," Anna
said gently.

Constanza was still unused to the trammelling effects of
embarrassment. She came forward with a movement of
affection. " Mama, *cara*, you look quite miserable. And now
you must tell me all about it! "

Anna was surprised, then faintly pleased. " My darling child," she began. " You are all I have now." Then she told her: " I have left your father." She told about the Legal Separation; about the finality of everything.

" But why, mama? For God's sake, why? "

" That is the hardest part," Anna said solemnly. " I have thought and thought.... I have come to the conclusion that I should not tell you. You have always known me to respect the truth? "

Constanza thought she had.

" Well then, you must believe me now that there is the gravest reason. Your father has done something very, very dreadful——"

" Something I don't know? "

" Something you had far better not know," said her mother. " Your father has acted like a villain, a faithless man. I shall not speak of it."

Something so dreadful, asked Constanza, that they could not go back?

" Yes."

" I can't think of anything dreadful enough for that. Papa hasn't murdered anyone? "

" My dearest child."

" If he had, we should have to help him and it would be he who would have to flee the country. No, mama—I cannot understand it."

" I am not asking you to understand; I am asking you to believe."

At length Constanza said, " And I? I am not to see papa? "

It was best so, Anna said. At least for some time. " And it is my wish." She did not reveal that she had legal sanction to enforce it. She began to cry.

" I do see that it's all very dreadful." Constanza suspended her own feelings; she needed time. She quickly told herself

that there was a way out of everything—if it came to the
worst one could always run away. She said, " My poor
mama." Anna responded.

" But are you sure you've got it all quite straight? Two
heads are better than one. Why don't you tell me about it?
I'm used to knowing things."

Anna said, " I don't want you to know this about your
own father."

Presently Constanza said, " But what will we do? What
is going to happen to us? I suppose we shall be going to
America."

Anna, who had not yet turned this over in her mind, said
instantly, " We are *not* going to America. I shall never go
back to my native country. Return *now*? Inflict this shame
on my family? You do not realize our new position—everything will be different. We are no longer. . . ."

" No longer what? "

" What we were. We are——"

" Outcasts? Mama, will you be a divorcée? "

" Certainly not."

Constanza tried, " *Déclassées?* "

" Alone," Anna said. " Two ladies alone."

" As long as we are not maiden ladies," said Constanza.

" Mother and daughter," Anna said, " mother and
daughter," she repeated as if she liked the sound of it,
" in exile."

Gradually she became calmer. They might as well live
in England, she said. It did not matter *where* they
went.

" We *could* go to Brazil," said Constanza.

They—that was she—would live very quietly. For herself, life was over.

" Oh, no," said Constanza earnestly.

" And for you, my poor child, it will be different from
what it might have been; you have your father to blame for

that. This utter change, this break—it is very hard on you, and I shall do my best to make it up in any other way I can. When I was young I was very happy in London." She changed to a note of cheerfulness. " Now what do you think you will be doing with yourself? "

" I think I've finished with education, don't you? " said Constanza quickly.

" Well, one's never quite that," said her mother. " You mean no more lessons? "

" What's the point? If I'm not going on with it . . . I'm not going to have a career? "

" Not unless you very much want to."

" I don't think so," said Constanza. " I can't see it. People are supposed to regret it later on, but I've never met anybody who had one, I mean a woman."

" Miss Hill."

" I don't count governesses."

Anna made the automatic rebuke.

" Yes of course, mama. I only meant it doesn't apply to me."

Anna winced. " One doesn't have to put such things into words," she said. " At any rate our circumstances *have* altered. Perhaps I ought to warn you that we shall be a good deal poorer."

Constanza said, " Too poor for me to marry? "

" Darling. I only mean we shall not be able to live in quite the way we used to. Which reminds me, you ought to carry some money." Constanza never had; clothes were sent to the house, she was known everywhere, besides she was no shopper; when she did want some cash she turned to the nearest parent who would dish out a handful. " And you had better have some charge accounts," Anna said, " at Harrod's and one or two places I will tell you about, it's quite easy."

" All right, mama."

" Very well then, no more lessons. You know that
Jonathan is at the National Gallery now? "

" Benvenuto di Gentile," said Constanza. " Good for
him."

" And dear William is at the British Museum."

" Which he is going to show me, no doubt."

" It might be as well for you to cultivate some interests,"
said Anna. " As things are, you may not have the same round
as other girls your age. It will mean more leisure for you,
more freedom, and of course more responsibility. People
over here, as you will find, have rather large ideas about
many things and are quite strict about others. I'm sure
that you will always know what to do. I should like to see
you develop a certain independence. You will know when
you can go out alone and when you might take Mena or
another girl. I do not believe in chaperones. I find the
system degrading. I am sure you can rely on your own
judgement and good sense. And when you are not certain
ask me."

" Is it all right for me to go to restaurants with Mr
James? "

" Quite all right. And now you must think of what you
want to do with your time."

Constanza said: " I'd like to hear a debate in the House
and go to Oxford next Saturday to Monday and I want to
meet some interesting people and I want to hunt." She left
out the race-meeting.

" Blood sports," said Anna. " But very well, darling,
hunt if you want to, I know you'll be good at it. It sounds a
nice programme. Do anything you like, my angel, only keep
up your reading."

When Constanza was gone her mother was left with the
conviction that she still had something to offer to the
world.

Constanza, for her part, was left with a good deal to think about.

This utter change, this break—Anna had called it. It was all of that. Yet in Constanza's case there were some factors which modified its nature. The first of these was a misconception, puerile enough at first, but the effect upon herself she was never quite able to shake off in later life; it was a misconception about her father's guilt, the dreadful thing he had done that was too dreadful for her mother to divulge. Now Constanza was nothing if not a girl of quick intelligence and one who was in many ways forward for her years; she knew life as it went in a Roman slum and on an Italian farm and life as it was seen in a Roman drawing-room, and life in books, but there were gaps in her experience, vast gaps. She lacked some raw materials and so she had to attack some human problems with the logic of a child.

Giulia and her father, and the tales of her father's attachments to attractive women, were within Constanza's range, they even added to the bond, made an under-current to the affectionate pride the prince and his daughter took in one another; she could not remember a time when she had not known, and hardly one when she had thought about it twice or thought about it in terms of her mother's place within the pattern; this was part of that unexplored half-knowledge children, even uninhibited and lucid children, keep aloof from when it is about their parents, part of the tacit accepted half-knowledge shared in such circumstances by the persons most concerned; it was more than that, it was in the air, it was part of the general half-knowledge, half-acknowledgement, of society, part of the great Italian split between sensuality and the Church, between doing one thing and believing in another, of saying yes to two views of life. That her mother could have kept herself wholly outside that circuit, appeared to Constanza, now tackling it at last, incredible. That her mother was an outsider, was in a measure ' different ', she was well aware; the true extent of Anna's frigid distastes, of Anna's complex edifice of self-delusion, Anna's insatiable demand on life at an idealistic peak, was as yet beyond Constanza's faculties.

The talk that had buzzed round her during the last hours before leaving Rome, she had taken to be roughly the truth; now she became convinced that it had been far from it. She could see her mother outraged, wounded, difficult, kicking up an unholy fuss; she could not see her mother—a just woman and attached to the train of things—smash up their lives because she had found out about an old infidelity. Such action, for such reason, appeared to Constanza, at that age, as entirely improbable. The very dreadful thing, then, that had driven them from home must be some crime. A hidden crime, she hoped for her father's sake. And kept hidden with the help of mama. One thing she had said gave the clue: " Perhaps I ought to warn you that we shall be a good deal poorer." It was money. Papa had taken money. Mama's of course—who else's?—and she was covering it up. He must have changed something on a paper or given a false signature, perhaps to pay a card debt, but no, wives had to pay these openly, and papa never gambled much; perhaps he had taken it, this large sum, this capital (for Constanza it was already that) to be on the safe side or to put something by for Giorgio later on, perhaps he had bought some land or given it to a woman. Fraud. And this explained it all. People could be carted off to a filthy prison for picking up a five-lira piece, and in America if you were in business and did that kind of thing, you were finished—Constanza was able to see that to her mother it was a shattering blow. She had helped her husband; she could not forgive him. Constanza herself had been inclined to hold that tampering with money was outside the pale, now she saw how wrong one was to think in abstract terms. Papa must have had his reason, must have wanted the money—there is but one life to live—and mama, as became daily clearer, did not miss it or at least needed it a great deal less. Constanza was very, very sad for him to have been found out. Yet if she did not judge her father, she did not judge her mother either, for her unforgivingness nor her flight, it was the way she was made, *paziènza*. Constanza was grateful to her for not having exposed her father, rather admired her courage, and for her, too, she felt sad.

As to herself, Constanza resolved that she also had better keep her mouth shut, and for the rest to bide her time.

She sat down to write her father some explicit reassurance but, once before the paper, found that this was not within her powers, then that it was not necessary. So what she sent was a brief loving message.

Soon it was November. There were fogs, the days were short, the light was always grey. December came, blustering, misty, wet. Constanza hardly noticed it. Climate was nothing to her; she had soaked up enough Italian sunshine to last her through some years. Constanza hunted. She had not before experienced anything equal to that strenuousness, that abandon of limb and blood and mind, and it seized hold of her. Part of the time she was talking her head off to a score of new acquaintances, but her main absorption, her passion, during all of that first winter was the hunting. She went from country house to country house, asked by her contemporaries, mounted, cosseted and admired by their parents and their parent's friends, a mascot in the library and field. Her hybrid status proved an advantage rather than a hindrance. Her beauty was still slightly epicene and so she could be treated by who wished as one of the youngsters, a precocious child; others took her for older than she was and stuck to the notion that she had been out in Rome. In any case she was a foreigner, a guest and the daughter of a highly valued mother with eccentric views, a fugitive now from some mysterious tragedy.

Anna, acquiescent, told Constanza that she could not go on sharing other people's maids. " And if you insist on continuing with this activity you ought to have at least one hunter of your own."

" I'd love one, mama. But can we afford it? " She was asking out of curiosity rather than concern.

" I've written to Jack." The principessa's brother-in-law was one of her trustees. " We're trying to make some changes. I may have to go into capital."

" Should you? "

" There are many demands on my income," Anna said, looking uncomfortable.

" Yes, of course."

" But do get that horse. Get a decent one. The horse is a drop in the bucket. Where are you off to this week? "

Constanza told her. " It's in Gloucestershire."

" I know them well."

" Mama, darling, why don't you come? "

" The skeleton at the feast."

" Nonsense."

" I don't consider it fitting."

" It wasn't *your* fault."

" No, my love. But the situation of a woman in my position is a delicate one."

" Why? "

" You know very little yet about the world."

" Mama, you are not intending to spend the rest of your days at Brown's? "

" I am not *quite* alone. I have my visitors. One or two faithful friends from the past."

Years later, Constanza used to say: " Of course it was

fantastic. I don't know what got into her head. It was all above mine; and alas I was too busy then to sort it out. I believed her. I didn't help her much. Not enough. Perhaps it comforted her to add social eclipse to her other woes. But there was nothing in it—she could see whom she wanted —and in her own fashion she did—the only ones she did not see were the people she kept deliberately away. She had a notion that she was no longer *persona grata* with the older women, so she asked men only to her *conversazioni*, as if she were a famous actress, or worse. They came in droves, you can't imagine how charming she looked, even then. . . . Yes, utter nonsense, pure imagination. Oh I'm not saying there wasn't a breath of scandal: between my efforts to cover up my guilty knowledge and mama's dark hints, I don't know *what* people thought! There were all kinds of rumours, all a good deal worse than what it really was. And there were still a few houses—remember it was before the war—where a woman would have been dropped for having left her husband for whatever reason. But not mama. Mama always had a special place, and it was just in the eyes of those people that she could do no wrong. There were others, naturally, to whom mama at Brown's Hotel was *not* the same as mama the Roman hostess; but there were plenty of pickings left even for those, it wasn't as if mama ever went back to calling herself Howland or anything like that, in spite of her not being able to pronounce my father's Christian name. Oh, she became more Italian every year. Brown's and the furnished houses later on were her own choice." Constanza added: " Like so much else."

§

Constanza got her hunter, picked for her by two of her new friends, and the maid arrived as soon as Mena had tele-

graphed for her. She was Mena's sister's child, whom Mena
was glad to place. The girl was not much older than Constanza, and on their journeys it was Constanza who had to
take her by the hand and look after her, but she could sew
and pin and keep in bounds Constanza's already then
extravagant untidiness. Her name was Angelina; she, too,
had never been out of Italy before and she, too, took to
England kindly. It would seem that the pangs of Mediterranean longings are mainly felt by those of Northern
birth.

In the spring the principessa allowed herself to take a
house for a few months at Regent's Park. Hunting was over,
Constanza plunged into London. When she had first
arrived, sheer material novelty had made her younger than
she had been in Rome; now she was growing up fast. Her
first English summer was nearly as exciting, as delirious, as
had been her winter. It was made by people—every kind
of people, new people, points of view, tones of voices:
undergraduates, riding partners, authors in their prime,
colonels who had loved her mother, young men who went
off to work in the City and young men who already spoke of
nursing a constituency, K.C.s, radicals, fast girls, spectacular
old women, aesthetes, dons. At odd moments Constanza
missed her father and thought of him affectionately, ruefully,
as a child might think of nanny during a wild and glorious
holiday. For exercise, she danced.

Chapter II

One afternoon as Constanza slipped in to change her clothes, she found her mother on the landing saying good-bye effusively to a retired brigadier and his exceedingly plain wife who had been having tea.

Constanza flung herself into a chair. " Goodness, mama, why do you keep on seeing these dingy people? "

Anna said, " They're on my side."

Constanza looked about the room. She did not easily notice things of that kind but the room did not look right to her, it looked dreary. " I'm sorry," she said, " I couldn't lunch today. Have you had someone nice? "

" Only Humphrey-Kerr."

" *He's* on your side all right. Darling, you do choose the dowdiest confidantes. I wonder why. What's the matter with this room? "

" The flowers," Anna said. " It's those lazy English servants." Nobody could run a house more exquisitely than Anna, but she was not running this house.

Constanza got up and gave her mother a kiss.

Anna said, " I *had* to see Grace and the brigadier today. There's been another," she pinched her lips, " communication from Rome."

" About me? "

" Through the lawyers. A certain person has given up molesting me directly."

" Mama, when can I see my father? I must. I want to. I will."

" You don't understand," said Anna.

" What is there that you can tell those dried-up people
that you cannot tell me? "

" He and Grace have a great experience of life."

" I doubt it. Mama, I'm beginning to believe that it's
you, and only you, who wants to prevent me from seeing
papa."

" It would kill me."

" Oh, please," Constanza said softly. " Couldn't we——"

" Don't speak to me of him."

Constanza swallowed and waited. It was the unkempt
room that got her. " Mama, is there nothing I can do for
you? If you hate this place, we can take another. I agree
we ought to get a proper cook."

" It doesn't matter," said Anna.

Constanza seldom carried a watch, but she felt it was
getting late.

" What are you going to wear? " said her mother.

" I don't know; Angelina will have put out something."

" She showed me a red dress of yours! "

" Oh yes," said Constanza, " I got that one myself.
Rather nice, isn't it? "

" No," said Anna.

" Oh. What's wrong with it?"

" The colour. Chiefly."

" That's what I liked about it. Mama, it isn't . . . it
isn't because of the *déclassement?* "

Anna herself these days wore only autumn colours.

" Gracious no. You have your life before you. Because
it is the most hideous common red."

" Well whatever you say, mama. Shall I tell Angelina
to burn it? "

" I gave it to her," said Anna.

" Good; she liked the colour, too. But how very undemo-
cratic of you, darling." Taking advantage of her mother's
easier mood, she said quickly, " What answer did you give. . .

what message did you send to Rome? I really ought to
know."

"I am leaving it to the lawyers. *There will be no change.*
And Constanza, if you love me, do not re-open the subject."

"Mama," said Constanza, "I do love you." And so she
went upstairs, threw off her clothes and let Angelina help
her into a very well-made dress which she herself found
rather dull. Not that it made much difference to her what
she wore; nor, as she was beginning to find out, did it to
other people.

It was true. Constanza had begun to love her mother. And
this love was the first serious emotion of her life. Its seeds
had lain partly in their new isolation, their sudden and
essential dependence upon one another, the shared passage
of two *voyageurs sur la terre*. Some of Constanza's feeling
sprang from gratitude. Her mother was the anchor, the
one tie, the fixed ground from which it was possible to explore
the new; more than that, she was the protectress, the giver,
the fount quite literally of everything that now made up life.
Once again it was owing to this stiff-necked, this intransigent
woman, that Constanza had been given the freedom of a
world. The same defects of vision that made Anna such a
mill-stone as a wife, made her—at least from a temporal
point of view—a parent of unique desirability. One second
look, one gesture, and the bright new magic could vanish.

Gratitude was an element. Not the only one. There was a
compassionate side to Constanza's nature, a streak of
chivalry; she had also reached the stage where one has to
love. Like many people who have discovered sensual love
early, and with ease and gaiety, the scope of her emotions
was left free. Again, Constanza had lovers. The setting
was less pastoral, but she managed. In fact she was (for her)
almost methodically careful. It was because she so entirely

despised the rules (only a religious, a supernatural sanction might have made them acceptable to her instincts and her reason, and in that version of the supernatural she could not believe) that she was so determined not to be tripped up by them. The men who attracted her were vigorous, detached, subtle, gay; sturdy arcadians whose spirit matched her own. A rake herself, she looked for brother rakes, and even in that England found them. With these she was generous. She gave and expected sensuality, a measure of passion, *gentilezza*: a light tenderness, and comradeship. Any one attachment while it lasted—for some weeks, some months, a season—held her entirely. When it was over, it was over. It was not that she was flighty (as she was to be called), but a realist who from early youth chose to obey her instincts. Men were her accomplices and brothers; her unengaged emotions she turned—at that time—towards her mother.

Before August they had to face some of the immediate aspects of their situation.

" So we move again. But have you any idea where to? "

" She doesn't know herself."

" Have you any idea of what she'd like to do? I mean what would upset her least? " Constanza herself had arrangements for a string of (sagaciously spaced) visits.

" We used to go to Scotland at this time of year," said Mena.

" And now you're so much nearer. It seems a pity not to take advantage."

" She won't go."

" I know," said Constanza.

" She says not this year."

" *This* year? That's one step better. What about a house in the country for now? "

" Not her."

" The country here isn't at all like Castelfonte. What about Switzerland? A lot of her cronies are going to Vevey. I'd go with her—God knows it doesn't suit my book."

" She says her travelling days are over."

" I know. But she can't stay put in London all summer. Not that we are staying put—that move! I suppose it will be back to Brown's at the end. Well, Brown's *is* convenient."

" We have every convenience here," said Mena.

" Yes, it's a jolly house."

" She can't bear it."

" I know."

At last Anna decided to go to Brighton for a while.

" Will you like that, mama? "

" That is hardly the point. Mena adores it. Brighton is her favourite town in England."

" We never sent Mena back to her village at Udine."

" Mena doesn't care for Udine. Constanza, I don't like that giggle, it's so like your—— It's a silly Italian habit. I was not making a joke, Mena has left her native country to follow me. The least I can do is——"

" Make it up to her."

" It's no more than my duty," said Anna.

Constanza, with whom love was not blind, asked herself whether her mother might have some pleasant secret reason for choosing Brighton. It was possible but, as she had to admit with a heavy heart, it was not probable.

" I'll take you there and I shall come to see you all the time."

" That'll be lovely, darling," said Anna; " but don't let it interfere with your engagements. I so much want you to make some friends in England."

In Another Country

§

The end of September was the time settled for Giorgio's first stay with his mother. Again there had to be plans. Many people were urging the prince not to send the boy, but his lawyer wrote to Anna saying that he was carrying out their agreement to the letter. Anna took a house in Hampstead, in the Vale of Health, and engaged some staff. The suggested *quid pro quo*, a visit, *ex gratia*, of Constanza's to her father, she ignored. There arose some correspondence as to who was to accompany the little boy on his journey across Europe; it seemed difficult to find a person capable both of coping with the trains and looking after a child of three.

Then Constanza heard. Early one morning she and Mena stood in Anna's door. " Papa is coming! Papa is bringing Giorgio himself—papa will be with us in a week! "

Anna did not stop her. " How did you hear? " she said. " Did he write to you? "

" No, Mena heard. Angelina's mother wrote, she has it from Socrate. But it's true."

" *Madonna!* The Signor Principe is on his way, they are packing at the palazzo."

" Mama, *carissima*, papa is coming to England—just like the other time when he came to marry you."

" The first time in nearly twenty years that *Eccellenza* has left Italy! "

" A good omen," said Constanza.

Then they saw that Anna was about to faint.

They ministered to her. When she was in possession of herself again, she said: " People here cannot realize what a tremendous thing a journey like that is for a man like him."

Once more she took to her room, was not at home to

friends; but it was not as it had been the other times, it was not the same, Mena said, not the same at all.

" You think she might . . . she would. . . . ? "

" She is getting ready for the change."

" Do you think papa will snatch her up and carry her off to Rome by storm, like that picture we have in the dining-room? " It was a Rape of the Sabines.

Mena signed herself and smiled.

Confirmation came. It went through the lawyers and was addressed to Anna. The prince was taking the boy to London personally; the principessa could rest assured that no attempt would be made on his part to approach her or disturb her peace; the prince merely hoped to be permitted to spend a few hours with the Signorina Constanza.

Anna burnt that letter. Her next action was to inform Rome that she would obtain a court injunction against the prince's seeking access to his daughter; if he persisted, he might find his way barred by a policeman. Then, stony-faced, she told them: " Your father is not coming, he has changed his mind."

" The Channel," Constanza cried, " I should have known it was too much—papa couldn't love us enough to cross the Channel."

Mena and Constanza were wretchedly disappointed but able to pay but small attention to their feelings; they were in for the worst time anyone had had so far with Anna.

In due course they learnt that Giorgio would be arriving accompanied as far as Calais by Signora Rossi and all the way by a courier and a *bambinaia*. Constanza spoke her first harsh words: all very well for him to be so gentlemanly over Giorgio, he *has* let her down; I suppose that is the way he really is.

In Another Country

§

To Constanza many doors were open. She realized that she could choose, and chose. In the years that followed she still hunted but she also found her circle, circles, a place among the young in the intellectual and political world of the day.

These years for her were splendid ones; they were perhaps, and by the nature of the times she lived in, the best she was to have. To her they were the most magical, a fulfilment, a substantiation of so many speculations, dreams and fires that had animated her first youth. The images raised by literature, by history (that passionate curiosity so casually engendered by two or three men of perspective turn of mind in her eccentric Roman school-room), life, the sense of life, as she anticipated it reading Stendhal, reading Byron, the breath of affairs, the roll of destiny in Gibbon, Pitt and Burke, her own *penchant* for Lord Melbourne, her Fabian hopes, the whole heightened image of England itself, all of these, in some subtle, unhoped-for way had been made manifest, made flesh, had been transmuted into the stuff of life. In the gallery of the House of Commons, at Covent Garden standing in tears after the first performance of the *Chapeau de Tricorne*, alone, confronted by the first intimations of the new writing, the new poetry, and her first response, she felt that all that mattered was within her grasp, knew that she was near the hub of things. London gave her what she could have been given nowhere else and not by London at any other time.

A Liberal Government was in power. These were the years of the great reforms, of social legislation. The Bill curtailing the power of the House of Lords had been passed; now came the passage of Lloyd George's National Insurance Act; controversy was bitter, party feeling high. Constanza, though still interested in socialism as the seductive solution, was more under the spell of Mr Asquith than of Keir Hardie, and her spontaneous affinities were with the Liberal Radicals, not exactly with Winston Churchill's " prigs, prudes and faddists ", but with many of their ideas and most of all with Winston, Radical Minister as he then was, himself and his friends. It was one of the worlds she lived in. The parents of one or two of her most intimate contemporaries were in the Government, a few of her older young men were in Parliament themselves or the secretaries to men in office. In the House she heard the orators of the age, she heard Lloyd George, she heard Churchill speak for Irish Home Rule, for Prison Reform, and she heard F. E. Smith. Her mother approved of her political friends and leanings, and shared them; and this became for a time one of their main adult bonds. Gradually Anna unbent so far as to accompany Constanza to some of the debates and to do again a measure of entertaining, evenings at home after the Italian pattern and luncheon parties for her daughter's friends. She still refused to make a permanent home, but the houses she took then were at least central and the refreshments again in accordance with her own instincts of hospitality.

When German naval building caught up with Churchill and moved him from the Home Office to the Admiralty and turned him into the champion of re-armament, Anna and Constanza looked to Lloyd George, the pacifist and the reformer. Nothing, they held, should be allowed to interrupt or even slow down the present unique course of internal social change; and the best way, they were convinced, to avert war, to stay at peace, was by staying peaceful.

To the Suffragettes—clamorous and evident—they gave their nominal support.

Many of her daughter's other enthusiasms, the principessa did not share. She, too, became rather excited by the Russian Ballet, but was not really able yet to develop an eye for Cézanne and Picasso, or lend an unprejudiced ear to Stravinsky or Debussy. To writers (the new ones, to whom Constanza had soon shifted her curiosity and allegiance), Anna's reactions were more definite. Snugly fortified by her Victorians—Thackeray, Trollope and beloved Dickens were also on her side—she had once told Constanza that Madame Bovary was unnecessary. Her objections now, she said, were not against the *new*. In her own time she had been ready to laugh with G.B.S., and more than ready to read, welcome and extol Mr Galsworthy and Mr Bennett. H. G. Wells she held in awe, nor had she ever found—she was able to point out—that he went too far. But what she saw no point in was formlessness, ugliness, obscurity. When she found a copy of *The Voyage Out* on Constanza's table, she inquired serenely about the beginning and the middle and the end. The novels of D. H. Lawrence were incomprehensible to her (to tell the truth, so they were then also largely to Constanza), and those of E. M. Forster pointless and rather drab. Marcel Proust she declared affected; but it was the poetry that Constanza in due course was to bring so triumphantly into the house—Eliot, the Sitwells, Pound, Gerard Manley Hopkins, "a contemporary of *yours*, mama"—that fared worst of all. Amateurish, Anna said; and of course not poetry at all.

"*We shall see*," said Constanza. "I'm not holding it against you, darling—whatever should I have done without you? if you hadn't had me educated? Reading d'Annunzio now, no doubt."

"A very fine poet," said Anna.

Once a year Giorgio came to spend a month with them. The principessa's feelings about this child of hers were as ambivalent as they had been from the first. She often spoke of her son in Rome, his existence was a consolation to her, the one tangible sign that all had not been in vain. But when he was with her she could not identify herself with this dark and pretty little boy. She did not know how to take him, what to do with him. Naturally she was nice to him, and she spoilt him. She did not go out to buy him toys, she had never done that, but she told Mena to take him to the shop and let him choose. Mena for some reason was not dispensable and Angelina was entrusted with the expedition in her stead, and she, too, being young and foolish there was no-one to check Giorgio's greed. Constanza and the men from the delivery van happened to coincide in the hall. (They had just moved into a house near Princess Gate, and she had been walking in the Park.) " Good gracious," she said, " what are we doing with so many tricycles? "

Giorgio, who had been watching for his loot, began to take possession.

" Have you got a gang, *bimbo*? Are you going to equip them? "

Giorgio, unused to this kind of joke, scowled at his sister.

The delivery men re-appeared.

Constanza took another look and her more frugal instincts began to stir. " It isn't as if I were just seeing *double*," she exclaimed.

Giorgio let out a howl; Constanza said to the men, " It isn't your fault, I know, but that stuff has got to go back."

She went to enlist her mother. Anna came out on the landing. " Giorgio, dear——" she said. Her son had entered his full whirl of fury and was spinning like a top. " You don't *want* all these. . . . One clock-work train is much nicer than four. . . . Do believe me. Isn't that so, Constanza? "

Constanza looked disgusted.

Giorgio had started grabbing things and throwing them about.

" I'm afraid he is not clever," said the principessa.

" Come on," said Constanza to the men, " give us a hand, you can see this won't do." They obeyed her. The toys were borne away. Anna withdrew. Giorgio calmed down and sulked. He sulked the whole day, the next day, he sulked for the whole of his visit. Constanza said he was still sulking when he came back next year. She said that she never knew Giorgio when he wasn't either in a tantrum or in sulks; but perhaps she was not fair.

On an earlier occasion, her friends had clamoured to see the Italian brother. They took him out on a ride. Giorgio was eager enough, but the first thing he did was fall off.

" Can't you ride, *bimbo*? "

It turned out that he had never been on a horse.

" *Ma che?* Didn't papa take you? "

Giorgio shook his head.

" Doesn't he take you riding with him? How very odd. What can papa be thinking about? "

School, Anna kept saying, school—she was sure it would be nice for him to start going. " The Jesuits, I know, like Carla's boys; well, they *are* first-rate teachers."

Constanza said she wondered what her grandfather— whose essays she had just been reading—would have felt about a grandson of his having a Jesuit education.

" *Autre temps, autre mœurs*," said Anna.

Constanza never became a débutante. When the point in time was reached, the point in fact had long been passed. Her mother's heart was not really in it and Constanza took advantage of this. " Too late, darling," she told her, " I've been out to so many intents and purposes that it would only start questions in people's minds."

" I am not giving you what I had," said Anna.

" We seem to have put ourselves into a slightly different

position from everybody else and they've accepted it. Let's
stick to it."

" Are you sure you don't *want* to be presented? "

" Quite sure," said Constanza. Tales of her mother's
presentation—by the American Ambassadress, at a *small*
Court, the Queen's expression, Edward VII behind the
throne as Prince of Wales—had regaled her childhood. She
had no wish to repeat herself the contemporary version of this
experience.

" The pageantry. . . ." said Anna.

" I had some of that in our Church."

" All the same," said her mother, " there is a meaning
in it."

" Well, you know mama, I'm rather anti-monarchy. Yes,
yes, I know it's extremely *mal-vu* here, a republican is worse
than a socialist—I can't help it. Constitutional monarchies
have their uses, but why keep the trappings? Like
primitive *and* organized religion, and it's all so bourgeois."

Anna said, " You haven't seen their jewels."

" Perhaps I'm prejudiced because ours is so very jumped
up. You can't expect *us* to venerate the House of Savoy."

" They are very fine people and the Crown has given a
sense of unity to the Italians."

" A nice sentiment for a daughter of the American
Revolution."

" Fiddlesticks," said Anna. " You have no more respect
for the United States than you have for your own Royal
Family. I've heard you poke fun at both. Roman irreverence, that's all it is."

Constanza said, " *Meno male.*"

If for her daughter Anna put a bright face on things—much
of the time—she did not do so for Mena. Whenever Anna
was in her implacable or disconsolate or her restless mood

Mena bore the brunt. When Mena had a sad time with her, which Mena felt, Anna would try to make it up by giving her a present.

" That's a nice bright new alarm clock you have," said Constanza. " Mama? " Mena nodded. " Oh, dear." She examined the clock. "Not a very big present, that's a mercy."

" I didn't spend it all on the clock," said Mena; " I put it by for the nephew's land."

" *Oh, dear*," said Constanza.

" We are in for another move soon. They've asked her to sign a lease."

" It's high time."

" She can't bear to feel she's settled."

" Better than having no home at all."

" She misses her own."

" *So much?* "

Mena said, " She thinks of nothing else."

" Poor mama."

Mena added loyally, " *Era magnifico*."

" Yes——" said Constanza. " I suppose so. *Was* is the word, it doesn't bear thinking about what the house must be like these days. It was always cold, even with mama's steam heating; and so dark. I'm thinking of the painted ceiling, with luck it was supposed to have held for another eighteen months, two winters; that was when we left. The estimates for saving it were astronomical. With the ceiling gone, they'd have to shut off the *salone* and the rooms beyond. I cannot imagine how papa has the heart to go on there."

" My sister writes that everything is in the best of shapes in the palazzo," said Mena. " They're always having workmen, Socrate tells her, everything is in repair."

" All *bella figura*. Socrate *would* spread that to save face. I know them." Secretly Constanza thought it possible that her father was still prosperous with the embezzled money.

What surprised her was his spending it on a house he did little except sleep in, and not on Castelfonte.

Mena said, " If I were the Madonna and had the ordering of things, I would make the Signora Principessa live in the palazzo and you could live at Castelfonte with *il babbo*."

" I do miss Castelfonte. But I don't think I want quite that now."

To their relief, Anna took to travelling again. It was too strong an instinct, and someone had the inspiration to speak of it as her wanderings. From then on it was that. When Anna went off to Montreux in good company, on a Scandinavian cruise or a round of country visits, she was able to chalk it up as part of her burden, a stretch of her life sentence.

Now and then Constanza broached their most stormy subject. Anna always fought it with her own unhappiness. One day Constanza said: " I am going. What kind of daughter have I been! To papa, who has always been good to me. What does it look like? "

" What will it look like for me if you go to him against my wishes."

" Your wishes are not reasonable. I am not a child. I am a grown-up woman."

" You are not twenty-one," said Anna, " you cannot go. I have your legal custody."

" Yes, I gathered that. Surely, mama, that's a scrap of paper. What *you* say goes—and you wouldn't prevent me from seeing my father now? "

" Don't force me into something," said Anna.

" Signorina Constanza—don't do it to her."

" How can I do it to her? And how can I explain to papa?"

" *He* knows her," said Mena.

" He used to say, remember? ' That's the least we can do—poor woman, all alone in a foreign country! ' "

Constanza and the prince wrote to each other. It was a meagre exchange. They were poor correspondents; they had no life in common; there was too much that each believed he must keep from the other.

§

Constanza came of age in the spring of 1914. At once she made her arrangements. Giorgio was spending the whole of May with them, this time it was she who would take him back. She presented her position simply. " I shall spend this summer with papa. I did not go before because it would have offended you too much; if I do not go now I shall be offending him."

" And what will the world say if you rush off to him the minute you are free? "

" What you tell it to. It always has."

It became their first clash of wills. Anna went into the now familiar cycle. She kept to her room, refused trays. Soon poor Mena was beside herself. " She really doesn't eat. One day she will starve herself to death." Constanza went ahead.

Giorgio had a wretched visit. Constanza took pity on him. She led him to a nearby mews where some of the stables had been converted into garages. Giorgio came home late for his supper, covered in black grease and full of exciting lore. He had made friends with the chauffeurs, his days were no longer a problem.

"How does he get all this stuff about pistons and gaskets?" said Constanza. "He doesn't speak English."

"Oh yes, he does!" said Mena.

"We thought he had forgotten."

"He is *furbo*."

"That's what they said of me."

"Ah, well. . . ."

Constanza had telegraphed Rome. Then three days before she was due to leave, Giorgio started mumps. In the event no-one else caught the disease, but they all stayed in quarantine for twenty-one days. When these were over, Constanza had capitulated. Fate, she believed, had given too strong a hint; she allowed herself to compromise. Giorgio left without her. The Roman journey was postponed until the autumn. The principessa was jubilant, revived, grateful. Constanza for the first time in her life felt deeply uneasy.

Six weeks later Europe was at war.

To Anna and Constanza it was the bitterest blow, the reversal of everything, an end. "So it has come," they said, "it *was* possible." On that first night, the night of the day on which Germany had declared war on Russia, they talked little about sides, about who was right, who was wrong, about the Kaiser, England's entry or neutrality; they hardly touched on outcome, the future; they talked of what had happened, was happening now, this night, to men and their women, to men entraining, marching now, with rifles, with bayonets, to tear each other's living flesh.

"Don't they see it, these decently brought-up gentlemen round their tables, as what it is? Physical blackmail, direct, brutal, primitive blackmail—Give up this, apologize for that, or we'll burn your crops, starve your children, shoot your people to pieces. All blurred by numbers, fine words, divided responsibility, abstract thinking. *That* is war. War as an instrument of policy. If individuals dared behave, or even talk, like the representatives of nations they'd be shut up and put away."

Mother and daughter cancelled their engagements, stayed in London and stayed in. They sat together, on that Saturday, in their drawing-room. It happened to be the same house again at Regent's Park that they had lived in during their first summer. The curtains of those tall windows were undrawn against the long twilight; Anna sat mostly silent, listening to Constanza's raving.

" Has everybody gone mad—blind—stupid? "

Anna said, " Who can want it? The people cannot really want it? "

" Fat lot of good that does them. We see now that the people have no control over peace or war."

" They should control the men who have."

" But they can't and they didn't and some of them didn't even want to. From what we've seen in the last week what they want is yell and hate and feel they belong to the biggest puddle with the largest cannon, the biggest place on the map, the brightest flag. Hate, vicarious self-love and the pleasure of being in it."

" I shall never get over the Social-Democrats in the Reichstag," said Anna, " voting for the war credits."

" And the crowds in Paris."

" *They* had 1870 to remember. War breeds war."

" A fine prospect. Mama, unforgivingness breeds war; exploited resentment, treasured grievances. If we don't learn to forget a wrong no sooner than it's done or said, if we don't all of us—privately and collectively—draw a line below the past every day of our lives, we're going to be sunk. We *are* sunk."

Later on, she said, " I'd like to stand back and wash my hands."

By ten o'clock Mr James joined them. He thought, he said, he might find them in London. They welcomed him.

" Did you think it could happen? " Constanza asked him.

" In my mind—yes."

" How did it happen? "

" As it always does: concatenation of circumstances and men's very considerable propensity for evil."

Anna had a couple of bottles of wine fetched up for Mr James and themselves. It was a Moselle. Nobody noticed this.

Mr James said, " Here's to civilization."

Constanza said, " No toasts."

" Is there any chance at all that it can still be stopped? " said Anna. " If the British Government and my country and the Pope and the Scandinavians were to make an appeal——? "

" No."

" There is no chance," Constanza said, " of the crowds smashing up the Chancelleries and the women lying down before the mobilization trains? No chance of the men stopping in the factories, the soldiers refusing to shoot and the General Staff tearing up their plans and bursting into tears? No chance of Poincaré and the Czar and old Francis-Joseph and Kaiser Bill having second thoughts? "

" No."

" We were near it in 1911," said Anna, " and it didn't come."

" That it has happened is never proof that it had to happen," said Constanza.

" It didn't look at all inevitable even two days ago," said Anna.

" When I was a child I used to wonder why God never spoke to us when necessary in a direct loud voice. Today would have been the moment."

" One more voice in the wilderness."

" Mr James, what is wrong with human affairs? "

" Too many, discovering too much, too soon."

" Giorgio. Millions and millions of Giorgios, equipped with high explosives, printing presses, wireless telegraphy."

" What can we do? " said Anna.

" Learn to be wise and kind," said Constanza.

" Wait for Evolution," said Mr James.

" Meanwhile break the machines," said Constanza.

" Giorgio wouldn't stand for that."

" It *is* the abyss? "

" An instalment," said Mr James.

" Is it the worst thing that ever happened? "

" Quantitatively speaking, it may turn out to be. *Intentions* have been worse, a good deal worse; it's the material power now that is so immeasurably greater."

" Must power always be for destruction? " said Anna.

" That has so far been largely the experience."

" Torture was worse," said Constanza. " Judicial torture, every form of torture. But is it so very different to be wounded and maimed in a war? "

" You are a hero and belong, instead of being a martyr or a criminal."

" Or a conscript. Don't forget that the French, the German and the Russian are all conscript armies. You haven't seen our people at Castelfonte being marched off to military service."

This gave their thoughts a new turn.

" I pray that Italy will not come in with the Germans," said Anna.

" I pray that Italy will not come in," said Constanza.

" Tonight," said Mr James, " we, the three of us here, are neutrals; three neutral nationals. . . ."

They sat up late, drinking their wine. At one point Anna spoke of her father. They felt tender about one another, each lucid and tender about the others' vulnerability. When Mr

James left, he said he would walk. Constanza let him out. He kissed her.

" Your coming of age hasn't brought you much good so far," he said, " has it? "

" No," she said, " I've thought of that, too. Well, luckily, I was never one who could not wait for time to pass."

Chapter III

Throughout the war Constanza remained, and called herself, a pacifist. Some people broke with her, she quarrelled with a few of her friends, with some she quarrelled occasionally. Many bore with her, some did not take her seriously, others became of her mind; she made new friends, slightly shifted her circles. In other respects her war was like the war of most young women of her London world. The immediate surprise of things going on as they were, the adjustment, the shock of the first losses; things no longer going on as they were and the adjustment to that; the tension, the heightening, the drabness, the excitement, the dark stretches, the waiting, the routine; the acceleration of living, emotions, decisions. She worked at a canteen and later for an organization in aid of prisoners of war, sent parcels to the front, helped entertain enlisted men, fell in and out of love more rapidly and violently than she had done before and often enjoyed herself very much. Half of her friends, half of the men she knew and loved, were killed. The war from any concrete point turned out infinitely worse than she or anybody had envisaged. The sense of revulsion, the inner conviction that all of it was wrong, outside the scheme of sanity, never left her, she was never quite without some consciousness of the split between her life and that of the trenches and the men in them. Yet she did not feel again with that intensity, that clarity of detached despair that had united the three of them on that first night at Regent's Park.

Some weeks after the German invasion of Belgium, Anna

said, " Forgive my bringing this up. I don't want to involve you in these things, Constanza, but I should like to have your approval and it does concern you too. I'd like to talk to you about my investments. You see, Jack writes he wants to change them; he says the events are bound to be reflected in the United States economy. He wants me to switch over chiefly into steel, and Mr Baxter, the dear vice-president of our bank, I mean I remember him as vice-president when I was a girl, actually he's been president these last twelve years, and now the dear man is dead and his son, who *is* vice-president, is the new trustee and he wants us to keep pace and anticipate the boom he foresees in certain heavy industries, and I don't feel that I ought to——"

" Mama, can we get this clear? Are you supposed to change your investments because of the war or because of the new Mr Baxter? "

" Well, both I suppose."

" And you object to making money out of the war? But not to the new broom? "

" Jack says he's brilliant. I'm glad you see it my way. No, I don't want to put a cent into something that may turn into a war industry. I don't mean I don't want to *give* to the war, Constanza; I cannot see that we have any choice now except to fight and beat the Germans; but I don't want to profit by it. As everything I have will come to you—and Giorgio, if he proves himself capable of responsibility—I want to know how you feel about it."

" You know my views, mama."

" I am very glad," said Anna. " It may mean a heavy loss."

" Well, we can't think of that," said Constanza. " What are you in now? "

" A good deal is in Russian Railways and in soap."

" Soap? "

" Apparently it does very well. Not the soap we wash with, darling. Laundry soap."

" I thought that was made at home. Obviously not. Let that pass. I should keep the soap, then, and get out of the Russian Railways. Get rid of those. Somehow, I don't like the idea of them at all."

" The old Mr Baxter was very keen on them. *I* felt it was bolstering despotism."

" Well, tell the brilliant young Mr B. that Russian Railways are out. He can buy more soap. Do they listen to you? Do they have to? "

" Perhaps not strictly under the terms of the trust, but I hardly think they'd *like* going against my wishes. And there is another matter I want to talk to you about. I wanted to break the trust—they won't let me—it seems it can't be done—my father and the uncles made explicit provision against that. Now I want to go into capital."

" Haven't you? " said Constanza.

" That was Aunt Emily, the bit that was not tied up. They won't let me sell out anything else, or only driblets, and we can't live on the income."

" Do we live too expensively? "

" We live simply," said Anna, " simply and decently."

" We may not live like millionaires, but I'm under the impression that we live like the rich."

" You know nothing about such matters," said her mother.

" I'd be quite good at figures, if you gave me any. Mama, if we ought to retrench, as they say, let me help you."

" You don't even know what things cost," said Anna.

" I don't know what they cost, but I have them. If that is not a definition of riches."

" I don't want you to pinch and scrape. You can help in another way. When I die the trust is dissolved, it goes absolutely to my heirs."

" Capital and all? "

" Yes," said Anna happily. " All yours, in the bank to
draw on. Well, I thought as you are twenty-one and my chief
heir and gave your consent to our using a little capital now
and then, it might help with those stubborn men. If not,
there's always my overdraft, people here are so very nice to
me about it."

" Darling mama, naturally I shall sign anything you
say."

At that time, the English in Italy were coming home for the
duration. One evening in September Constanza was asked
to a party to meet a young man arrived from Rome the day
before. Constanza was much involved with a Greek poet at
that moment, and as often she was late. She entered a
crowded room where things were in full swing. She strolled
up to a group of people who were clustered round a fair,
tall, lanky young man who was holding forth. He had a
rather ugly, rather charming face, a little like Boswell and
a little like a pug. He was sitting on the floor, rocking to and
fro, nursing his knees and enjoying what he said. Constanza
thought she heard a name she knew and stopped.

" A beauty—a Veneto-Roman beauty—nothing like those
Bronzino-faced Bolognese—not in her first youth mind you:
autumnal; but the way she moved, and of course *so* like their
paintings, Tintoretto, Giorgione, it was all there—so I gave
good Professor Pestalozzi the slip whenever I had the chance
and nipped down to Rome. In vain! Don't let anyone tell
you Rome is the New Babylon. The morals and domestic
customs of those people are too touching to be believed.
The fidelity! The sentiment!

" Well then, there she was stuck with this beau of hers, it
must have been going on for a quarter of a century. Sweet
old boy, actually—he tried to carry me off on a shoot—lives

in one of those vast barns off the Piazza Farnese and puzzles over the Risorgimento. Well, one fine day his wife—one of, those straight-laced American ladies—found out about it and upped and left him, favourite daughter and all. Since then my autumnal beauty has been tied to him for keeps. There isn't a dry eye in Rome when they tell you this story—poor Giulia, they say, so devoted, so loyal—and he's heart-broken and spends morning, noon and night moping in her drawing-room. The poor marchese, that's *her* husband, is *driven* to his club and if old Rico didn't go duck shooting once in a while he wouldn't have palazzo to set foot in."

Nothing would have made Constanza sneeze or slip away, she only longed to turn into a mouse. But at this point came a stir, people had become aware of her presence. Someone quietly named her. The young man looked at her, she at him; there was a fraction of the expected silence.

" Strike me pink! " said the young man.

Constanza laughed out loud. " That was the best thing you could have said."

" So that's *you*," said the young man.

" The favourite daughter."

" It's not fair. I somehow got the impression that you were a child."

" The *bambina*," said Constanza.

" *Già*," said the young man. He was a perfect mimic.

" You know, I could tell you one or two things about the Risorgimento that would puzzle *you*. What were you doing at Bologna? "

" Cramming for the F.O. Polishing up my Italian."

" *Is* there a Professor Pestalozzi? "

" No. I made him up. Plenty like him. You know, I ought to have known you anywhere, you do look like the marchesa." He appraised Constanza seriously. " What is called a generic likeness. But *you* are not all Venetian School, for one thing you are too tall, then you have more lightness—there's a good bit of Gainsborough in you. Of course there's English blood."

" My straight-laced American mama."

" Quite," said the young man. " I've seen it so often, the fining down of the Titian/Veronese type, it shows in the hair, too. It's very interesting."

One of their friends said, " I say, Simon, you are the most impudent man of your age I know."

" I shouldn't give it that limitation," said Constanza. " How old *are* you? "

" Twenty-one," said the young man.

" A fatal number. If I were you I should be careful about everything you do for the rest of the year."

The young man made a mock sign against the evil eye.

" *Don't*," said Constanza. " Were you by any chance brought up in Italy? "

" Two years as a boy with an Aunt and Uncle near Genoa. The uncle was a parson, I had had pneumonia, *paziènza*."

Before they drifted apart, he said, " As a matter of fact I've got something for you, your father gave me a present to take over. He said, ' Tell her it's a birthday present, I meant to give it to her myself, but with the war now we don't know when she'll be able to come.' I was going to send it to you."

" How *like* papa," she said, " how like us. It would never occur to us to send anything by post if we can help it. I don't think I ever put spit to stamp before I came to live in England."

" Well you know, the marchesa did hint it was something pretty valuable, ' For the love of Heaven, don't lose it, *caro*! ' Post indeed: There's a war on. I had a nightmare of a journey myself."

" So it *is* possible to get to and fro? "

" Not *to*. And I shouldn't advise it."

" Have you got it with you? "

" Your father's present? It's locked up at home."

So Constanza had to name a day for him to come to tea at Regent's Park.

Constanza's Greek poet had enlisted, and she knew better than to interfere. People, even people whom she loved, were separate entities to her and she left them to their own convictions and decisions. But she was going through an anxious time. It was only when she came in late one afternoon and saw him sitting with her mother eating nectarines and drinking Sauternes that she remembered having asked the young man from Rome.

" I am most frightfully sorry," she said.

" Constanza," said her mother, " Mr Herbert has been waiting for you for an hour."

" In delightful company," he said.

" I hope you will forgive me, I was seeing a great friend off to his Depot."

" Catch me ! " he said.

" I shall light a candle for him tomorrow, dearest," said Anna who *in partibus* adhered strictly to Catholic observance.

" Yes, do, mama."

" Mr Herbert has been telling me all about himself, he is going to read for the Bar. And do help yourself."

The young man filled his glass. " It's so clever of your mother to know about Château Suduiraut. Most people in this country have never heard of anything beside Yquem, and as they can't afford that or are too stingy, you seldom get a decent drop of Sauternes in England. I love it at this hour, don't you ? "

Slightly huffed, the principessa said, " Oh, we do have some Yquem. One or two of my friends like it."

" May I call myself that ? " said Simon.

" You certainly may have some Yquem," said Anna.

" I'll take you up on that," he said. " And here it is,"

he turned to Constanza and produced a small sealed packet.

She took it, her mother's eyes following her. " Thank you, that was most kind." She put the package in her bag. Simon, too, had watched her. " And why the Bar? " she said.

" Oh, I never meant to go into the Foreign Office, I only said yes because it meant snatching a couple of years abroad. That's all up now and I have to present some sort of plan to my people. The Bar is the quickest, and the least expensive. My people don't hold with their children drinking *premier crus*."

" That's always such a mistake," said Anna seriously.

" Princess, you are a parent after my own heart."

" Can you see yourself at the Bar? " said Constanza.

" Darling, what a question."

" It's the way I ask myself about things."

" Just: Addressing a British Jury. I might enjoy it. Standing up to the judge. What I shan't like is being thrown in entirely with men. But there is room for all kinds at the Bar, it isn't all stuffy. What I'm most interested in is painting. But I can't paint and don't want to, I want to look at it."

" Then you want to write about it," said Anna.

" Not too much; not for a living. There isn't much you can write about anything without it becoming a racket."

" So you'd rather stick to the Bar? "

" Oh, stick. I haven't started, you know. I shall next week."

" Are you an only child? " said Anna.

" No such luck. Two big brothers, great hulking philistines, one of them already in France, and a very dull sister."

" But you don't live with them? " said Constanza.

" God forbid," he said. " No nice cosy family life, Signorina, no nice warm cosy Italian family life. The *famiglia* live in Northumberland; for me it's been boarding school, college, Professor Pestalozzi; now it's rooms, or rather look-

ing for rooms. *La mamma* is Ulster, connected—not remotely
—with trade. It comes in very useful to keep up the fences
as *il babbo* has got a big hulking brother too, but she's had
to live it down, poor woman, ever since she came. Now she's
more like the rest than the rest. They loathe me, but wouldn't
admit it. When I ran away from Eton——"

" You ran away? " said Constanza.

" I didn't have a bad time—if you are *débrouillard* you can
get away with it—one day I just had enough. But I didn't
run home, I made straight for an aunt. My mother's sister
who married a man who turned Liberal. *That* was never
forgiven either. Darkest England—innocent ladies in
London can have no idea."

When he said good-bye, he said, " Don't forget the
Yquem."

" I shall not," said Anna. " Do come again, I'm always at
home," and she named the evening of her *conversazione* and
two other days.

When he was gone, she said: " Poor boy."

" Poor boy nothing," said Constanza.

Later, alone in her room Constanza undid the package from
Rome. When she opened it, she saw her father's Indian
ruby set extravagantly in a ring. It gave her a shock which
she did not forget; and of course she cried.

Chapter IV

Constanza tried to see all she could of her Greek poet, and besides there was her war work. Anna (the courted representative of two neutral powers) was active on a number of committees; this helped, but it took more to keep her occupied and reasonably cheerful. So when her poet was up on embarkation leave, Constanza was very pleased to find that the young man from Rome, as she still called him in her mind, was practically living in the house.

Running up the stairs, with half an hour not to spare to have a bath, she would catch glimpses of them, him and her mother, bent anxiously over an ailing potted plant, or sitting over a tome of Anna's excellent collection of art books.

" No. That's the other Giovanni."

" Who was he? Have I heard of him? "

" You needn't," said Anna. " He was Cosimo's son, not *the* Cosimo's, the nephew's."

" *I* know. The one they called Giovannetto to keep him apart from Lorenzo the Younger's second——"

" That was another one again. Oh good evening, Constanza, do sit down if you have a moment, but I expect you don't. Il Giovannetto was killed at San Gimignano three years before the Cavalcade."

What they were dissecting was a reproduction of Benozzo Gozzoli.

" Your mother is telling me all about the Medici cousins, she knows every one of them."

" And he's telling me that the Donor on the mule looks like poor dear Humphrey-Kerr."

At other times Constanza, passing, would find them teaching each other a new patience game or reading Tennyson, or Simon carving a pineapple, Simon opening a bottle. Every time he would say something agreeable about the principessa.

" Guess what we just had? A clam chowder. Your mama had it cooked for me specially."

" You silly boy," said Anna, " it was only an oyster chowder; I can't get clams."

" Any rate it was delicious, and I do like the way you say Oyster. Say ' Oyster '." Anna did. " Now you." Constanza did not. " Spoil sport. Well, you needn't. I bet you say it English. It's a great test word, that and Squirrel. That's something I'm fascinated by, voices, and why. Your mother's has remained so very New England, and yours is English English. Not a trace of Italian; not a trace of American, oh yes: sometimes. An inflection, a turn of phrase—but then I have a very good ear."

" Part of your private zoo? " said Constanza.

" I love the Zoo," Simon said, " I'm going to take you some day."

When he first saw her ring, he said : " *What* a stone! Mind if I have a look at it? "

" That's what came in your pocket."

" She insists on wearing it," said Anna.

Another day she was greeted with, " I wonder if you have any idea *how* good your mother's food is? But then Italians have no palate."

Constanza could not let this pass. " *No palate?* I can tell if two leaves out of a dish of spinach have been picked the day before yesterday."

" That's about the extent of it. *Poverina*; and how do you manage to get your fresh blade of grass in London? "

" Mama."

" *Ecco*."

Or it was: " Your mother really does know every column
in Rome."

" And how do *you* know? "

" I know enough columns to know that she knows more."

" You aren't half conceited," she said, " are you? "

The first time she caught him alone, Constanza told him:
" Don't think I minded what you said at the party that night,
it's what we all say about people we don't know very well;
I didn't hold it against you, but I'd like to ask you something
now. Is it true what you were saying? about my father?
That he was heart-broken when mama left him? "

" It was about you they said he minded most."

" Is it true that he is so very sad? "

" You know how they talk."

" But how did *you* find him? "

" He seemed quiet."

" Gay? "

" Not very gay."

" But you liked him? He's rather a dear."

" He was frightfully nice to me, he put me up once or
twice. I seem to make a hit with your parents."

" You stayed at our house? " she said. " You actually
stayed there? "

" Only for a night or two when I was supposed to be at
Bologna. What's the matter? You look queer? "

" Have you told her? Have you told my mother? "

" What about? "

" That you stayed at the palazzo? "

" I did not mention it."

" Much better not."

" I thought so."

" Of course you know the story. Does mama talk to you
about it? "

" Oh yes. She told me she's been through a tragedy of
betrayal. She thinks that you don't know."

" The real reason for her leaving my father? "

" That's what she said. But you do know. I didn't tell you anything new that night."

" Is that what they're really saying in Rome—mama found out about that old love and went away and took me with her, and that was the reason she went? "

" That's what I heard."

" Nothing else? "

" Oh yes, you know. Chorus girls . . . other women."

" Nothing else? "

" Not in Rome."

" Can you believe it? " she said. " As a child I was almost sure she knew; that was just an impression I had. Can you believe my mother doing that? "

" Easily. The women in my family would; *if* they dared treat their men like that and weren't so afraid of scandal. Your mother is someone used to having her own way."

Constanza said, " Do you think I could get to Rome before winter? "

" You know how uncertain it is about civilian travel. I daresay if you pulled strings and if there's no offensive. Then there'd be the question of getting back. Nobody knows which way Italy's going to jump."

" Did you hear I was supposed to go this summer? "

" Yes, and how cut up they were when you didn't appear. Scarlet fever or something. But I shouldn't dream of trying to go now, it would drive your father out of his mind. He said as much. He has very odd ideas about travel. Not that he hasn't got something now. I should wait; the whole show can't last long."

The Greek poet was shipped off to the front. Constanza was sick with fear for him. Every time a glass broke or a bird came to the window she saw it as an omen; she was not certain yet about the ruby; some stones do not take to change. As it was a thing with her not to talk about her lovers while they were her lovers, she had no-one to share her anxiety; besides she felt the times were miserable enough. So she only tried to console Angelina who was in the same position, and accepted her mother's concern for all young life and for her friends, whom she chose to call Constanza's protégés. When Anna asked her to come to mass with her one Sunday, she said simply yes and went. She looked back a little ruefully on her proud and bracing atheistic days. She would have called herself an agnostic now, a sceptic, sad and mild, with a sharp aversion to the Church of Rome and hardly any feeling about the Reformed. Her own conviction that this life was all there is to it, a single chance, now seemed to be occasion for mourning, humility and tolerant good sense in living it, rather than for crowing. So she drove with her mother to the Oratory and lit a candle for her poet. She prayed. She made a kind of vow. Hardly in words: a mere line. Let him keep his life; never mind about me. Let him stay alive, I shall ask nothing for myself.

Simon had moved into Regent's Park. " So much more convenient for him," said the principessa. " I'm arranging the morning-room for him to use as a study." Constanza found it rather a comfort to have him about. He was always ready to walk with her, often late at night; he was gay like an Italian but with fewer reversals of mood, and his range of interests was not exactly limited.

There was not one novel or play written after 1699, he told her, that would not be immeasurably better for a cutting.

" Why 1699? "

" The death of Racine. Have you re-read Stendhal? Recently? Well, do. You'll find a staggering amount of sheer tosh. I started cutting *La Chartreuse* the other day— such an improvement."

" How is your work going? Or don't you do any? " said Constanza.

" Nobody works for the Bar exam. Nobody who's going to be the slightest use."

" Simon, what are *your* reasons for not going to war? "

" Number One apart, because it's a plot between the old, the stupid, and the wicked. And they are going to be hoisted by their own petard."

" That's no consolation."

" No consolation," he said, " at all."

Simon was not her type, far from it. She had never much liked fair men, and she had no patience with the to her ridiculous predilection of English and American women for tall ones. Height appeared to her of little use, off a tennis court, and aesthetically not an asset. But she did find him a comfort and a good companion.

The Greek poet had not been out a fortnight when he was reported missing. For a week Constanza dared hardly breathe. She took on extra shifts at her canteen, even so the day had many more hours. Again Simon, who always seemed to know without letting on, was a great help.

Then she learnt that her Greek was at a base hospital. And soon she had a letter from him—rather disgruntled— saying that he had a splintered elbow and was being shipped to England. She and Simon set off for a long walk across the park. It was a November day with a low sky and not cold; Constanza was like a creature released.

Suddenly Simon said: " One of the things I love about

you is the way you wear your beauty lightly. Like a sable coat flung on like so much sacking."

" The Veneto-Roman type fined down by English blood? "
He said: " You are ripping."

" Cut it out, *caro*," Constanza said. " One at a time."

" What can you mean? *Good God*——! " He was taken aback, even shocked. " The principessa? She's old enough to be my mother."

" You told everyone how madly in love you were with Giulia Monfalconi. You didn't object to the autumnal. She's older than mama."

" That was in another country," he said.

" All my tutors used to be in love with mama."

" I am devoted to her, I worship her, as she would say. *And quite true*. She's an angel to me and great fun to be with. I look on her as an aunt, the most delightful one I ever had. If *she*'d been my mother, I daresay I might have turned out a good son."

" She has a son," said Constanza.

" Yeah: the little boy in Rome. What's he like, your brother? "

" A little boy," she said. " He came too late."

" The marchesa was the ideal," said Simon. " She was the fore-runner. A logical step. Let's keep it in the family."

" I don't like that kind of talk," said Constanza. " You might leave papa out of it."

" What unexpected prejudice in a wholesome pagan."

" Wholesome pagans have taboos," she said.

" You know what I heard people here say about what drove your mother from Rome? "

" What? "

" A pagan taboo, all right."

" What? "

" Incest."

" Great God! Who said that? They must be mad."

" That brigadier's wife for one. Broad hints—something indescribably terrible . . ."

" *Mama!* Oh, if only mama could learn to call a spade a spade. My poor father. And with *whom* for heaven's sake? "

" Hasn't the prince any near female relatives? "

" What next? Don't make me laugh. What do they take him for? The Italian Lord Byron? "

" That's what your mother thinks *she* is: Lady B. One cannot carry on the way she does without a precedent."

" Don't say that, I can't stand that woman; the moral Clytaemnestra, she's one of my *bêtes noires*. Mama is not like her. Burning the memoirs—I can never get over that."

" Don't you see the principessa doing exactly that? "

" And you say you're devoted to her."

" Most women would burn a manuscript. And don't forget that Lady Byron is supposed to have had great charm. A well-bred, well-educated woman of high principles, strong character, by no means all narrow views, and a great deal of charm. Apt to surround herself with a crew of malefic flatterers. Yes, my dear, let it sink in."

" I'd rather not," said Constanza.

" *You* wouldn't burn a manuscript. That's another thing that fascinates me about you—just as much as the Veneto-Roman looks—your strangely masculine code. And your being such a compound of Mediterranean and Anglo-Saxon elements."

" One of your interests," she said.

" Yes indeed. I know you're occupied at present. Never mind, *I shall apply again*."

" One day, Simon Herbert, you'll go too far."

The Greek poet was home. Constanza made several tedious and uncomfortable journeys to his hospital somewhere in the North-East. She found him grumpy, monosyllabic and uncouth. His wound was not much but it was unlikely that he would be able to bend the elbow joint of his left arm again. Quite soon he was passed unfit for active service. By the end of the month she was out of love with him.

§

" A wonderful Christmas present, my darling," Anna said. She did not call it Christmas, she said *Natale*. " The very best you could have given me."

Constanza looked blank.

" I am so very happy. Happy, for the first time in I do not like to say how many years."

" What about, mama? " Constanza said, making her voice cold.

" You need not tell me, darling," her mother said, " I know everything."

" Know what? " said Constanza now in considerable alarm.

" We won't speak about it yet if you don't want to. You were always a reserved girl. I don't want you to feel rushed, I want you to think that you can take your time. Not like *me*, who was fatally rushed into everything. . . . *I* had no mother to stand by me and advise. Well, we won't say another word now. But I shall treasure it as my lovely secret Christmas present."

" Oh for God's sake, mama, come out with it," said Constanza.

" Well, darling, Simon has spoken to me. Brilliant boy though he is, he has an old-fashioned side. So he came to *me*."

" *Simon has talked to you?* What did he tell you? "

" I need hardly repeat that—but of course you want to

hear. How much he admires you, how much you mean to him, that he has reason to believe you will consent to marry him."

" The cad! "

Anna turned colour. " Don't tell me it isn't true? Oh, don't say he's made it up. You don't love him? Constanza! "

Taken by surprise, Constanza said, " Oh, I do rather love Simon."

Anna breathed intense relief. " There, there, darling. What did I tell you, you mustn't be rushed."

Constanza said: " There hasn't been one word of marriage; and there won't be."

" But dearest girl, why? "

" One doesn't marry like that," said Constanza, " just like that. For a bit of love."

Anna chose to laugh. " You don't know yet, my dear, what one marries for."

Not at all nicely, Constanza said: " Perhaps you can tell me? "

" I was dazzled," Anna said, and a soft look came into her eyes.

" Oh, you were then? Ah, you see—it isn't the best reason, the best way to marry."

Anna's voice was still dreamy. " I was dazzled by Italy."

Constanza later recalled that her mother's manner at that moment was so unlike her usual self that it came to her in a flash that this was the first time she had heard her mother speak the truth. It was as if Anna had gone into a kind of trance. The next minute she was as before.

" And now I am so happy, you've made up so much for me; and for the present we won't say more. I only wanted you to know how glad I am—and of course, you silly girl, you can marry for love: I shall see to it that you can. I told Simon that much. Oh! it's a lovely American marriage!

With dear Simon having his way to make—just two young
people starting out in life."

Constanza was very angry. She was so angry that had it
not been for the thought of her mother, the thought of
taking away her new companion, she would have put an end
to it then and there and asked Simon to leave the house.

" It is unforgivable," she told him. " You don't know
what you started. It's a disaster. And you do know: you
haven't even the excuse of not knowing her. You know her
as well as I do, better, and I am beginning to know her too.
It was a wicked, heartless thing to do. Why did you? "

" To give her pleasure. To provide cover for some of our
indiscretions."

" To gain an ally," said Constanza.

" Yes. Yes of course, that too. Darling, I admit I've
stolen a march on you. But what's so monstrous about it?
Where's the disaster? Ah, if you were *not* going to marry
me."

" Simon, let's get one thing quite clear: I've no intention
of marrying you."

" Why so absolute? "

" It's not the kind of marriage I can see for myself."

" What kind do you see? "

She said seriously, " I always meant to make a *mariage de
raison.*"

" By that, do you mean money? "

" Not necessarily. I would think of money if the situation
of either of my parents made that desirable, or if they told
me so."

" You, yourself, don't care much for money? "

She considered this. " No, not for money in itself. But
I live on money. We all eat, even the ones who don't cook.
I've had no experience of having no money, not *enough*

money, because that's what it really is. Even paupers get
some money. The way I've been brought up, enough is quite
a bit. I could still change, but it'll have to be soon. I'm not
afraid of work—but who'd pay me for what? I've read a
few books and I can milk a goat. I could run a farm, an
Italian farm, at a small loss. But if I were poor I wouldn't
have a farm."

" Would you mind where the money came from, from
you or from your husband, as long as there was enough? "

" I wouldn't care two straws."

" Then what is your marriage of reason? Position? "

" That doesn't come into it. I would want a man to have
a place in the world, but it wouldn't matter what place and
where as long as it was part of himself; it could be outside
the world."

" An outsider? "

" Oh yes."

" *I*'m an outsider," said Simon.

" I don't think so," said Constanza. " Only in Northumberland."

" You're still not awfully definite about your reasonable
marriage."

" It's only an instinct I have. There must be some
community of interests, perhaps a common aim, great liking
for one another, appreciation, tolerance——"

" It sounds like a description of us," he said.

" It is not."

" You left out love," he said.

" Love does not last. And when it's gone it leaves the
wrong kind of residue for a life in common."

" You are not looking forward to a life without love? "
he said.

" Mutual tolerance *is* an ingredient of a marriage of
reason," said Constanza.

He said, " Sometimes love does last."

" Not with me. Not so far. And unless I'm much mistaken, Simon, not with you."

" I'm going to settle down once I'm married."

" I shall not," said Constanza. " And now, may I turn the tables? Why are *you* so set on marrying me? If I am your marriage of reason, you had better think again. For one thing it is not reasonable to marry a woman against her judgement; for another, if you are thinking of money—you *are* thinking of money——? "

" It has its alluring aspects."

" I shouldn't put my trust in that trust fund. I'd back mama against any bank in the United States."

" I'm aware of that. We shall have to leave it with the brilliant Mr Baxter; meanwhile it will be awfully jolly while it lasts."

" You are not telling me that you are going to make, or trying to make, thousands at the Bar? "

" I am not telling you that," said Simon. " Nevertheless I might."

" You'd better look for some poor heiress, *caro*. If you damped down on your insolence just a bit you would be so successful. And I think you know how to temper your manners to the shorn lamb."

" The heiress might not have a mother to throw in. No, Constanza, *you* are my marriage of reason. Almost everyone else is a sham, like my beloved principessa, which is interesting, but I don't want to marry one, and I would never want to marry a woman who was not a beauty, and I couldn't stand a beauty who simpered, who was a Miss or thought about her complexion or her figure, and I couldn't marry a fool, or a woman who couldn't talk back to me—you are what I want and I've enlisted your mother's help and I shall insist and insist again, and I love you very much and would marry you with the trust fund down to the last dollar if I could manage to borrow five hundred pounds, and we will

have a roaring life and wash our hands of the bloody mess
other people've made and enjoy ourselves."

Constanza said nothing.

" Anyhow who is this ideal husband of yours? *Where* is
he? "

" He isn't an ideal husband, he is just a man I should be
proud to marry."

" Have you met him? "

" No. Not even in fiction. I have no idea what he'll be
like. But I shall know him when we meet."

" *That* sounds like love."

" So much is," said Constanza.

" And meanwhile, darling, you had better take me."

" Meanwhile," she said, " is for people who do not know
when to wait."

The next day was Christmas Eve of the first Christmas of
the war. Simon had said he'd be damned if he went home
this year and serve them right. Of course, dear boy, Anna
said, you must stay with us. She, in her eclectic way, had
kept up with some and discarded other of her native customs.
Christmas had never meant much to her. So during the
years in Rome, she usually gave a large dinner-party for
Thanksgiving but was content to go through Christmas as
the Romans used to, doing a little eating and drinking,
visiting the flowered festive churches. Her only personal
contribution had been the fussless giving of some excellent
presents. So Simon found himself spending the whole
festival without a carol, a cracker or a suet pudding. On
Christmas Eve the three of them with Mr James sat down
to a well-cooked dinner which ended with fresh fruit. Later
on the ladies drove to midnight mass, and on their return
there was very hot *soupe à l'oignon gratinée* and some vintage
champagne. (Since it is always a pleasure to record such

things: it was Krug 1904, and because of the onion soup it was Extra-Dry, not Brut, and there was as much of it as anyone might drink.) Simon learnt from an envelope that he had been given what amounted to a blank account at his booksellers. " I always think it's nicer to be able to choose oneself," said Anna.

" I do agree," said Simon in a loving voice.

December 25th and 26th were much like any other days except that, none of them wishing to venture out, they played some three-handed bridge. There was also a large Strasbourg pâté which Simon and Constanza ate up in one sitting. Anna was tactful and did not say a single hinting word. She was bustling and smiling in a way that reminded Constanza of her mother in the early days, and this new serenity struck fear into her heart. She would look at Simon, sunning himself in full favour, and could not forgive him. Simon felt he had never spent a more agreeable Christmas.

Chapter V

Constanza was defeated. Things were slipping and she did not stop them. Too much was tempting. Her growing guilt about her father made her feel that anything salvaged from their whole situation would be so much to the good. Fate had placed her so that she could do nothing for him now; instead it had given her what looked like a chance to heal her mother's life. The death in France (and her own defeat last summer) had unstrung her sinews, she no longer held her own destiny so dear. There was one more thing that weighed with her, pointed in Simon's favour: he was Hermes, he was the messenger, it was he who had come to her with the ring from Rome.

Simon, pleased with himself, was off to Northumberland to bear his news. "Your turn soon, darling. Unless they cut me off with a shilling."

"You see what you've let me in for, Darkest England."

"If they take to you, you may find a fire in your bedroom, but I bet the bath will be the coldest you have ever been in."

"At Castelfonte there were lizards and no water."

"But a marble tub."

"Oh yes, marble tubs. *Will* they take to me?"

"Never been known to do so. Oh, my father'll be civil."

"I'm just writing to papa."

"Will *he* take to me?" said Simon.

"You say he already has. Papa doesn't like change."

"What about my being a heretic?"

"Not a thing that would occur to him."

" All the world belongs to the True Church? "

" Naturally."

" Aren't you going to tell him? "

" One step before another."

" But we're going to Rome the minute the war is over. I want to be the son-in-law: *il genero*."

" It isn't over. I said one step before another."

" Would you like me to become a Catholic, my sweet? "

" That will be quite unnecessary."

" I would, you know, like a shot. Just to show *them*. I'd love to see my mother's face. A Papist! "

" Things done to spite usually turn against one."

" What did you say to your father then? "

" I haven't got very far."

" May I see? "

" If you want to. It isn't much."

Simon took the sheet of paper from her table, looked at it and crowed with laughter. " Listen to this,

' Darling Daddy, I hope you are well. It is very cold and Simon and I went to the Opera on Wednesday. The singing was very fine. This morning we saw a horse——' "

" *That* isn't what I said. Give it to me! And you know it's in Italian."

" I translated freely . . . for you to grasp the point."

" I told you it wasn't much."

" *It's the letter of a child of six.*"

" Papa and I never write long letters."

" Does your father also make spelling mistakes? "

" I shouldn't think so."

" Does he write demotic grammar? "

" Oh, come."

" *You* do."

" How do you know? " said Constanza.

" My dear, I *learnt* Italian. It's very good. Bolognese."

"Like mama. Hers is beautiful and Tuscan. I *am* Italian."

"Yes, my sweet, a real Italian, a real illiterate Italian," and Simon began to dance about the room on one foot.

Constanza said: "*No!* It must be true. *All* my lessons were in English. I never had anyone Italian to teach me. I suppose mama simply never thought I ought to learn to write my own language. It never occurred to any of us. I haven't been taught Italian grammar or syntax or composition—it was just forgotten."

"A curious omission," said Simon.

"I'm an Italian Illiterate. Well, strike me pink!"

"You know: I never said that in my whole life before that evening; and I don't think I ever shall again."

"It *is* for startling occasions."

Simon came back from Northumberland deflated and relieved. "They have *not* taken to you," he told Constanza, "and they *have* cut me off without a shilling."

"Sensible people. What happened?"

"To begin with, they were in rather a grim mood. My eldest brother has just got his commission and he's going out and so is my only cousin, and they feel I'm a disgrace before the neighbours. They positively prefer to have their children blown to pieces. For another thing, some poison-pen had already spilt the beans. They've been told I've formed a most undesirable connection in London. Two foreign women of doubtful reputation. I hardly know how to break it to your mama. To Northumberland she is an Italian adventuress with a bogus title. When I pointed out that she was an American, they didn't think it an improvement. And *you* move, it appears, in a very bad set. Fast. When I told them of my cherished plan, they threatened to cut off my tiny allowance. Now it's either or."

" Any hope of your following your parents' excellent advice? " said Constanza.

Simon simply went to Anna.

" Free, white and twenty-one," she said. " There's only one thing for you to do, you must marry at once and live with us."

" That's what he's been doing, mama."

" You would prefer a house of your own? " said Anna. " Shall I start looking for one? "

" What next? I am going to stay with you."

" I hope I shall be as nice to him as mammina was to me," said Anna. " Simon, wouldn't *you* like a house of your own? English people do."

" No thank you. Cosy Italian family life for me."

" I'm seeing to it that Constanza gets a decent allowance."

" How will you manage that, mama? "

" Oh those men are being unexpectedly pleasant about it. It seems there is provision for the contingency as they call it."

" Trust funds within trust funds," said Simon.

" I wish I'd known," said Anna. " Well, whatever it is, it may not be very much. If you get short the way one does, you must always come to me."

One thing Constanza asked of Simon: No wedding. " Now that your people are staying out and I don't have to think immediately about papa, let's cut out the Oratory and the rest of it. You can have no idea what it would entail; a mixed marriage needs a lot of working out, and I want to steer clear of all that just now. So a registry office *e basta*. I don't care what people say here, and papa need never exactly know."

" Suits me," said Simon.

" That leaves mama. I count on *you* to square her."

It was now that Constanza decided to put the straight question to her mother. Her own doubts had begun long before she heard Simon's story.

" When you left my father—did it have anything to do with money? "

" Money? No, of course not. What makes you say that? "

" Isn't it time that I heard the whole of it? " said Constanza.

Anna was quite ready. " You're old enough now, it may even serve you as a warning. Thank God, my darling, you are marrying an Englishman."

But it was not Anna who was able to pour out the tale. Constanza did in one sentence and two names. " And that was it, mama? and that was all? "

Anna had covered her face. " *All?* " she groaned.

" And you never knew before? "

" He lied to me for seventeen years."

" Politeness," said Constanza. " And you never tried to look through it—at the truth? "

Anna's face was exposed again. She pursed her lips. " I do not have that type of mind."

Constanza was silent. Then she said without anger, " What can I say to you, mama? What can I ask you? You heard that he was sleeping with another woman and you left him? "

" Your language, Constanza."

" Never mind that. You left him——"

" Any other woman with the slightest self-respect——"

" I am not asking about other women, I am asking about *you*."

Anna did not answer.

" What was it you could not forgive? You are not small,

mama. You did not believe that men are always faithful to
their wives? Do you really feel that people own one another?
You condemned my father for enjoying himself in a way that
excluded you? Do you like to be selfish and possessive——"

" Constanza, stop cross-examining *me*. Have you no moral
sense? What your father did was horrible. . . ."

Constanza said in a hard tone: " Mama, this won't do.
Mama, you must grow out of this. And you calling yourself
a Christian! "

" Can this be my own daughter? " said Anna.

" Papa must have been wretched. Speaking of him as a
criminal. Think what you did to *him* . . . to us all."

" I thought you loved your years in England."

" Yes. *But I was not asked*." Now Constanza thought of
something else. " Then you must have left papa very badly
off, all of a sudden."

Anna blushed.

Constanza said, " I was a proper fool."

" He is all right," said Anna, " he is not badly off. I
happen to know this."

" How do you? "

" You must believe me, my dear."

" Oh mama! How can I? " And it was Constanza who
began to cry. " How could you—how can you be so
unforgiving? "

" *He* never asked me to forgive him," said Anna.

" Oh, Signorina Constanza! "

" You heard? "

" I listen when her voice begins to get . . . that way. You
shouldn't have said the things you said. It is no use."

" One has got to tell people. As long as one loves them.
Oh Mena, dear Mena, *I* feel I can never forgive her."

" It's not her fault, poor woman, it's the way she is made."

178

" What is it, Mena? "

" Some women get to hate their men. They don't know until something happens. With her it was Giorgio. That reminded her."

" Oh, of what, Mena? "

" Of having a husband. They do what is required, they don't mind too much, but they don't like to think of it, they feel they are too good. We had a poor soul in my village who gave ground glass to her man. He died, and she'd had four sons from him."

" Is it the *bambini*? "

" The *bambini* are part of it, my lamb."

" Mama doesn't hate men. She spends her life with them. Look how she dotes on Simon. She patronized papa but she seemed fond of him."

" That was when she didn't have to remember."

" All the *more* reason for not grudging him to Giulia? "

" She loves the Signorino," said Mena, " the Signorino Simon. She is happy with them as long as there's no danger. Don't spoil it for her now."

" If I went away and left them together——? "

" That would not do at all. Oh Signorina Constanza, *don't* change your mind now! "

" I'm afraid I cannot," Constanza said. " Because if I did it would be revenge."

Simon managed to square the principessa. " I told her it was a war wedding. It worked like a charm." They were married, as Constanza had wished, before a registrar. Their witnesses were Mr James and Anna.

Mr James, the night before, had taken Constanza out to dinner. " He ought to be taking *me*," Simon said. Constanza pointed out that it was not he who was about to lose his freedom.

They went to the Carlton Grill and waited for the mood that might develop.

" Isn't one supposed to go over one's whole past like a drowning woman? "

" Too early for you," Mr James said sternly; " much too early."

" I feel you are disappointed in me."

" I am," he said. " I would have backed you as more selfish."

" Whatever prompted me was not my guardian angel. And to be alive these days is quite selfish enough."

" Your mother," said Mr James, " is one of my oldest friends—but I am not in her confidence. She has never chosen to speak to me. I have not—shall we say?—the right temperament."

" Oh, how fond I am of you! "

" Will you take something from me, my dear? What you are trying to do is not wise."

" I'd take anything from you; but shouldn't you have spoken a bit earlier? What I'm *trying* to do? At this point, isn't it as good as done? "

" One does not like to . . . meddle. And you did not give us much time."

" And I am . . . meddling? "

Mr James drew a deep breath.

" Do let's have it out," said Constanza.

" My dear, dear girl. I have found that what one does is likely to work out in a certain pattern. It's a question of leverage. If you go too far away from yourself you increase the leverage, but it also becomes less accurate. To change the metaphor, at long range you aim at one thing and you hit another. You *can* choose for yourself; you cannot choose for others. If you do, you are only manipulating them."

" I'm not one for power," said Constanza, " I have no wish to *manipulate*."

He said, " The things one feels obliged to do against one's inclination are often the most harmful. Chalking up the cost to oneself is no kind of guarantee. One contracts a debt one may be unable to meet in the long run. Choosing for oneself in twenty years' time is another form of over-reaching."

" That means *every* marriage, *every* contract, career, *all* planning."

" Some people have come to that conclusion," he said. " It is not a popular one."

" And so? Go on."

" Keep to the middle course. Beware of ulterior motives. Do not attempt to pin down the future."

" Even good ulterior motives? "

" Especially those."

" You talk as if it were all in *my* hands," said Constanza. " I did not start it. Well, except in one way ... I'm not the king-pin in this cat's-cradle—to change the metaphor."

" You are the one who is choosing to be fitted into the pattern."

" And so the most to blame? "

" Not the *least* responsible. The other two are out for themselves. You are standing aside. Discounting A (A being you) for the sake of C, and not thinking of B at all."

" So Simon is the Excluded Middle? " said Constanza.

" You still muddle your terms," said Mr James. " Though it serves: Simon is hardly to blame, and it is not very fair on him."

" *Il l'a voulu, Georges Dandin.*"

Mr James said, " It was your attitude to Simon which ... baffled me. You and he get on so very well."

" You see? What right have I got not to marry a man with whom I get on so well."

" That was not what I meant."

" Can you tell me in words of one syllable? "

" I expected better things from you."

" Is this an incitement to stand up Simon at the altar, or what serves as one? "

" I don't go in for drastic measures, as you know. It might be in your line."

" I cannot do it," she said. " *You don't know*, you haven't lived with it. It would kill her."

" Yes: I *can* hear her say that."

To cheer themselves up, he said he had never told her the story of Mena's wine. It showed a side of the principessa's character which he found, well as Simon would put it: interesting. Many years ago, then, the principessa was in England on a visit; it was the first time that Mena had come with her, and they both put up at Brown's Hotel. Anna—you know her way—asked Mena if she was looked after properly and if the food was all right. Mena said the food was not too bad, but what she minded was that there was no wine. No wine, said Anna, why how unpleasant for you, we must see to that. So Anna went and spoke to the waiter or whoever it was who had charge of the table-d'hôte at Brown's where the lady's maids and couriers ate, and told him that Mena was used to it and must have her pint or two of wine with meals. So out they brought for her their *Médoc Supérieur*, and very sound stuff it is in its unassuming way. A few days later Anna asks her, does she get her wine? Oh yes, says Mena, they give her wine, but pretty poor thick ink it is, *paziènza*, all puckery in the mouth, one might be drinking tea. Now our Anna caught on to that at once. She learnt to drink good claret in her father's house and she still, to give her credit, serves it at her dinner parties; but she, too, has acquired quite a taste for that nice light red Italian lemonade they all swill down whatever they may be eating and not a second thought—and so have you, my dear: don't pretend, you'll never make a claret drinker, and that'll be a grief to Simon for the boy has a nice taste in wine, a very nice taste indeed for one his age—Valpolicella, Capri, Colline

Senese, and very easy and companionable too, kind on the liver if you have one, but they're to the product of the Gironde what baby prattle is to Plato."

" Simon says Italians have no palate."

" Well, it is not tuned to Bordeaux. What they cannot take to is the tannin. So down went Anna to speak again to that waiter. Italian wine, she insists, it must be *Italian* wine. The waiter is doubtful, he doesn't think they have any. Anna sends for the dining-room head-waiter, for the wine-waiter, the manager. Long faces. They have quite a nice little cellar at Brown's and they don't clutter it up with great stacks of straw-clad flagons. No demand, they say. But of course they bow to Anna. The *sommelier* promises he'll do his best. So out they nipped down St. James's, and soon they found a merchant who was able to oblige. *He* did not have his cellar full of straw and hand-blown glass either, but he had a few bottles of something that came from Italy all right. It was the Barone Barbasoli's Private Bottling straight from the Gaiole Vineyards, *Gran Riserva*, *Stravecchio*, *Classico* and all the rest of it, and they sent it round."

" It was good? " said Constanza.

" They let it have a rest on its side at Brown's, they drew the cork at the proper time, they decanted it, and stood the decanter in front of Mena's place. It wasn't what Mena had expected, but she took to it; she took to it so well that repeat orders had to be placed in St. James's and in Tuscany, and they began stocking it at Brown's. Mena reported she had never tasted better wine come out of a carafe, and she drank it every noon and night. Since then they've always kept some against her visits, and even now your mother is getting it for her by the case from Brown's. I shouldn't mind having some myself, if it weren't that it's worth its weight in *Mouton*."

Constanza for once was not amused. Perhaps he was right, she said, she did not know enough about real wine, but it seemed to her that it had been very nice of mama to have gone to a bit of trouble.

" I think I must end by applauding Simon's decision not to earn your living," said Mr James.

After the ceremony the next day, quite a lot of people had been asked to Regent's Park. Simon and Constanza arrived in high spirits. Simon was as merry as a grig and had been mimicking the Registrar practically to his face. Constanza had suddenly decided to enjoy her wedding-day; in consequence all had passed off in a gust of what Anna called Roman irreverence and Italian giggles. Anna, too, looked as if she had swallowed a good deal of the cream. Most of their guests were puzzled. Such men present whom Constanza had turned down looked at Simon with distaste and astonishment. The ones who had not been turned down were more astonished still. The absence of the groom's family did not go unnoticed, and the women were most intrigued by the nature of the wedding. It wasn't as if Simon were being whisked off to war, they said.

But that was *it*, someone said, " He *is*. They all know about it at the War Office. He's to be off on a most hush-hush job."

" *Simon?* "

" Oh, that defeatist jabber is just a blind."

" Yes, I suppose with all those languages."

" They're sending him into Turkey."

" But what has Simon's going for a spy to do with their cutting out church? Church is just as quick."

" They're not allowed to put foot into Constanza's and they don't want to *afficher* the fact."

" Oh? "

" You see, after all those dark doings in Rome they excommunicated the principessa."

" Papists in bad standing. The Herberts can't like that at all."

Someone had lent them a house in Wiltshire. Simon loudly complained that it had to be that, not Paris.

" I've never been to Paris," said Constanza.

"Provincial. I long to take you one day. Will you come?"

" How charming of you to put it in the interrogative," she said.

" I forgot," said Simon.

" *That* was charming."

Their fortnight in the country went off like the picnic it was. Angelina looked after them; Anna had paved the house with hampers. Simon unpacked these himself, saying that it made him feel that he was loved. Constanza managed to get hold of a couple of horses and, although Simon said that this was his least favourite way of getting about, they went for long rides. One afternoon they found themselves in Somerset. " There's a house I know quite near here," Constanza said, " I only saw it once, an Italian house, I'd like to see it again."

" *Italianate*," said Simon.

They went. They looked down the drive at the honey-coloured façade. " I can't bear it," Constanza said, " it's too lovely. I mustn't start falling for houses, like mama."

" It is rather to *my* taste, too," said Simon drily.

" Let's call on them. The time I went it was night. I was staying in Dorset and we all drove over for a dance, you know how that changes a house. Let's go in and look."

" We won't," said Simon. " *I* know them, too. It belongs to my uncle. My father's brother."

" *This*—house? Simon! Why did you never tell me?"

" It isn't mine, is it?"

" I shall not get used to the English. If it were *my* uncle, we'd all be living with him."

" Come on," said Simon, " the horses are getting cold."

Chapter VI

1915 was a long year. Constanza, doing something more responsible now than filing forms, was kept busy at her job; at night she and Simon went to parties. There were always people on leave, people about to be shipped off, news of people killed. They seldom left London. After Italy had entered the war, most of her conscious thoughts were there. She read the letters from home and the letters that came for Mena, she read the *Corriere* and the Vatican paper and she read the casualty lists. In England she felt one with her friends, in Italy with the whole of the people. She could feel what it was like to be inside those thick and ill-made uniforms, those bulging puttees, she could breathe the dust of the summer roads, she felt what they felt about going, the jokes, the fatalism, the shrugging, the fear, and the desperate patience of the women. Two boys of Giulia's, the coal-man of the Via degli Specchi, Carla's eldest, Mario the carpenter's son and Mario of the Via Monserrato, the whole of the Campo di Fiori gang, half of Castelfonte. . . .

" I feel I can hold up my head once more," said Anna.

And Constanza tried not to nurse her other grief, which was her gradual turning against her mother.

Simon stayed at home most of the day, reading for the Bar. Constanza came and went as she used to do in her parents' house as a girl. Only towards the autumn, when the baby she was expecting began to show, she stayed in more. She found she could hardly read. " So much for that resource," she said. " Mama, I wish you had taught me to sew."

Anna did not sew either. The baby was not very welcome. Simon referred to it as the pram in the hall, and spoke wist-

fully of a sage-femme he knew of in the rue de la Tombe
Issoire and wondered if her likes could not be conjured up
in England; Constanza, cross and impatient though she was
about the business, would have none of it. The principessa
was only conventionally pleased.

One night, it was one of Anna's charity occasions and a
very glittering one, Constanza saw an exceedingly slim youth
in Italian officer's uniform walk into the ball-room. She
went towards him.

" *Tu!* "

" Constanza! "

When their *duetto* had dwindled to recitative, she said,
" How is it possible? "

" Military Mission. Youngest member."

" Safe and whole! "

" Safe; not whole." He laughed, he beamed, he tapped
his ankle in the slim and polished boot. " A bullet. Not
even Austrian—our own! A recruit dropped his rifle—San
Vincenzo must have guided his hand—and in my very first
week out. The ankle isn't much good any more. Now I have
a staff job. Did you pray for me, Constanza? "

" How not! " she said.

He gave her a swift appraising look. " *Sposata?* "

" What else? "

Simon, in a white tie, hovered, now came up. " Go away,"
Constanza said, " the *tenente* is a very old friend, I want him
to myself." Simon walked on.

The lieutenant followed him with his eyes. " A *jealous*
inglese," he said.

" Oh, surely not. He's my husband."

" *Figurati!* That's no reason."

" These days it is," said Constanza.

Simon passed the first part of the Bar Examination as he

had said he would, effortlessly and well. News of this, and news of the coming baby had seeped into Northumberland; so had other reports shedding a rather different light on the principessa. The family began making overtures. After a fortnight they were at a stage at which Simon had lunched with his father at his club, his father had called at Regent's Park, Simon's mother had written to Constanza asking her to stay, and Constanza had accepted for a later date.

" *That* doesn't help them out of their dilemma," Simon said, " which is the neighbours' knowing that they haven't met you before this brat is born. Their first grand-child. That's the trouble."

" Ask them here," said Constanza. Simon said he might. He had other things to think about. Conscription. " It's bound to be here by the New Year."

" Conscientious Objector? "

" You'd like me to be one, my sweet? "

" Yes."

" I don't see myself. Goodness knows why. I object enough."

" Could you face it? "

" I could face it all right. It's the sort of thing I've been up against at home. It's just a feeling I have; perhaps I wouldn't be much of a credit. Let's leave it to better men."

" An exempt job? "

" Would you like that for me? "

" Yes. I would do everything to help you get one."

" Perhaps not *my* thing either. I'm *better* than that. Oh, I'm not thinking about the bloody country, I wash my hands of the mob's war, the politicians' war (*why* won't they let Asquith stop it). I'm thinking about my friends, in the end one's got to do as one's friends do. When I'm old I want to be able to sit and drink my wine with them in peace. If any

of them will be left—if *I* will be left. But I have a feeling
I shall. You will bring me luck, Constanza."

" *Don't,*" she said.

Simon said, " You're as superstitious as a savage."

" I know. I can't help it."

So Simon went and got himself fixed up with a commission
before the Military Enlistment Act became law. He was off
training when Constanza's girl was born. He did not like
his new life; but he was twenty-two years old and he had
a tough streak and he was fascinated by some of the military
goings-on, and his spirit was not crushed one bit.

" Rather a mercy it is what it is," he said, when he came
home on a forty-eight hours' pass, " it'll keep my people's
paws off it."

" Girls don't get involved with inheriting and that sort
of thing," said Constanza.

" There's nothing to inherit," said Simon.

He was quite interested to see it and stood a long time
watching. " Helpless creature," he said, " give me a young
monkey any day. It isn't even a *bambino*, it's all fair like
me."

" Hair at this stage means nothing," said Constanza. But
the baby's eyes were unmistakably blue.

" Pure Howland," said Anna. " Every feature. A rever-
sion to type."

" It'll be a bit young for Giorgio to play with," said
Constanza, " we do seem to manage things badly."

When they were alone Constanza said, " Mama is having a
Catholic priest in to baptize it."

" All right by me," he said.

" All right by me," said Constanza.

" Doesn't it have to have a name? "

" It does."

" Most English girls' names are of a frumpishness——"

" I wasn't thinking of an English name. I want to call her Flavia."

" Doesn't sound too bad. Please to explain? "

" It was my father's mother's name. She adored mama, so mama can hardly object."

" I get it," said Simon. " As near as you dare."

" Well, you would hardly want to call her Rica? "

That Christmas either they did not go to Northumberland; but soon after, Constanza kept her promise and they went up to spend two nights. Simon, who was now on embarkation leave, insisted that it must be no more. His last days on earth, he said. It was all much as he had described. He remained himself, and Constanza, who knew more now what it cost him, admired him for it. She herself had been used to a certain measure of philistinism and as it had never interfered with her own life, it troubled her much less. What did get her down was the emotional blankness.

" Ought we to conclude then," she said, " that they're all smouldering cauldrons underneath? "

She and Simon were alone in his cold dressing-room, but he had boldly taken up a decanter of brandy from downstairs. " I shouldn't bank on it," he said.

" Goodness, *caro*, your sister pulls a long face."

" She's every reason to, poor thing."

" If she doesn't hurry up, it'll stay that way. Your family reminds me so of mama's *secret* friends. You never knew the worst of them, a poisonous old crow who hung out in Rome for our sins. We used to call her la Trommo-Vailé. I expect you never ran into her? "

" Run into her? Run away, more like! *You* don't know

who she is, she is a relation of my mother's, oh quite distant, but as she's fearfully rich—she *is*—and childless and all that, they made her my sister's God-mother."

" *Misericordia*," said Constanza. " Does that mean Flavia is a blood relation of that woman? I really must begin to make it up for her as mama would say. And talking of revelations, *caro*, when you came to us with no cuffs to your shirts—I mean metaphorically; you were always beautifully dressed, darling, much better than I—we took it that you were brought up in the poorhouse. Well, the food here *is* like that, but they say it's the war and perhaps they really get no jam and bacon in Northumberland, and no coal or petrol either. But: the house is not *small*, and even if all those servants *are* as old as they look they must get *some* wages, and you can't have so *many* Daimlers under dust-sheets if you're really poor. I've come to the conclusion that your parents must be quite rich; like Mrs Throg."

" It'll all go to my brother Tom," said Simon, " the rest of us have been told to expect nothing."

§

Simon went to France. For Constanza there came again a time that was suspense and nothing else. Again she dared hardly take a step or breathe; above all she did not dare let go. It was as if she had to hold on to a thread that had to be kept taut. Her bond with Simon was of a nature other than anything she felt for him when he was present; she hardly thought about him as a person now, and of herself not at all: what she had before her night and day was Simon's life. The sense that this strange vigilance was necessary never left her and the strain was very great.

Simon wrote to her every day he could, and often a second

letter came for Anna. They were good letters; Constanza could hardly bear to read them.

Once that winter, a Northumberland Herbert was on the casualty list. It was Simon's second brother, Harry, killed at Verdun.

In March Simon got wounded. When he was back in England, he talked as he had used to, he had kept his talent for putting himself across as himself. He was self-confident, almost radiant. " Constanza—*I've done it*: Honourably wounded; and out of it." His knee was badly smashed. " I'm damned if I'm going to lose my leg," he said, and he did not. To Anna he sent this word: I'm going to enjoy my convalescence, please, *cara*, send me all the good things you can get hold of.

To Constanza he said, " Still hurts like bloody hell. How I hate pain. Poor old Harry, poor chap—but then he was a real soldier, a professional, confound them. Not that *they* ever dreamt of this." He told her: " It was much worse than you and I imagined, *much* worse. May I only remember it in my nightmares. People going through with it is the final proof that we are all insane. Or hypnotized. I couldn't have stood it much longer, I would have cracked up soon. The relief of it now! *And* being able to look forward to a serene old age. Do admit—I was lucky."

By summer Simon had a job in Whitehall. Everybody said that he was brilliant at it, and he was promoted almost at once. Approval agreed with him and he began to work extremely hard. Constanza seldom saw him. He was living again at Regent's Park; in daytime they were at their separate offices and at night if Simon did not work they often went to slightly different parties.

Simon's leg had remained stiff, and when he began to walk again he did not use a cane, but immediately acquired a very rapid gait that seemed to be propelled rather than impeded by a light, rhythmic limp.

His father came up. They ate another luncheon at his club and the outcome of it was that Simon was offered and accepted a rather decent allowance.

Occasionally Constanza was able to call for Simon at mid-day, and they would eat their sandwiches together in St. James's Park.

" It's nearly as much again as we have from the trust fund," she said.

" They're beginning to be kind to the survivors."

" I was thinking perhaps we shouldn't let mama pay for everything any more."

" She doesn't mind," said Simon.

" Even Flavia's doctor's bills are sent to her."

" I thought the creature was never ill, like you and I."

" Oh, babies have to be looked at from time to time."

" We never were," he said.

" Yes, Simon; and you never stop complaining about your childhood."

" *You* don't really love me."

" I brought you a bottle of *Graves*," she said.

" Tepid? "

" Not to the best of my ability. Here."

" Damp newspaper," said Simon. " You're almost as clever as I am."

" Your mother has written again about the Nanny question."

" Tell her to shut up."

" I have told her how nicely Mena and Angelina are looking after her. No-one could be better than Mena."

" She means an *English* nanny," said Simon.

Before they had to be on their ways, Simon said lightly, " You were awfully late last night? "

" Dawn," said Constanza.

Suddenly furious, he said, " And where were you till . . . dawn? "

" Where I told you, where you knew I was, dancing, at the Grafton Galleries."

He snorted.

" Why didn't you pick me up? "

" I have work to do."

" So have other people."

" Who did you dance with? "

" I didn't make a list. What's the matter, *caro*? aren't you being a slight idiot? "

But he did not respond.

" You are more than a bore," she said, " and this isn't the first time. I won't stand for it, you know. It's . . . unseemly."

" Your fine words," he said. " Well, I have work to do. *Thank God*." And off he walked.

Another time they were coming home together late in a taxi. Simon said to her, " You treat me as if I were a member of your gang."

" So you are, darling, and a nice thing too."

" I want more than that," he said.

Simon was rather drunk and so she let this pass.

" Everybody knows that American women treat their men like dirt . . . even half Americans. I am your husband."

" Yes, *caro*."

" But you don't love me. You don't love me for myself, you didn't want to marry me," and he burst into tears.

Next day he apologized. Overwork . . . too much to

drink. . . . They both felt it was a time to be polite rather than dot i's, so they exchanged a few jokes and let it go at that.

" What's come over Simon? " Constanza said to Mr James.

" Well—his war, short though it was, must have been a big strain. Reaction. And as you know he is a very spoilt boy and you are a very run-after woman."

" He wasn't spoilt much," she said. " Well, until now."

" In the new jargon," said Mr James, " he was longing for a mother and a father. Now he's got your mother and his own father—don't tell me he doesn't feel flattered—not to mention all those Government Offices treating him like a prodigy. All very different from the cheeky rebel he was two years ago."

" And how do I suddenly not fit in? "

" Simon has a lot of things to be proud of now, but the story of his marriage to you is not one of them. And you've become the wrong kind of wife. You are still a feather in his cap, but he's not sure he can count on your staying put. Will you? "

" I stayed put so far. What *does* he want? "

" Assurance for the future. Being looked up to. His own way."

" We have so many same ways," said Constanza.

" He may want to lead."

" Simon was not like that. I always thought Simon was different from anybody else."

" My dear, very few people are that," said Mr James.

" Simon is one in a thousand. His mother wants us to have an English nanny; now you say he wants an English wife."

" How fast you go, dear girl."

" Yes—too fast. I don't see sweet gay Simon with a Miss Mouse."

In October there was talk of Simon being sent to Washington on a commission.

" Interesting? "

" Oh enormously," he said, " I'd love to go."

" Good."

" I suppose you'll be glad to be rid of me."

" Simon."

" Well, how do I know? How do I know I can trust you an inch? "

" Simon, this is folly! Dynamite. Never say that to anyone. Don't say it twice to me."

" All right, *cara*, all right," he gave her a crooked smile and lay back in his chair. " Though I can't even figure out if we're supposed to be a *mariage de raison* or *d'amour?* "

" Idiot," she said. " Bit of both, don't you think? "

But her answer failed to soothe him. And soon after they had again what can only be called a jealous row.

Simon did not go to Washington. Before the end of the year Constanza started having an affair with someone, and within the same fortnight, prompted by some obscure sense of fitness, she did what she had never done before, she started a second one. This instantly made her feel more light-hearted. It also complicated the time-table of her life and made her tell so many circumstantial stories, where before she had hardly deigned reply, that Simon's suspicions slackened and things between them became a good deal easier for a time.

They had reached the third winter of the war. Asquith had

resigned, Lloyd George was Prime Minister. It was the winter after Ypres, the Meuse, the Somme, the winter of the U.S. Peace Note and Unrestricted Naval Warfare. None of the news was good. " And if it stopped this instant," Simon said, " nothing would be the same again. A shrunken England. . . ."

" They must be saying that in France."

" And in Germany."

" It will *not* stop this instant."

" No miracle."

" America must come in," said Anna.

" Then they can say it there."

" I'm ready to accept anything that will help to end it," said Constanza.

From Italy it was the same kind of news. Carla's eldest killed, one of Giulia's missing; only one of the Simonetti boys had caught double pneumonia, pulled through and was now invalided out. " How cold they must be," Constanza said. The winter on the Austrian front below those mountain passes had become one of her obsessions.

" I think I'll stay in tonight."

" No, you won't," said Simon, " I want to show you off to my dark horse. We're meeting him at the Eiffel Tower." The dark horse, he told Anna, was also a bit of a rough diamond, a bloke he had come across in a dug-out in France. "Ware, Captain Ware, that's the name he goes by. Nobody's got the least idea where he's sprung from. Hard to describe him. Well: shaggy."

" A bohemian? " said Anna.

" Not the opposite. But he's got grit. And bright, frightfully bright: knows everything, has read everything; I've never met a man with less prejudices. Makes *me* feel like Little Lord F."

" An intellectual? " said Constanza.

" Self-made. Writes. On pictures. That's where I

came in. Though he seems to be doing other things as well."

"A gentleman?" said Anna.

"Technically, no. Just thirty and he's made a packet—and lost it again—buying and selling, guess what?"

"Scrap iron?"

"Rare books?"

"You're warm. Impressionists. Picked them up when he was the age of a school-boy. Now he's on to some starving Spanish chap who does cubes, Juan Something. Well come on, Constanza, pick up your rings, off we go. He's got five days' leave and we're only half an hour late."

Constanza put on the rings she had slipped off and scattered on the table in front of her; said oh very well, kissed her mother and went. Anna, punctual to the minute, drove off to a bazaar.

The war had not been unkind to Anna. The general ban on travel had done much to ease the private anguish of her exile. She was busy, she was sought after, she had scope for her emotions. Many young people were fond of her. She had reverted to her life-long habit of having a few men of her own generation dance attendance, but since the episode with Sir Charles their attentions had been merely formal and implicit. The chief meaning of her present life was Simon, and making a home for Simon's family, and he never failed her in courtesy and affection. The child, too, she was beginning to enjoy. It had begun to speak, its hair showed signs of staying fair and the likeness to herself was striking. Constanza she often found rebellious, harsh and lacking; but she had never liked to think too much about her daughter. Simon was a safer field. If Anna's views of it were not conformist, she was yet too much of her age not to love success: and though it had looked anything but a brilliant marriage people were beginning to tell her that Simon would go far.

Before that spring Constanza had cut loose from her second young man and changed the first. And when that one, who was a science man who had joined the Navy, was posted to a laboratory in the North and their opportunities for meeting became rare, she let it end itself and refused replacements. Her heart was not in it. There goes another resource, she would have liked to say but there was no-one she could say it to. She and Simon had some difficult times together and some good ones.

America was in the war, the Czar of the Russias had abdicated, the second battle of the Aisne had started. Together they read the anti-war poems that were coming out in little magazines.

" *I* shall leave Europe the day it's over," Simon said. " Central America: Savage architecture and no present history."

" Quite a lot of local history."

" One can cope with that. And no utopia or group business for me either—just off."

Like everybody else they talked about the revolution in Russia. Constanza, with reservations, put her hopes on Kerensky.

" A liberal ideal," Simon told her, " he will fail. People are not liberal, they are beasts. In England: smug beasts."

" People who make constitutional revolutions are not beasts," said Constanza.

" That's why they fail."

" They didn't fail in England or America."

" They didn't have to cope with vast masses then. *Nous avons changé tout cela.*"

When the Bolsheviks took over and they had to face that

news, Constanza was appalled. " What a way of forcing the brotherhood of men down each other's throats. Like the Church at her worst."

" What could you expect? " said Simon.

" It would seem that in history it's never a tooth for a tooth, but a thousand, a hundred thousand for one." She asked Mr James if it would end by affecting the whole world like the French Revolution?

Mr James thought there could be no comparison. Russia was an undeveloped, semi-barbarous country, as good as outside Europe.

" I always believed socialism would begin in the United States," Constanza said. " Certainly not in a backward agricultural country without political institutions. Karl Marx must be turning in his grave. Well, so far they are at the easiest stage: smashing and murdering."

" According to our press," said Simon.

" It'll run itself out," said Mr James.

Only Simon was not sure. " That's been said of every new movement one dislikes and fears. And it'll need very very careful handling on our part, by which I mean the Allied Governments. And of course they'll bungle it. Now if *I* were——"

Simon often talked this way these days and Constanza liked it least in front of Mr James. She interrupted him with an impatient gesture.

" I didn't mean Number 10, darling, I shall never want that. I only meant the Foreign Office."

Not long afterwards, Constanza was able to say to Mr James: " Miss Mouse has entered our lives. I must hasten to add that she's Miss Mouse in tiger-skin—quite a beauty. Very dark; flashing. Her mother was a Greek or something, the looks, Simon's kind of looks, are taken care of. But she's being Miss Mouse all right with Simon, she dotes on him and shows it. Everything he does is perfect."

" My dear child. And your husband? " said Mr James.

" Purrs. What else? Except for her devotion to him, she's perfectly lively and easy-going; and she's most presentable, in fact rather a big catch: rolling rich. So of course he's delighted."

" Who is this paragon? " said Mr James.

" She has a war job as somebody's secretary in Simon's Department. Her name is Mary——" Constanza supplied the surname. " You know, old Thingummy's daughter. Newspapers."

" A Newspaper Empire."

" *Già.*"

" My dear child," Mr James said in a shaken tone, for he loved Constanza.

" Yes? "

" Isn't this rather . . . perilous? "

" These things often are. If you mean, will Simon up and leave me for this heiress? I think not. Everything is possible. But Simon isn't interested in oceans of money, all he wants is to be comfortable and perhaps buy a picture or two. And he is comfortable with us. As long as mama doesn't manage to spend all our money."

" And what does Mary . . . Miss Mouse want? "

" Oh, Simon. Tooth and claw. That's not admitted yet. For the moment they're having a rather jolly affair."

" Are you sure of that? " asked Mr James. " Most young ladies don't."

" You're wrong," said Constanza.

" Dear girl, aren't you being rather cool about it? "

" What else? The double standard? I never pretended to Simon that I expected a hard and fast marriage. Besides he's enjoying himself—when you think *how very nearly* he might not be here to do that. And I have had my schooling, I have

seen how to behave and how not. I have my rules, *and* shall
stick to them, same as mama."

Early in 1918 Simon's cousin was killed in action. " Poor
devil," Simon said. " He was the only civilized one of the
lot. *So* handsome, too. Poor devil. He was engaged but
didn't think a war marriage was fair on a girl. How right he
was. What a waste. . . ." He also said. " He was father's
only brother's only son. Winner takes all. That house,"
he named it, " will go to Tom now."

" The Italian—the Italianate—house? "

" Yes."

" Will your brother Tom love it? "

" No. It might just as well be Scotch Baronial. But he'll
like the money: there's a lot that goes with it. Well, long
may he enjoy it."

" *He* is all right? " said Constanza.

" All right in Egypt. Yes, darling, as safe as anyone.
Safer."

Constanza touched her ruby.

After that spring Simon talked no more about going to
Mexico and Guatemala; he said Germany had lost the war
and it was time to think about one's future. He told Constanza he would not go on with the Bar. " I might try my
hand in politics, an interesting life if one's financially
independent and not too ambitious." People were forcing
constituencies on him, he said, and sketched for her the life
he saw. What fun it could be; how he would keep himself
free and never hesitate to say boo to the Party Whips, or
think he was indispensable, or work too hard. He said for
the first years he'd like to be the *enfant terrible* of the House;
and of course he would always *have* to be right.

" *You* would like it? " he asked her.

" Very much," said Constanza.

She asked him if Miss Mouse approved of his new plans.

" How not? " Simon teased her. When they were by themselves they often called Miss Mouse Miss Mouse; it re-assured them.

" You used to like being talked back to," Constanza said.

" I find the other more restful—now that I'm getting old and important. Mary hasn't got as many principles as you have, she isn't New England."

Constanza found this a huge joke. " But *am* I so opinionated? Do I force my opinion on you? "

" No," he said, " but you always have one."

Simon's father came up again, and took him out to dinner. He gave him vintage port. It was the only wine Simon did not really like, but he appreciated the gesture. He reported, " The old miser has taken to my going into Parliament, and he's going to see me through."

" Does he know that you're not going to be a pillar of the Tories? "

" He doesn't *know*. He suspects. He'll swallow it when the time comes. One step before another."

Chapter VII

By midsummer Simon had asked Constanza to give him a
divorce. He did not quite put it in that way. They both
had been too young; he was looking differently at things
now; the war was going to be over soon; it might be a good
moment to start with a clean slate. " So if it's all the same to
you? "

After she had agreed, he said, " I thought you would.
It isn't as if— Ah well, no use going into all that again.
Now that we know where we are, there's no hurry, no hurry
at all. So many people involved, it's going to be rather
complicated."

" Not like our wedding? "

" No."

" Simon, one thing: Mama." Constanza almost daily
judged her mother, but the affection was still there. " Have
you *thought* about telling mama? "

" Haven't I? " he said.

They shelved it for a week or two. Then Simon came to
her very much depressed. " I was an ass not to think at once
of the laws and customs of this ante-diluvian country. I
told you there are too many people involved. I want to
marry Mary as you know and all that. Well: if you divorce
me and name her as the intervener, her people are going to
kick up the most awful row. The seducer. I may not get
horse-whipped, but what do you say to a political career that
starts off with one morning, one evening and a Sunday
paper against the candidate? "

" *Caro*, you must quickly seduce somebody else and I will name her as the intervener."

" *Furba*," he said. " Well and good, that still leaves *me*. I'm the person most involved. As the Guilty Party to a divorce, I might squeeze into Parliament, but there'll be small chance of office, nor could I ever be a judge."

" I thought you were giving up the Bar? "

" I shan't practise. But I might as well eat my dinners, I'd like to have been called. And it has its uses. But that's neither here nor there."

" Did you say Guilty Party? " said Constanza.

" Hmm. *We* haven't got Desertion or Mental Cruelty, we haven't any of those accommodating outs they have in your mother's country."

" I believe they only have those in the newer States. And in my father's country we have no divorce at all."

Simon said: " A bright idea! What about an annulment? It'll cost plenty, but that ought to be no problem. Yes—let the cardinals do it."

" My sweet oaf, we would have to be properly married to get an annulment. Married before a Catholic priest. In their eyes we aren't married at all."

" Damn," said Simon.

" Darling, it *would* make a difference if you were the injured party? "

" All the difference."

" Very well then, that's simple enough. I must seduce somebody and you divorce me."

" That isn't so well-regarded either," Simon said.

" Your *crime passionnel*. You'll carry it off, you have the jealous streak. Unfortunately."

" *Is* there somebody? "

" There is not." She nearly added: as it happens.

" I must know the truth."

He looked tense and wretched. " There is no-one at all," she said.

" Swear."

" You know I don't do that. But it is true."

" Well I'm glad," he said, and looked it.

" You're as bad as mama."

" *You* are like your father. What about last year? What about ——? and ——? " he shot names at her.

This time she decided to lie.

" You are a queer girl," he said. " Now why this? Why do you suggest taking a lover to help with my divorce? "

" Because it seems a friendly, sensible way. *I*'m not going into the House or sit on the Bench."

" Women will any day now."

" One step before another," said Constanza.

" I won't have it," Simon said, " not as long as you are married to me."

" A dilemma," said Constanza.

" I wasn't saying it was not a tempting proposition."

Then she asked him, what about Flavia?

" I don't want her," he said.

" I know. She'd better stay with me. For better or for worse."

" No use having her bundled to and fro the way your little brother was before the war. It's not as if my people were good with children. Yours being an R.C. makes it rather awkward for them, and what they're keen on is sons. She really doesn't fit. Anna'll look after her."

" *I* will look after her," said Constanza.

" Either way, better start with a clean slate here, too.

Tom's going to marry as soon as he gets home. I can always get a peep at her when I come to see Anna."

Next day Constanza said, " I've got it. Since you're so finicky, why not make it a *divorce blanc*? You know the way men fix it up by going to Brighton with a tart. Can't we rig up something like that for me? Spend the night at an hotel with a man we know and have the chambermaid come in with the breakfast tray? "

"And *who* is going to be this partner of our white divorce? "

" You may choose him, *caro*. It shouldn't be difficult. Let's ask one of our friends who doesn't like women, we seem to know so many of them lately."

§

It was very difficult. The men who did not like women took alarm at the thought of spending a night with Constanza at an hotel and being dragged through the Divorce Courts for their pains. Others had to think of their wives or mistresses or their careers, and not one of them thought the proposition very creditable.

" So much for friendship," said Simon.

" My sweet, you *will* have to leave it to me."

" I will not," said Simon.

And how right he was, Constanza told him presently. " I've realized, it will have to be a *white* divorce or nothing. Mama. If she leaves me, she'll be all alone, poor woman. I don't expect you'd have her to live with you and Mary? "

But Simon, shrewd as always, absolutely forbade Constanza to let her mother in on it. " She'll have the King's

Proctor on us. And *that* would be exposure, scandal, all
our plans in ruin."

" *Your* plans," said Constanza. Nevertheless, she promised
him to leave her mother in the dark until it was all over.

Then Simon came home with the solution. " Lewis. Lewis
is on leave again, *he* won't turn a hair. Lewis Ware, Captain
Ware, remember? My dark horse. He's a sport and a good
friend, I'm going to ask him today. All right by you? "

Perfectly all right, said Constanza.

Lewis did not turn a hair. Thursday, Simon told Constanza.
" He hasn't got much leave."

" What a waste for him," she said. " We can't accept
that."

" I told you he's a good friend."

" What do I do next? "

His detectives were on, Simon said. For the rest she
was on her own now. " You'll have to make the arrangements. I've got to keep out of it."

Captain Ware—very considerately, she thought—telephoned. " I hear I have the pleasure of taking you out of
London. Where shall it be, Mrs Herbert? "

Constanza said wouldn't he prefer a London hotel so that
they could go to a theatre or something.

Very thoughtful of her, he said, " But London isn't such
a good idea for what Simon has in mind."

" Brighton, then? "

" Can you think of a place people *don't* go to? "

" Wouldn't that be awfully dull for you? "

" Mrs Herbert," the Captain said, " we are supposed to
be doing a job. Will you please do as I say."

So Constanza named a small inn not far from Cambridge,

where she had stayed once or twice in her unmarried days.
Captain Ware told her to leave the booking to him.

They met in the hall and the captain signed the register.
Constanza had not thought they might remember her, but
it became apparent that they did.

" Did you put Mr & Mrs? " she asked.

" Captain & Mrs."

" Isn't one supposed to try to be discreet? "

" Best to play it simple," he said.

It was not the shortest evening and night she had ever
spent; but Captain Ware was easy and open without asking
questions, and she liked him for doing what he did. Before
dinner was over she liked him very much. They ate in the
hushed dining-room and the food was indescribably and
wilfully bad. Captain Ware drank whisky.

" Would *he* be the detective? " Constanza said, indicating
a table with a single, bald man in mufti.

Captain Ware gave him a glance. " No. Corner opposite.
Second table from the left." When she could, Constanza
turned and saw another bald and single man in mufti.

They had no friends in common except Simon, and, unlike
Simon, Captain Ware would not talk about his own existence
in the war, so at first they talked about the technicalities of
their situation. " Why did we come *here*? " Constanza
asked.

" Your choice."

" You made me choose. Why? "

" It's got to look right, hasn't it? "

" So Simon tells me."

" Who would know the kind of place a woman wanting to
spend a night on the quiet with a man on leave would go to,
except the woman? "

" How were you sure I'd know? "

" I took a chance on that."

Suddenly he began to tell her stories about America. About Chicago, about the West, Colorado, the Arizona Desert, California, the motion-picture studios. He made it all sound fascinating, wide, larger than life.

" But you are not American? " she said, " I only ask because I am; half."

" No, I'm not American," he said. He did not volunteer where he was born. " I knocked about a good deal on the other side before the war, *regrettant l'Europe aux anciens parapets.*"

Startled, she said, " Rimbaud."

" I read him in France. He stands up."

" I read less now," she said. " I've taken rather to Horace."

" I learnt French in Belgium—oh, long before this show— there's no country where I could have picked up Latin."

" You mean you didn't go to school? " said Constanza.

" Not what you'd call school."

Then they did talk about the war. Captain Ware said it had brought opportunities, as well as interruption—he had begun to write a book. " About a customs man who's painted some very rum pictures. Rum and beautiful. Still, if it weren't for the war I should not have met people like you and Simon."

" You always would have met people like Simon and me."

" That's what *you* think."

" We should have met after you'd written your book about the customs man's pictures."

" This way is quicker," said Captain Ware.

Presently they were left with nothing except empty tables and disapproving stares. " What shall we do now? I'm a noctambulist."

" So am I," said Constanza.

" The bar shuts at ten."

" We could try the town."

" There is no town."

" I don't remember that."

" I bet you don't."

They went upstairs and talked some more. Captain Ware had brought a bottle. Constanza, who hardly ever drank spirits, thought the least she could do was to be companionable and had a little in the other tooth-mug.

At length he said: " What a way to spend a night with a woman. A woman like you! "

" Same here," she said.

" Now look," he said.

But she said, " I have apologized to you before. It's got to go according to plan. There are several very good reasons."

" Very well," he said. " I didn't think you were one to change your mind. Only——"

" Wrong time," she said.

He got out a pack and they played a few rounds of some two-handed game. Constanza had learnt to play piquet and écarté with her father, but she had never had much card sense and there was no use pretending she played well. They did not pretend.

" Any rate poker is the only game worth sitting down to," he said.

" You are a rum man," said Constanza, " like the customs man's pictures. Which sides are the pose? "

He gave her an appreciative look, but did not involve himself in answers.

Through the rest of it, including witnessed breakfast the next morning, they got with tolerably good grace.

Captain Ware was off to an early start by himself as he was going back to France that day.

" Good God," Constanza said, " your leave? "

" It isn't up. I want to put in a few days in Paris. Iron or two in the fire."

He came in again, dressed and shaved, to say good-bye and before doing so, he proposed to her. He added, " I've no idea of course what your commitments are, but there's no harm in asking."

Then he said: " *I see*. Well, there hasn't been much time. Only let me put in two points quickly: You are exactly the kind of woman I want; and I should have asked you in any case to wait for a year or two. I haven't got a bean at the moment but I expect I shall be able to look after you quite properly in the not too distant future."

Constanza was feeling very sad that morning and her mind was not on Captain Ware, so she held out her hand and said a little vaguely, " You are a very nice man."

" I shouldn't have put it that way," he said. " Now remember: the offer stands. Good-bye. I shall keep it open—within reasonable limitations."

Constanza took her time getting back to Regent's Park. When she let herself in, she found that Simon had already left his office and was waiting for her.

" According to plan? "

" According to plan," she said.

" Anna is out."

" Thank God."

" Oh, Constanza."

She sat down. Simon took her hand. " What do we do now? What's the next step? " she said.

" I am supposed to react. I must either turn you out, or leave. I shall have to leave you—walk out of the house."

" If you don't? "

" Then, my dear, I shall be deemed to have condoned the

offence. If you had helped me more with my law-books, you would know. We'd have to start all over again."

" Not in Cambridgeshire," said Constanza.

" But I haven't been notified. At this hour I am the injured but still unsuspecting party. Darling, this is Friday afternoon, that detective's report can't come in before Monday morning at the earliest—we have three more days. I am *not* going to walk out now."

" Oh, Simon," she said.

At one time in the course of that Sunday, he said to her: " Constanza, *tesoro*, you're the only one for me. If you say one word, I'll throw them all over. We can still go to Guatemala, you and I."

" Which word? " said Constanza.

" A magic word. Potent magic. If you could ever make me feel certain of you! Don't think that Mary—— I often wish I'd never set eyes on her. Don't think I don't see that she's a poor copy of you. But she loves *me.* Once you've had that, it's hard to do without." His voice began to tremble: " *You* hardly wrote to me when I was at the front. Scraps—— I felt you didn't bother to read my letters. It was your mother who wrote to me. I can never forget that."

On Monday morning Constanza came down to breakfast. Simon had gone through the post. " Nothing," he said. " A reprieve." A few minutes later their English parlour-maid came in with the long envelope. Simon looked white as he signed. " By hand. Damn them."

He swallowed some tea. " We can pretend it came in the afternoon."

" Simon."

" Ought I to leave now? Have I got to walk out of the house now? "

" I am not driving you out," said Constanza, " and don't cry, my sweet."

" All right. I am going. Mena——"

" Yes, Mena will see to your things."

" I have to go up to Anna now and break it." He had promised to do this.

" Yes," she said, " we must keep our strength for that."

It took him more than an hour. When he came down again, there was a cab at the door, luggage in the hall, and they were no longer really alone.

" How did you tell her? "

" Involved."

" I must know. Let's meet somewhere this afternoon."

" I'm not supposed to meet you," he said.

Constanza went out to the cab with him and he was able to manage a few words. " I'm afraid I had to make you the nigger in the wood-pile. I told her I had just received some very terrible evidence against you; she doesn't believe in the truth of it, but she believes that I do. So now you know the line."

Constanza did some very fast thinking and said, " It was the best you could do." They had no chance to say more.

§

In the months that passed while Constanza was waiting for her divorce, it was her relation with her mother that was intolerably strained. That Anna was shattered goes without saying; the new element consisted of her not knowing, this time, where to turn or whom to blame.

" Poor woman ! " Mena said to Constanza, and Constanza said to Mena. But this did not change matters or help either her or them.

What the principessa held was, with some vacillations,

this: If Simon was convinced that Constanza had spent the
night with a man in Cambridgeshire, he was right in what
he was doing; where he was wrong, catastrophically wrong,
pig-headed, to blame, was in not believing that Constanza
had merely appearances against her. The principessa had
believed this with to Constanza almost shameful ease.

" Mama, it was not what it looked like, I can't say more,
but you must take my word for it," she had flung at her
mother in a tone of barely concealed irony, and her mother
had chosen to believe her on the spot.

All the same she was beside herself with grief and anger
at Constanza's conduct and she raved at her, not so much
at the folly of having got herself entangled in such appearances at all (Anna was certain that a daughter of hers could
have done so only for good and sufficient reason), but at her
refusal to *explain*, to *make up* to Simon, to *exert* herself. She
accused Constanza of being shallow, wilful, flippant and
unfeeling.

" You are a *femme fatale*," she said, having this notion of
the term, " you are ruining your life and his and mine—
all over again—and you're not thinking of your innocent
child."

Constanza took on more overtime at her office and told
herself that if she were a man this would be the moment to
enlist in the Foreign Legion.

Naturally Anna's informers told her of the existence of
Miss Mary Mouse. Anna said that Simon was being vindic-
tive and was being got at: these people were known schemers
who shrank from nothing, and she stormed at Constanza for
allowing her husband to fall into the hands of designing
women and the Yellow Press.

Simon was very good about one thing, he came to Regent's
Park every other day or so to be with Anna and to draw her
thunder. They did not get anywhere. Anna would tell him
at new length why he must believe Constanza and above all

herself, while Simon would sit drinking brandy-and-soda after brandy-and-soda and put in from time to time that he couldn't help it, he still felt that Constanza was perfectly capable of being unfaithful to him.

To this Anna would say: " Dearest boy, you got these notions by staying so much in Italy."

They got nowhere: but these visits made things bearable for Anna. *She* at least saw Simon, and it saved her from any attack of pitched despair. In some ways, it also helped Simon.

Simon and Constanza spoke a few times on the telephone.

" I'm getting some very black looks these days. Have *you* been talking? "

" What do you mean? " she said.

" They say I am treating you shabbily. What *do* you tell people? "

" Nothing unless I must. That we haven't quarrelled, that marriage wasn't our thing."

" Oh God," he said, " you're hopeless."

Another time he said, " My lawyers tell me it's going to be sticky about the custody, the court is going to look on you as a loose woman."

" Simon, I will have Flavia; I shall insist on that."

" That's the point, darling, you're not in a position to insist on anything. Well, I shall try to do my best."

Mr James was not a solace either. Never had Constanza found him so uncharitable and so cold.

" I shall never forgive Simon. I shall never speak to him again."

"Things aren't quite the way you think they are," she told him.

"Whichever way, I cannot forgive Simon. And don't imagine that I haven't got a pretty shrewd idea of what you've been up to."

"If you have, why the fuss?"

"You take too much upon yourself," he said. "*As* I told you before. You are an inverted romantic. My poor benighted girl, I never thought I'd see *you* stand in for Don Quixote."

Constanza said lightly, "Oh, not all women treat their men like dirt. Not even all American women."

The divorce came on early in November. Next day a paragraph in small print appeared in *The Times* (the Yellow Press kept—relatively—quiet).

Mr Simon Herbert of *** Terrace, London, was granted a decree nisi in the Divorce Court yesterday because of adultery by his wife, Mrs Constance Herbert, with Captain L. C. Ware, D.S.O. The petition was not contested. Judge Morell awarded the custody of the only child of the marriage to Mrs Herbert's mother, the Princess ***.

Afterwards, Constanza said that she would not describe it as the happiest day of her life. "I ought to have been warned. I had no idea judges talked that way. . . ."

At the time, she telephoned to Simon in savage anger. "How could you let the child go to mama! It was sprung on me: I didn't take it in before it was done."

"My dear, you don't know how these old boys feel about adultery. It was that or *my* mother. In the eyes of the law I am now a single man with a sixteen-hour-a-day job. It was the best we could do."

Constanza hung up on him. She went at once—and too late—to get legal advice; in different words they told her the same.

Four days later the war was over. So it has come, they said, the Armistice. How we waited.

" Prayed," said Anna.

People telephoned. Where are you?—London's in an uproar—we are waiting for you—we're all off to Piccadilly. But they decided to stay in.

Presently they were joined by Mr James.

" We are celebrating," said the principessa.

" An inveterate instinct. Hope springs eternal. And how do we start from here? Once the shouting's over? "

" The killing is over," said Constanza, " let us be grateful for that."

" A qualified celebration," said Mr James.

" I shall have to think of moving house," said Anna.

Telephone calls were still pouring in and at one time of the evening Anna was out of the drawing-room. " I think I ought to tell you," said Mr James, " I see you haven't heard. You didn't read the evening papers below the head-lines? "

" What is it? "

" Major Thomas Herbert. Died on his transport home, it only says, of the after-effects of dysentery."

" Brother Tom—how ghastly. How ghastly for all of them. And poor Simon. . . . It won't be easy to be the survivor, and to that extent. Those poor poor people. I suppose Simon will be expected to go to Northumberland. The strain. . . ." Then Constanza said, " Don't tell mama. Not just now, not tonight."

" That's what I thought," said Mr James. " Does she know about? " He named the house in Somerset. Constanza nodded. " Well, Simon will be the master of that one day."

" *He* never thought he would."

" Simon, all in all, will be a very . . . substantial man,"
said Mr James.

Constanza smiled. " *Substantial*—he'll like that."

The principessa came back and they began talking about
Clemenceau. Later on someone else telephoned. " It *is*
revolution in Germany: they are turning against their
officers."

" Whatever that means, they won't stand for another war."

" Nobody will that," said Constanza. Mr James said
he agreed.

He stayed up late with them and when he left, Constanza
saw him out. " It was good to have had you with us," she
said, " you must come more often. Well, here we were
again, just the three of us, like that other night."

" Four years ago," said Mr James.

" Four years and three months," Constanza said. " Simon
wasn't with us that time either. I had not met Simon. That
came a few weeks later. So it did turn out the way Simon
told mama: A war marriage."

§

Before the end of the year Constanza was in Rome. The
journey had been uncertain, long and cold, and she was
grateful more than once for her decision not to take the child.
At Dijon she and other passengers had to wait fourteen hours
for an engine to their train; at Turin, where there was
another long delay, they also ran into a waiter strike. Constanza did not care much: she felt herself at large, in the
world, in a detached way absorbed. She often thought of
Simon and what he had called his nightmare journey in the
opposite direction in the summer of 1914. If anything was

needed to bring the past war home to her, it was those trains, the crowded platforms and the icy waiting-rooms, these broken window-panes, the worn-off paint, the soldiers, the state of their uniforms, the look of the countryside, the looks on people's faces. Over Italy the sky was grey. Her father had been waiting at the station. He was a middle-aged man in an overcoat, shorter than she remembered. She was a woman of twenty-five who had lived all her grown-up years in one of the most accomplished sets in London.

It rained a great deal in Rome that winter. Copious cloud-bursts several times a day, one day after the other, water gushing through the cobbled streets, drops of water seeping through the ceilings. Constanza had forgotten about the Roman rain, and how long it was able to last. The palazzo was not in bad repair, but it looked unlived in and nearly everything in it had become shabby, and so were the drawing-rooms of their friends. The war, the war, the war—everybody was sadder, older, poorer, and now there were strikes, they told her, discontent, more poverty, black hatred, fear of socialism. The prince and his brothers-in-law made defeatist jokes about the future. Everybody talked about the Reds. Constanza's Aunt Maria had gone pious and talked what Constanza and her pals had used to call rosary talk. Her Aunt Carla wore an avid look and several people hastened to inform Constanza why—Fabrizio had gone off, the wretch, with a hospital nurse from Milan. Which Fabrizio? Constanza asked, and they shrugged and said, oh, of course, that was after your time. Constanza's contemporaries were either not demobilized or tied up sustaining widowed mothers. Younger people in all walks of life spoke of emigrating to America.

The foreign colony had melted, and such of her mother's friends who were still there, no longer came to the palazzo.

Constanza found the atmosphere provincial and the chatter dull. Her clothes, she dimly realized, though chosen by her mother, were looked upon as scandalous; not scandalous-glamorous, which would have given pleasure, but scandalous-simple, scandalous-emancipated.

Everybody was affectionate and the prince was kindness itself; but Constanza felt that she bewildered them. They had been surprised at seeing her arrive without her maid. She explained that Angelina was expecting a baby by an English soldier and had stayed behind to have things made all right for her. It was in fact one of the last things that Simon had done for them. He had found out the name of the soldier and his regiment, and he had pulled strings to get him demobilized. Now Anna was buying Angelina the goodwill of a sweet-shop, and the soldier was being quite content to make her an honest woman. At first Constanza's family were enchanted by this story and exclaimed at Angelina's luck. But when it transpired (Constanza having become careless in such matters) that the soldier was something called Chapel and there was little chance of their going before a priest, they could not understand at all. Then Angelina was *not* being made an honest woman? and the sweet-shop was just waste. They said less, but were a good deal more puzzled about Constanza's own situation. Everything the poor girl was, or was not, appeared to be cancelled out by something else. She was married and there was a *bambina*, what could be more felicitous. The husband was a Protestant, this was not so good but one lived in the world, mixed marriages were a fact and Constanza strong-minded enough to cope with one. But now she was not married any more, and this was neither good nor bad because it could not be. Why pretend that her marriage was dissolved when it was undissolvable? Only in Heaven and in Italy? They were in Italy and hoped to go to Heaven. Oh, they well knew that divorce was something practised in some countries, but it was a great sin and furthermore not valid. So why say she was not married when she plainly was? A married woman with a baby, just like Angelina, only that poor Angelina wasn't married yet, and never would be, and that her baby had not yet been born.

To cushion her divorce, Constanza told them about the registrar. After this they asked no more. They thought they understood. No marriage. No divorce. A child. The child —no wonder it had been left wherever it was—remained the concrete fact.

Soon all Rome knew, Mrs Throg having done the rest. The man's parents, she told them for a fact, had not been to the so-called ceremony.

" Clever of her," the Romans said, " to have taken that plain foreign name."

" Mrs Herbert? They have special arrangements for that kind of thing over there."

" Is that what they call a courtesy title? "

" Something like it."

The prince treated his daughter tenderly. He was worried by the thought of Anna. " Has she been difficult? " he managed to ask.

The same question, in another spirit, was being asked everywhere. " How did *Anna* take it? "

Here, also, an answer was supplied by Mrs Throg. " La Trommo says Anna took the man's side; the man's been seen constantly in Anna's house."

This many people did not believe.

It was while she was in Rome that Constanza heard that Simon was a Member of Parliament. The result of that General Election—the large Liberal defeat—distressed her very much; Simon, who had stood as an Asquith Liberal, was one of the few who had got in.

People asked her, was she back for long? had she returned to live? Constanza said she did not know herself. Presently the implications of some of the things unsaid came home to her. She spoke to Carla. "What's all this preposterous stuff about Flavia? What next?"

Carla said, "Well, *carissima*, it is confusing."

So Constanza patiently explained it step by step.

When she had finished, her aunt said, "Yes, as we thought, *paziènza*. No visible father."

"I was thinking of bringing her up here," Constanza said. "At Castelfonte."

"*Who* would they think she was?"

"I know papa wants to see her."

"He doesn't face what it will be like." Then, more warmly, "Does she look like you?"

"No," said Constanza.

"You know what you must do," said Carla. "You must marry. Then you can have plenty of children and come back with all of them."

All in all it was a slow sad winter. Constanza asked what had changed, the times? herself? Was it the end of youth? She was cold, she had little to do, she was alone. For the prince she felt much love but she found she could no longer talk to him. And all the time, bitterly, she missed Simon. Before it was March she told them she must go, she must go and see her daughter, she must go and see. *Figlia mia*, said the prince. Then they said *già* and let her go.

PART THREE

Voyageur sur la Terre

Chapter I

In the ten years or so that followed many things happened to Constanza that were not wholly shaped by and do not belong to this story. She returned to London, found her life both altered and unaltered by the fact and circumstances of her divorce, and for some time she lived plunged in the general post-war life of the Twenties. There was much in that current then that suited her affinities, as well as drifts already alien to one who had entered the adult world in the decade before the war. She was wild, but never destructive or self-destructive. She never got drunk. She always maintained the privacy of her love affairs. She did not think about manners and some of her elders found her unconventional, but she had manners. As far as her circumstances permitted she often exercised a kind of peasant frugality towards herself, dimly supported by a notion that what she did not buy today, and very likely lose or wear out, might come in useful some time for Flavia.

She was seldom without what is called a man in her life. She was slightly in love or much in love, once or twice very much in love indeed. But it always ended. It was not what in the last resort she wanted: it was not enough. And so there was no other marriage, or serious plan of marriage.

After her divorce from Simon became absolute, Constanza who did not like mysteries had told her mother about the arrangement made between them. Anna never forgave her. For doing what she had done; for telling her about it. Anna did not forgive Simon either, but her implacability was intermittent and she did not break with him. It would

have been too much for her at that stage, and too diffused.
Life at last had forced the principessa to put her wrath and
her affections into several baskets. She declared herself as
living for her new responsibility, her grand-child, or as she
preferred to call it, Simon's girl. She also tried to pin new
hopes on her son Giorgio and sent for him quite frequently.
Above all she clung to Constanza. She often spoke of her as
my unfortunate daughter, and she blamed much on the
Italian strain.

Simon's affluence and growing reputation in the House of
Commons did not help. Anna, bitter now where in the past
she had laid her lightest touch, used it mercilessly.

Constanza exercised a patience, a withdrawal and a cold-
ness that had not been in her first nature. She never lived
quite separated from her mother, nor ever again entirely
made her home with her. They moved often and in varying
combinations. One year Anna with a household and the
children (Giorgio on long loan to make up for his absence
during the war) would live in a largish house while Constanza had a mews flat in Mayfair; the next, Constanza
would take a small house for Flavia and herself in Chester
Street, and Anna, alone with Mena, moved to Brown's.
Then Constanza might be off in Spain for a long stretch
with nothing more than the *poste restante* by way of an address,
and Anna with her dependants settled in the Engadine.

At least once a year Constanza went to see her father. If
Italy was not recovering politically, the Italian spirit was.
Constanza came when it was warm and stayed only a few
weeks. She did not again experience anything like the alien
desolation of the winter of her first return. She had learnt
to travel light. In her youth she had looked at fate as the
bolt from the clear sky, now she recognized it in the iron
rule of time on all human affairs. Today is not like yesterday; the second chance is not the first. Whatever turning-
points are taken or are missed, it is the length of the passage,

the length of the road that counts. She realized that she would never again entirely belong, but also that a large part of her belonged nowhere else. Once more she basked, volatile and melancholy: the sun, the fruit, the colour of the stones were her inheritance as well as the sad pagan creed of *carpe diem* and stoicism for the rest.

Life was still good to her. Exceptionally good. She had what all mortals pray for and unfortunately few are given. She had health, she had looks, she had money for her needs. If she was free, is too large a question, but it can certainly be said that in terms of our common lot she was her own master. She was equipped to appreciate, to derive entertainment, connotations, pleasure, from almost any situation she happened to find herself placed in. She had the power to inspire love. And she was not unhappy; there was only a vague disquiet, a nagging question: What is it for? What have I made of it? Where is it going, where can it go?

Her mind was often on Flavia, her own daughter, in whom, too, elements were mixed, more mixed perhaps; and Constanza wondered. Her field here was limited by the (polite, unspoken) resistance to the child she was up against in Rome. Had she fought it, as she might, she would have had to fight her mother. The principessa so far had chosen to treat her custody of Flavia as a matter of form, nevertheless Constanza shrank from putting the issue to a test, and with her sporadic tendency not to impose her will on what might be designed, she let the matter be. When she left the child with her mother, as so often happened, she did it with an easy heart, holding that the association could only be to their mutual advantage: Anna's influence, she remembered, on the very young was wholesome and benign. (Here she was mistaken.)

§

Giorgio, on his first re-appearances after the war (a boy of twelve, thirteen, fifteen, dressed more like a young man), spoke English and seemed disposed to make up to his mother. With Flavia it was war on sight. He looked down on her, and made this plain. Flavia ascribed it to her own inferior sex and age and found it not unfair. All the same she confided to Mena that she did not find *il fratello* quite *simpatico*. *She* spoke Italian.

" He's not your brother, my treasure, he's your uncle," said Mena.

The principessa promptly bought Giorgio what he wanted at that moment which was a gold watch. Presently he flashed it at Flavia, telling her what it had cost. Flavia's main concern was to be shown the works. Giorgio would have none of it.

" Please, *Uncle* Giorgio."

" I am not your uncle," he flared at her. " Don't you dare call me that again! I am——" he rolled out a sonorous string, " And you are just a bastard."

Flavia would have made little of this incident if Mena had not surged up and slapped Giorgio's face. Giorgio slunk off and Flavia inevitably said, " What is a bastard? "

Mena drew her on her lap. " Nothing you need concern yourself about, my little angel."

Flavia went to her grandmother and repeated the question.

" Well, darling," Anna said, and, believing that she must have read the word somewhere, launched into a fascinating explanation that came straight out of Shakespearean drama.

" Are bastards better than real princes, *nonna*? "

" Well, some of them cut a great dash and were extremely brave."

Flavia withdrew having conceived a high romantic notion of herself.

Often Anna preferred Giorgio who was her own son and would one day have her house in Rome. When he told her that he wanted to go to America later on and see her country, she felt pleased and flattered and saw him to her credit. At other times she remembered that he was his father's son. Flavia, moreover, showed signs of being clever, which Giorgio obviously was not. When it was found out that Flavia could read, Anna began to give her a few lessons, but soon grew tired of it, saying she was too old. Her memory was as excellent as ever and the dates of the kings of England were still firmly hers, she felt no kind of excitement though in making them Flavia's as well. The whole thing had palled. Constanza had been her educational masterpiece, she was not up to bringing off this *tour de force* a second time. So rather haphazardly she engaged and dismissed again a series of governesses whose comings and goings were more dependent on her own likes and movements than on Flavia's progress. As neither Anna herself nor Constanza had been sent to school, school was not envisaged. They were sure that any gap caused by Anna's present method could be made up by a child of theirs in its sleep.

Flavia, who was also a child of Simon's, managed to pick up, and miss, a good many things on her own and connect them according to her lights.

Constanza sometimes tried to do right by her brother but with him she seldom had a happy touch. She asked him news of Castelfonte, and found that he had none to give.

He never went there, he said, if he could help it; he loathed the country; farming was a mug's game.

"Then what are you going to do, *bimbo*, what are you going to live on, if you're not going to live on the land?"

"If you call me *bimbo* again, I shall hit you," he said.

231

" I'm sorry," said Constanza, " I didn't know you hated it."

" The steward can look after the land. I wish papa would sell the place. Not at once, of course; we must first get a decent road, then it can be built up for the tourists."

" You want the place to be like Florence on Easter Sunday? "

" Tourists bring money," he said.

" Are you going to work for the tourists . . . Giorgio? "

" I am going to marry a rich woman and race cars."

" Each will require a measure of skill," said Constanza.

His mother said yes to the first step. Giorgio at sixteen was handed the money for a motor bicycle. As neither Anna nor Constanza were given to much physical anxiety about their off-spring, Giorgio's tearing up and down the road to Brighton at all hours caused them no loss of sleep. Anna remained ignorant of the girls he picked up or took with him, Constanza merely shrugged about his taste. " Floozies," she said to her young man.

" Poor chap," said the young man. " Why don't you introduce him to some nice girls of his own age? "

" Do I know any? " said Constanza.

" Tell you what, let's take him to my cousins."

" Is it wise? "

" *They*'re a pack. Anyhow, girls know how to look after themselves. It isn't as it was in your day, Constanza."

" We didn't read Kafka."

They took Giorgio to the young man's cousins. Some of them were still in the school-room. Constanza tried to answer their questions for ten minutes and after that she only felt for Giorgio.

He came home, went to his mother and asked for money. He needed a new dinner-jacket, he said, and some cash; he was going to take one of the Radburn girls to dinner at the Savoy.

" Can he do that? " said Anna.

" Of course not, the idiot. Giorgio, you must know that you can't take little girls to dinner at hotels."

" Who's talking about little girls? " Giorgio said coolly; " I asked Artemis; she's been out for years."

" She's engaged."

" I know," said Giorgio; " to a very rich man."

" Has she accepted your invitation? " said Anna.

" How not."

" *Meno male*," said Constanza, and later on slipped him a fiver of her own.

" I'm not going to spend it all on *her*," Giorgio told her. " Nothing in it, no return. Girls in that world are the same everywhere. But it does no harm being seen. I may get to know some of her married friends."

Giorgio, when he put himself out, did have something. Only his sister could not see it. " *The chic*," she muttered when he presented himself to them in his new clothes.

" You mean he looks . . . common? " the principessa asked after her son had left.

" Yes."

" Oh, dear. Perhaps it's because you have become so very English? "

" Perhaps. I don't think it's got much to do with being English or Italian, it's a new look, it's the age."

Giorgio carried off his evening well. As he had said, there was nothing in it. During the first part of it, the girl, who was quite a prize and much admired, talked only of her engagement and the difficulties her people were putting up; later she talked about Constanza. Constanza seemed to fascinate her.

" All the boys at our dancing-class had her photograph, and we used to cut her out of *The Tatler*."

" She's not bad," said Giorgio loyally.

" When I was little I used to hear my parents' friends say that she came second only to ——" she named the English beauty of the age. " Of course they are entirely different types."

Giorgio sipped his *crême de menthe* and looked detached.

" Later on half the men one met were madly in love with her. There's something queer about her, though. You know what people said during the war? All Constanza's young men were all right. They all came back, not one of them was killed."

Artemis looked up and was surprised to see her escort sign himself.

Giorgio did not consider the evening a dead loss, he had cut a fine figure and was left with some cash in hand.

§

Mussolini marched on Rome; the new regime took power and was consolidated less than two years later by the Matteotti murder. Constanza reacted to these events as she had reacted in the war: by instinct and by reason she became an anti-fascist from the start and never abandoned that position. This did not bring her any closer to her Roman family. There were of course a good many exceptions, but as it happened the prevalent attitude in the prince's circle was opportunism disinfected by a dash of cynicism. There was a lot of shrugging and washing of hands, they laughed at the new Caesar and his henchmen, but there were also fat sighs of relief: were the strikes not being put a stop to? were the brutal clowns not saving the country from the Reds? For the rest, Italy was a kingdom still, the clown and his mob were regarded as occultly held in check by the mystique of the House of Savoy.

" The Piemontesi *have* come up in the world," said Constanza. But it was no longer a joke.

She became mildly active. She carried messages and scraps of information across the border and brought back other messages and banned foreign newspapers. The underground she worked for was a rather professorial group—" liberals and doomed to fail," as Simon would have put it—and Constanza had little illusion about the amateurishness of the organization and the immediate hopelessness of its task. All the same she looked on resistance as morally and historically essential; if it ceased the Italian people would be lost.

The principessa, too, became a staunch anti-fascist; she simply saw the movement as an insult to the human race. Always at her best when events allowed her to forget the personal cage, she cracked jokes against the fascisti that were almost Roman in irreverence. If the blackshirts tramping over Italy filled Constanza with anguish and deep sadness, it animated Anna's fighting spirit and revived her. She was provided with the impetus and formula to return to Italy. Her place now, she said, was there. And indeed the principessa—with her name, her air, her imagined, but effective, American impregnability—protesting hard and loud against the regime on Italian soil was to a few at least a refreshing minor mercy.

She went to Lake Como, she wintered on the Ligurian Riviera, revisited Pisa, took a villa at Fiesole. The exiled-from, the unreachable, now became Rome, the seat of the arch-enemies, the fount of all iniquity. And when she spoke of it no-one was certain if she meant the prince or Musso. At any rate before Constanza had taken it quite in, her mother had almost completely transferred herself again to

Italy. Flavia, if she wished, was given the freedom of an
olive grove. Constanza looked on sardonically—the paths of
fate *were* devious.

Constanza's organization did not find her unuseful. One
day she was summoned to Milan and asked to do a job that
was fairly consequential and quite risky. If they catch
you——she was told. " Are you afraid? "

" Only fools are not," Constanza said, but of course she'd
do it.

She was sent away to think it over. She did and had to
come to the conclusion that they had not taken her British
passport into enough account: the worst that could befall
her, and the most likely, was her not being allowed back into
Italy. She was quite clear then where her duty lay: she had
no right to do something that might cut her off from her
father for a second time. She went back to the committee
and told them that the job was out. Family reasons. *Certo,
certo*, they said, but she could read their thoughts: These
people have no guts.

Inconsistently she went on taking smaller but quite
definite risks, and she never refused to carry a personal
message. She was never caught.

Financially Constanza was independent from her mother by
her mother's wish. After her divorce, the trust fund continued to pay her the allowance she was first given when she
and Simon married. It was very much less than what Anna
had or spent, but it was enough for her. Railway tickets,
books, a couple of rooms to herself, the minor freedoms, an
orderly existence of paid bills. Constanza had no acquisitive
instincts, or at least not for the things that were within her
reach; she could have dreamt of land, a family house.

Simon had disliked her hunting side, but it had run itself out; she did not take up serious hunting again after the war. She did not care much for motor cars except as casual conveniences, and she never learnt to drive one. About things that did not interest her she cultivated a vagueness that saved her boredom and much trouble, and one of these was clothes. Not unwisely, she let Anna get them for her and they were often more expensive than Constanza knew or would have liked. She had a tendency to adorn herself with things that glittered, but had no real sense of jewels. After Angelina (reasonably contented) was married in her sweet-shop, Constanza for more than a single reason gave up having her own maid.

Anna's unselfconscious extravagance continued. From time to time came rumblings from her hard-tried trustees, but they had cried caution so long and always paid her overdraft that she gave little heed. She would write back rubbing it in to them how well-advised they'd been by Constanza's hunch to get out of Russian Railways, and draw their attention to a fact which even they could not deny: Wall Street was booming.

The Italian villas Flavia now grew up in were rambling and enchanted and full of the incomparable vistas and glaring drawbacks that are common to Italian villas and mean not much to children and can in any case be partly overcome if there is a sufficiency of servants. There were enough servants; all of them Italian, and many of them talked. Anna also talked to, or rather before her grand-child. It was a habit she had formed during Flavia's infancy. Already at Regent's Park she used to have the child brought in to her in the morning and, while she let it taste a duck's egg or some honey, soliloquized before her. The theme was always simple if above Flavia's head: The villainy of men, the villainy that lurked in Italy. Beware of Rome, of treachery, beware of men. When Flavia herself was able to talk coherently, and presumably to listen, the flow of these tirades did not entirely cease during half-guarded moments. Flavia learnt that her grandmother used two distinct ways of communication. She either addressed a person or the air. When Flavia made her presence felt or asked a question, Anna would incline her head, bestow attention, say My darling, and answer everything with smiling deliberation. But when Flavia was in a book or concentrating on some food, Anna might lapse into a *sotto-voce* stream of warnings and abuse. Look out for lies . . . Never trust a man . . . Men are deceitful . . . Men are vile. Flavia half shut it out, half took it in.

After they had moved to Italy, Rome cast a spell also upon the child. The Forbidden City had a presence that loomed larger than prosaic Florence. Flavia supplemented what she heard with reading. She knew about the Borgias, she got hold of *The Cenci*. She loved the sound of all of it, she felt she had looked inside these palazzi, and her head was filled with dark dreams.

One day she asked Mena, " Is the prince in Rome a hunch-back? "

Mena had strict orders not to touch certain subjects and had kept to them for years. This was too much.

" What next!" she cried. The love that she bore Anna had never diminished her immense pride in the prince. " *E bell'uomo!* "

Flavia pricked up her ears. Quick to take advantage of the first breach in Mena's reticence, she pressed on, " What has he done? Does he stab his adversaries? "

But Mena had become like a clam again.

" Has he deprived his heirs of their Rights and Titles? "

" Off with you."

" Does he put poison in his guests' wine? Does he entertain a Guilty Love? "

" *Sciocchezze,*" Mena said, unperturbed.

Flavia saw herself complete with cloak and charger knock one day at the Sebastian Gate—she liked the name—demanding her patrimony and the truth about her ancestor. Meanwhile, other ways were open to research.

" What would be your idea of a *bell'uomo?* " she nonchalantly asked her governess. At ten, Flavia was a lanky child, very thin, with the fine light hair and colouring of her grandmother's; her features were like Anna's, too, but without Anna's porcelain prettiness, and instead there was an indefinable look of Simon, and she also had Simon's voice and Simon's laugh. Like most children, Flavia kept many things to herself and blurted out others. She was solitary rather than gregarious, but could hold her own in company, and when she showed reserve it was reserve, not shyness.

The governess, a rather stupid Englishwoman, said, " Oh, I suppose someone with a lot of teeth and smarmy hair, a kind of Don Juan."

" And who is *he*? " said Flavia.

Miss March hedged ineptly.

Soon Constanza was paying a visit at Fiesole.

" Mummy, I want to know all about Don Juan."

" *All?* " said Constanza. " *Mille e tre*. You monster of curiosity. He was loved by a thousand and three women."

" Oh, was he," said Flavia. " At the same time? "

" The timing *was* at fault occasionally."

" May I have the whole story please, mummy? "

" Certainly. There are many versions. Some day you may enjoy Byron's; meanwhile you could go to the Opera, they're putting it on this spring. Well then . . ." and she told the story.

" He went to hell? " said Flavia, " what a disaster. He oughtn't to have murdered the Commendatore." Then she said, " Mummy, people are sent to hell for *one* woman; if they're not married to her. It doesn't have to be a thousand and three."

The gulf of *déjà-vu* opened before Constanza. She said humbly, " You needn't believe all of that, my sweet."

Her daughter gave her a quick look. " I don't," she said lightly.

Flavia could be disconcertingly persistent. Before her mother was off again, she reminded her. " You will tell *nonna* that I may see Don Juan? "

" You just tell her you want to go to the opera, that'll be enough."

Flavia said doubtfully, " *She* only goes to Brahms."

" I know. Mendelssohn, Brahms and Beethoven. But Mozart will do. You can take my word for it."

" *Certo*," said her daughter.

Flavia went and was tremendously impressed by the whole thing. Afterwards she renewed her assault on Mena. " I believe he *is* a hunch-back after all," she said. It did not fail and Mena at last was goaded into her Leporello piece.

" *Tutte le belle di Roma, tutte le donne*——" All the ladies of Rome, and not only the ladies had been unable to resist the prince. " *Tutte!* " Mena cried, carried away, enraptured by the past.

For Flavia two and two had come together, and she also felt enraptured. There was one more test. From the floor, a finger in her book, she flung into Anna's musing a light, clear-voiced question:

" Like Don Giovanni? "

Anna was so startled by this sudden intuition, and so gratified—out of the mouth of babes!—that she held out her arms: " Oh, my perceptive child." Flavia was just as glad to hide in them.

But when her mother had returned, there was no conceal-
ment. " Mummy, mummy—you know what I am going to
be when I'm grown up? I'm going to be like the prince,
I am going to seduce all the beautiful ladies in Rome, and
other women, too, and I shall love them all."

" *Dio* darling," Constanza exclaimed, " you *have* got it
all wrong! That wouldn't do at all. Oh, shall we never
escape the muddling consequences of our family history? "

§

Giorgio had not been pleased at all by his mother's move to
Italy, he considered that it cut down his manoeuvring
room. He had much preferred circulating between Rome
and England, and besides one cut some figure running over
to London in June, while running up to Florence one did not.
Moreover Italy was finished.

He did run up quite often all the same (he now had a
Fiat and coveted a Lancia) with some demand or other, but
he generally sulked. In compensation one January Anna took
him to St-Moritz. It was not her kind of place—Anna
always went to *quiet* hotels—but Giorgio lapped it up,
Flavia liked the snow, a pleasant Irish Colonel attached
himself to Anna, and for a week or two all went well. Anna
sat with her Colonel where they did not have to hear the jazz
band, was almost persuaded to try a turn on skates again,
watched Flavia button-holing unguarded hotel guests—
" Have you tried freezing milk on your window-sill? " " Do
you know the difference between Centigrade and Réaumur? "
—and told herself that after all she owed something to the
boy.

Then Giorgio announced that he was engaged.

It cost Anna an effort and some courage to pull herself
back into reality. She managed to say to Mena, " Will you

tell him that he must speak to his father. He is not eighteen! "

" I shall do as you wish, *Eccellenza*." Mena who wept so easily was also an adept at clearing her face of any expression whatsoever.

Anna might have spared herself. Giorgio strolled in and dropped a few words airily. Mama, *carissima*, matters had not reached that stage at all, not at all—what was required at present was she, his mother, to smooth the way.

She telegraphed for Constanza. Constanza was going through one of what Anna called her restless times and again could only be reached by a *poste restante*. As a matter of fact she had gone to Naples for her underground. The telegram found her, she had finished her job and she took a train to Switzerland at once. It came natural to her to rally in a family emergency. But no sooner had she arrived and stepped into that plushy hall than she learnt it was all off. The facts, when pieced together, were simple. Giorgio had become acquainted with a family from Milan exhibiting the exterior signs of wealth. Obvious to all they were war rich. Giorgio made up to the girl, the girl fell for him, they came to an understanding. Giorgio's assets and lack of them were equally obvious; the parents were doubtful, alarmed, not unattracted, ready to negotiate. Then there came an hotel dance. Giorgio sat with his *Milanesi* and drank their champagne, but he danced once, and again and a third time with a woman from another table, an Hungarian countess. He sat out another dance with her; towards the end he disappeared. Consternation; covering-up. The girl swollen-eyed next morning, the father furious.

" And what did you think you were doing, guttersnipe? " Constanza asked her brother.

" They expect me to wait for a couple of years, can you see it—*il fidanzato?* Who can keep it up that long? What do we know about them? perhaps they aren't as rich as they look."

" You might have thought of all of that before."

" *Già*. It was practice. I have to learn to handle these things."

" Well, I congratulate you. You've made three people wretched. If you had to break it off, there were other ways."

Giorgio grinned at her. " I didn't know if I wanted to break it off when I sat down with them, I hadn't danced with the contessa then—have you *seen* her? "

" You are not going to make yourself very popular, *caro*."

" There are other fish in the ocean."

To her mother Constanza said, " The silver lining: we can now move out of this gilded cage."

They did. Giorgio dared not squeak. It was Flavia who protested. " *Nonna*, mummy, we can't leave, please let me stay, couldn't I stay on? I've just met such an *interesting* man, he is a . . . positive, a logical—— He's written it down for me, look: a Logical Positivist."

Anna found a new adjective for her son. Not responsible. He was, she said, neither responsible nor clever.

Mr James, during those years, sometimes came to stay. In his mid-sixties, perhaps a little fragile, he had remained the same to them.

Flavia liked him to tell her tales about her mother when she was a child.

" Well, she was a very pious little girl," Mr James would say. " Never without her rosary or whatever you are supposed to carry," and Flavia would crow with laughter.

" She was very foolish and slow at her lessons, and you know the most foolish thing of all? She liked to think that I was a philosopher."

" She asked your advice? " said Flavia.

" I can't recall her doing *that*," said Mr James.

" And what *are* you? "

" I have been called a dilettante."

" I know the word, but will you please explain to me exactly what it means."

He tried.

" Hmm. Not a professional? "

" Quite, my child."

" But I was told," she said, " that you taught at Harvard? "

" *That* was a very long time ago and quite brief."

" Still," said Flavia, " it must have been something. And you went to Oxford, too. I'd call it all very grand. Can women go to Harvard? "

Anna, who for herself was quite fearless in such matters, never let Mr James leave Italy without distributing half a dozen envelopes about his luggage—just to post abroad, you know—containing if not paramountly useful certainly quite compromising documents. Constanza, who could not bear to think of anything happening to Mr James, never failed to make them disappear again.

" Does he know you do that, mummy? " asked Flavia, who saw far too much.

" No."

" How do you manage it? "

" Substituting perfectly harmless envelopes," said Constanza.

" *Substituting?* "

" Putting one thing in exchange for another."

" Cheating? " said Flavia.

" Yes," said Constanza.

" Mummy, when is it all right to cheat? "

" I'm so glad you said *when*, not if. When one does

it for someone one loves. When one does not do it for oneself."

" I see," said Flavia. " Mummy, was the letter you put in *my* suitcase when we came back from Switzerland a perfectly harmless envelope? "

" No," said her mother.

Flavia said nothing.

" Does that puzzle you? "

Flavia's very blue eyes had a way of appearing to turn dark at moments of emotion. " I haven't worked it out yet," she said in a neutral tone.

" Let me help you," Constanza said. " If they'd found that letter at the frontier, nothing would have happened to *you*. Not like Mr James. They don't do anything to children. They would have blamed me. Do you follow that? " Flavia nodded and her face cleared.

She said, " You did it because we hate the blackshirts."

Constanza said, " That's not quite the right way round. I'm against the blackshirts because of the things they do to people, and make them do; and I mind that ultimately, because I love those people. Hate is nothing, even in politics, hate is only temper and unhappiness; it's an accident. It is stupid and unkind to let it overtake one. I don't hate men who wear black shirts, I sometimes hate what they do—can you see the distinction? "

" I think so," said her daughter. " I rather hate *nonna*," she blushed, " when she talks, you know . . . in that way when she's angry; but I do love *her*. She can't help it—poor woman," she added in Mena's voice, for Flavia was a mimic.

Constanza kissed her, then gave her a wink: " And now you must let me see to Mr James's packing."

Mr James was with them again when Giorgio made one of

his appearances. There was something in his buttonhole. It was the insignia of a Fascist Youth organization.

Constanza flung a word at him. He still feared her and with the look of a cat at bay, all insolence and deferred defiance, he slowly picked out the small enamelled thing and dropped it in his pocket.

" You could be sent to the Islands for this," he said, but in so low a tone that it was scarcely heard.

Behind his back, Constanza said to her mother, " What can you expect? He doesn't know any better, wretched boy, do think of the pressure that's being put on all of them. But I thought it was right to show him that it still isn't accepted in all human company."

Anna's reaction was different. If she had never given to her son the feeling she had given to her father, to Simon and to Constanza as a girl, he had also never had a taste of her full anger. She took her time. She sent for him. She let herself go. He was dazed, he was cowed; he was also rather impressed. Giorgio had always been impressed by his mother, while he looked down on his father (through a layer of affection), as a man in whose shoes he would do a good bit better.

It was at this point that Constanza gave up her opposition to Giorgio's transatlantic longings. Let him go, she advised his mother, it will get him out of this at least: he will learn how the decent half still thinks.

" It will be a wonderful influence for him," said Anna.

Mr James, who unlike her visited his native country frequently, hinted at some changes in President Coolidge's United States. " He may meet other things besides New-England probity."

Oh, very likely, Anna said. " Prohibition. That won't concern him much, he's an abstemious Italian. Constanza says——"

But Constanza, who saw America through the eyes of her

mother's youth but also through the novels of Dreiser and
Sinclair Lewis and a new magazine called *The New Yorker,*
did not know what to say.

Giorgio was buoyant. Letters were sent to Mr Baxter, the
trustee; to Arizona, to half-remembered friends. Giorgio
had a visa, more new clothes, travellers' cheques. There was
even a prospect of some instructive employment being found
for him in the automobile industry.

" You *are* interested in that, aren't you? " they asked
hopefully.

§

Giorgio had sailed. It was early summer. Anna had taken
her family to a small resort on Lake Garda. Constanza was
fond at that time of a man on long leave from the Colonial
Service, whom she had borne off from London. They were
at the hotel; Constanza's policeman, as she called him, had
taken a little house inland. Flavia liked him too, and Anna
did not mind him. It was a pleasant life. The lake was blue
and calm. There was some animation though the summer
visitors were yet few. The post arrived by boat, and people
walked down to the shore to meet it. The food they ate was
local, simple and dripping fresh. This was Flavia's word.
She was a water creature and most of the time was in or on
the lake or sailing a small boat with Constanza and the
policeman. At noon they put in at some bay and ate a picnic
in the shade.

" *Dolce far niente,*" Flavia said to her mother with the
policeman's accent.

" Yes, we *must* stop him saying that."

The governess of the moment had been sent on holiday.
She had not liked the place at all and come to Anna the first
morning with a list of her complaints. At night Flavia ate

dinner with the other three, and after Constanza and her young man had driven off to dance somewhere, her grandmother would read aloud to her. They often settled for Trollope. " Can we skip this? " Flavia usually said when they reached a love passage. " I find it so unreal, and I don't like this heroine. Let's skip *her*." Sometimes she asked for legal anecdotes. " You *must* remember some, *nonna*? " Anna said it was a mighty long time since Great-Grandfather Howland had practised at the Bar. " Anecdotes live on," said Flavia, and Anna found that this was so.

One morning Flavia was sitting in the open verandah with the principessa. Suddenly she saw her mother coming towards them through the garden very rapidly. She was not actually running but she moved as if propelled by some great urgency, her eyes were wide open and unseeing, her hair appeared to be streaming and her face was like a mask. When she had reached the steps she called: " Simon is dead! " The principessa rose and slowly lifted her arms in a speechless gesture. Then the two women passed into the house and the door was shut.

It was only some minutes later when she found that Mena was by her side and she in Mena's arms, that Flavia realized that the person dead was her own father.

Constanza had not believed that Simon could die. Since the war the thought had never crossed her mind. Much else, but never that. He and she were of the same age, almost to a day; Simon in her memory was life itself. Now she blamed herself for negligence. She was struck by his death; by death. It was not her own loss then that moved her, she hardly would have known if it was one. *He* was alive, now he is dead: that was the thought, the feeling foremost in her mind, it was what she told herself.

Simon! How was it possible, how could it be? Fuller

news came slowly. Letters, the English papers. It had happened in Somerset, in the Italianate house. The uncle, the owner, who now befriended Simon, had long been ill, his end often in sight. Simon and his wife had been living with him, Simon going up to London to be in the House, going up for committees (Simon had been returned at every election, holding then a Labour seat); he had a Bill of his own on his hands just then, he had been working extremely hard, he had not quite recovered from a severe attack of influenza in the winter and it had all been rather a strain. The uncle took a turn for the better; in their relief they asked some people down to stay. There was a night with Simon flushed and excited and everybody drinking a great deal. Later the men had gone out into the park, the night was chilly, there had been some argument followed by a wager and Simon, fully dressed, had plunged into the water-piece. When they came in again and Mary, his wife, had begged him to take off his wet clothes, he had sent for more brandy and told her to go to hell. Next morning he was half delirious but insisted on getting up. He got himself to London but collapsed at Waterloo Station. He was taken by ambulance to a nursing home. There they found that he was in very poor condition—worn out—and without any resistance at all. He did not last three days.

Constanza openly carried herself as one bereaved. She told her policeman that he must go.

He was flabbergasted. " Am I not to see you again? "

She did not know. Tears streaming down her face, she told him he must go at once. " It would not be respectful."

Flavia was able to say to her, " Death *is* very terrible? "

" Yes. Yes. Yes," said Constanza.

And when the child continued to look at her, " Because it is the end. It is the end for *them*."

" Mummy, don't cry so."

Constanza said, " One must cry for the dead."

She sent for all the English papers, read the obituaries, was assuaged by every tribute, deeply moved by the few words spoken in his memory in the House. She expected her friends to write to her. (Few did.) One matter agitated and distressed her—would they bury Simon in Northumberland? Would they? could they? she asked and wrung her hands.

" *They* mind? " Flavia asked lightly.

" We don't know. We must act as if we knew. We must do as we feel would please them. Anything else is impious."

Anna inclined her head. She had been very good throughout, gentle and silent. She thought it was wrong of Constanza to include the child, she preferred a degree of prudery about death, and she had never seen her daughter so excessive; but awed, she neither commented nor interfered. She was hard hit herself. Simon's death was a personal loss to her. He wrote to her quite often, and when she came to London he never failed to look her up. The reason was that he liked her. He had done so from the first. You old humbug, he would say and kiss her on both cheeks, and Anna would feel oddly relieved.

She had often asked him to see and speak to the child, but he had told her, No. There was no point—it would have to be more than that, or nothing. Constanza never saw him; they had run into each other once or twice and he had been very cutting. Simon had taken against her since their divorce. A version of it had leaked out and people thought the worse of him for it. Captain Ware, it was said, was a figment of the imagination, and in point of fact when he was to be put on the pensions' list he could not be found and there was no proof of his ever having existed. Men and women of all shades of opinion said that Simon had sacrificed Constanza to ambition; he himself had mocked ambition, and they did not forgive him. His new wife was not popular; their marriage had not been happy. Simon despised her and did not care who saw it, and that, too, did not go down very

well. His political career had been set back—not for long it
was said—by the decline of the Parliamentary Liberal Party
and his own change of allegiance. In other ways his father-
in-law had been able to be helpful. Simon, in his short life,
had already made a mark for himself as a collector of Italian
painting.

Presently news came that Simon had been buried in
Somerset with his uncle's people.

For days on end Constanza talked and talked about Simon.
What he had said about this, about that, their first meeting,
his plan to cut Stendhal, his views on the Russian Revolution,
how he used to rock himself forward and back in his chair
when in the grip of words, how he had known the classifica-
tion of the *Médoc Crus* by heart and would recite them like
so many lines of poetry:

Château Latour, Château Rauzan-Ségla, Château Rauzan-Gassies,
Château Léoville-Las Cases;
Château Ducru-Beaucaillou, Château Montrose. . .

It was a need to her and she felt it gave him substance.

People at the hotel pricked up their ears and tried to get
their two's and two's to match. They were mostly German,
and called Constanza the young widow. Sometimes Flavia
was accosted in her play and asked for confirmations.

Simon's uncle, advanced in age and very ill, did not
survive the new shock long. A few weeks later his death was
in *The Times*.

" If Flavia had been a boy," Anna said with a note of
reproach.

" Well, she isn't," said Constanza. " And don't put anything into her head."

" When you think of the advances we *have* made in
women's rights! Who *will* inherit now? Who will have the
house—? " Simon, so set against early children, so far had
had no others.

" Nobody knows. Some cousin in Canada, no doubt."

She was wrong. When Simon had died, his wife was expecting a child. After some months of uncertainty, it was learnt that Simon had a posthumous son. The principessa was back at Fiesole by then; Constanza was off somewhere on her own. Flavia was shown the newspaper with the two or three printed lines.

" *That* is my . . . half-brother? "

" Yes, darling," said Anna.

" He is not *your* grandson? "

" Not really," Anna had to admit.

" Shall we see him? "

" Not for the present, my darling."

Flavia knew of course by now that there was nothing in that bastard story, a fib cooked up by Giorgio when she was too young to know better; all the same she felt convinced that something was a bit odd.

The principessa had been informed of Simon's will, made at the time of his second marriage and containing several bequests by codicil of various periods. By one codicil he left his personal jewellery to Anna. By a later one (having meanwhile collected a library), he left her his art books. The books, cases and cases of them, arrived at Fiesole in due course. Anna was very touched. The jewellery had puzzled them, but when it, too, arrived (in a small insured parcel) Constanza said that she saw what Simon had meant. All of it—some links, some studs, a flat watch and chain, a pin— had originally been given to him by Anna. " And very nice they are, too, mama," Constanza said, kissing her, " I didn't take in at the time *how* nice. He must have loved them." Apparently he had never had or worn anything else. For a day or two Anna was nearly happy.

The third codicil had been made the winter before Simon

died. It was regarded in the nature of a bomb-shell by his second wife and her family, and they gave notice through their lawyers that they would contest it. Simon had left all his pictures absolutely to his only daughter Flavia. The bequest was written in his own hand and tone. In case the girl turned out a dud, he wrote, this legacy would at least keep her in husbands. If not, and if she sold it at her convenience, it would help her to have an interesting life to which he wished her luck. Until she was twenty-one he desired the pictures to be in the custody—he used this word—of Constanza, his first wife. She would look after them and at them.

Anna's solicitor's advised her of the other side's contention: The paintings had been bought through the financial assistance of Mr Herbert's father-in-law and on the explicit understanding of their going ultimately to the Nation.

" Yellow Press money," said Anna.

" Very well spent for once," said Constanza.

She had read at one time that Simon was bidding for a Tintoretto; she had scarcely believed this possible. Now they learnt that it had been true. The catalogue of Simon's pictures was awe-inspiring. Tintoretto, Veronese, a Bellini, two Mantegna, a Titian.

" Rather fabulous for him," Constanza said fondly. " It was very cheeky of Simon to leave them to the *bambina* and very sweet. She must hear of it one day."

" But," Anna said, " they belong to *them*? "

" There's no doubt. They belong to them. Lord Thingummy's money. A great pity. You must write the lawyers to say there is no need to contest."

" That's what I thought," said the principessa.

She, as Flavia's guardian, had to sign a mass of papers. When it was all over she was informed that there could be no objection now to letting Flavia inherit such pictures as Simon had owned before his second marriage. Arrangements were being made to have them delivered at Constanza's London address.

"That's easy," Constanza said, "he never had any. Poor Simon." And she remembered how she had prevented him from buying a Degas drawing. One thing drifted into her possession at that time. Someone sent her a snapshot of Simon. It must have been taken shortly after the war, and he was in wig and gown. Simon, as he had said he would, had been called to the Bar, though he never practised. He must have bought himself a wig or borrowed one, for here he was in it, new and snowy white, looking as pleased as punch. Constanza thought that she had never seen him look so much like himself.

§

Giorgio's American journey did not turn out a success. No single very serious thing happened, it was just one muddle, one vexation, after another. He spent too much money, borrowed more, failed to pay some bills, trod on people's toes. He took some of them on lordly sprees and made blatant use of others. He never seemed to know or care to know who was who and he made a good number of social gaffes. He proposed to girls and made love to married women; he never listened to anyone's advice, treated Mr Baxter, the trustee, as if he were the steward at Castelfonte, got into poker games on trains and never went within a hundred miles of that instructive job.

He was well-behaved, indeed charming, at his mother's sister's house in Arizona. Nevertheless his Uncle Jack took a poor view of him and presently wrote to say so.

Mr Baxter got tough, refused more funds, and Giorgio was home again before his year was up. He appeared unsettled, buzzing between Rome and Florence, his head full of

projects for making money. Some months later the principessa was in London, and one afternoon she told Constanza
that she would like to have a talk about her will.

" Oh, mama, are you going to make one? "

As a matter of fact, Anna said, she had. Ages ago when
they first lived in England. " Those men insisted. You see,
the trust fund——"

" Yes, mama, we've had all of it. It's yours to leave it any
way you please and I hope you'll do exactly that."

Anna went on to say that in the will she made then, three
quarters were left to her daughter and the remaining quarter
to her son. " You see the money will go absolutely to my
heirs—Mr Baxter says they can lose it in one throw—and
I did not know then how Giorgio might turn out. One quarter to him seemed, well . . . safe. Now I have made a new
will leaving everything to you."

" Ought you to cut out Giorgio entirely? " said Constanza.

" That is what Jack and Mr Baxter pressed me to do, and
I've come to agree with them. They wrote something about
his trying to buy on margin when he was over there, it's a
thing they do on the stock exchange, but Giorgio's scheme
made their hair stand on end. Jack writes it isn't that
Giorgio is a gambler, but that he has simply no idea, he just
does not know how things work. And Jack says he doesn't
want to bother to find out. He says it's ingrained and
invincible. They say that everything he touches melts
away. It's more than extravagance: he's not responsible,
he doesn't know what responsibility is. To leave anything to
him at all would be total waste. So I am not leaving
him anything. And I shall tell him that. I want you all to
know."

" You can't leave him with nothing," said Constanza.
" And wills are such public things."

"It's not as if he didn't have property coming to him, as
you know he stands to have the lion's share from Rome.

As it's not money, it will be safe." A gleam came into Anna's eye, and she added, " I know that he can never sell the palazzo."

" You know more than I do."

" And there are other reasons. Giorgio has already had a good slice of the fund, in one way or another."

" I've no doubt of that. So have we all."

" More's been done for him than you know," Anna said and blushed.

Constanza laughed. " Between the two of you! Now, why don't you leave him a share in trust? Surely a new trust could be set up for him? "

" They've gone into that and are against it—I must say it surprised me, I thought they were all for tying money up. They say things are too uncertain nowadays. Mr Baxter doesn't even trust the dollar. And we all think it's safe to leave everything to you. If Giorgio needed something to keep him going, you would look after him, wouldn't you? " Of course, said Constanza. " I look on you as the real future head of the family. Help Giorgio in instalments, they mean. They seem to have worked it all out; I've never had so many letters from Jack. They think that Giorgio is bound to marry, in spite of his lack of tact, well . . . the way Italian boys often have to marry, and then he will be looked after. And you may not." Anna gave her daughter a look in which there was disapproval, entreaty, interrogation. " When I think of the chances——"

" And I may not," Constanza said in her cold voice. " Let's leave it at that, mama."

" They don't let me forget that you have no other expectations—they boil at the way you have been treated by Northumberland."

" Let's leave it at that."

Anna changed her tone. " My poor child. And you were brought up at a time when women like you were not trained

to earn their living. *And* you have Flavia to think of.
With her English grandparents not even asking to look
at her! "

" Just as well. I don't want *her* to look at them: she might
be turned to stone."

Anna began to launch herself into a set-piece against
Simon's parents.

Constanza cut across. " They have lost three sons."

" A judgement."

" Mama, *I beg you.* Left with that dreary daughter, who
became what she is because they always showed how little
use they had for her. Poor people—prisoners of a code, and
nobody to show them early enough a way to walk out of it.
Poor man, believing himself on thin ice all his life because
he married into trade. Poor woman. It is such an unnecessary tragedy."

" You always find excuses for everybody, Constanza,"
said her mother. " It's moral laxity."

" If I escaped being shut into a code it is because I was
confronted by so many. When the whole point of a code is
that there can be no choice." Constanza smiled again.
" Well, I owe that to you in a way. Like so much else, mama.
Providence moves in a mysterious way."

It was Anna now who did not feel like going into it. She
almost snapped, " I know that I owe *you* some form of financial security. And this means that I have to protect you
from your brother. I'm ashamed that, as it is, there may not
be so much left——"

" Have you actually made this new will? " said Constanza.

" I have," said Anna, " and it's signed and sealed and
witnessed. I had Mena and Mr James in for it. Always best
to have people who know about one's affairs. It's on its way
to Mr Baxter's safe. It is *my* will and my intention, and now
you know it, and I shall not change my mind. I never
do."

Constanza left her mother feeling that on the whole her decision might be right. " How *many* disappointments she has had," she afterwards told Mr James.

" There is one thing I must say for her," he answered, " she never played her wills. Anna has never used her money as a weapon; and I don't think she is doing so now."

" She could have, I suppose? "

" That hasn't occurred to you? "

" Not until this instant. It never crossed my mind."

" And that," said Mr James, " is a very great compliment indeed to Anna."

§

In the course of the years Constanza's life in London became one of diminishing returns. Most of her friends had gone one way or the other, were settled in the country with a family, settled in their job, their college, absorbedly successful or mediocre; gone to live abroad, *en poste*, as dedicated writers, as failed writers. After a certain point everybody is housed, cased, fitted or misfitted; those who remain at disposal, are too much so. Constanza's present lovers were replicates and echoes, the Greek poet, the Latin youth, the young man with the ball at his feet. By thirty-five or forty most men have become what they set out to be or fallen short of it. The good writers seemed to work harder and talk less. The new writers appeared less good. The Liberal politics that had moved her so much in her youth were no more. Her early socialist hopes had been shaken by abhorrence of regimentation and distrust of bureaucracy. She had never been captured by communism; and thought she saw a human flaw in everyone over thirty years of age who was. She could not stand the Tories, and found much she could not sympathize with in the Labour Party. Perhaps it was too English. She felt that she was outgrowing everything or that it was outgrowing her. The times change and our lives change, but they do not always change in the same direction.

Constanza did not really take to abstract painting; it was not that she found it bad, but that she found the other richer, better. Her taste for music had never been more than that, a taste: good, slight, shallow. The ubiquitous use of Freud and all his works rather repelled her. She would not have called it unnecessary as her mother did (who now treasured *A la Recherche du Temps Perdu* and *Mrs Dalloway*); much of it might be true and some of it quite necessary. It was the solemn and indulgent tittle-tattle which she found unwholesome, tedious, ugly: a reduction to the mechanical and the ignoble.

Toward the end of the Twenties Constanza had come to feel that she must make some break.

" I spent one half of my life in Italy and the other half in England or based on England," she said to Mr James.

Mr James knew her too well to ask a factual question.

" I have a sense it's come full circle. I have a sense I have to go."

" Return to the first half, dear girl? "

" Not while the fascisti are there. Nor would they let me. I can only go as a tourist, a few weeks now and again."

" Any plans? "

" An instinct: Off with the old. That may well be the price of the future—to burn one's boats."

" Before seeing land? "

" That's the idea. Not that I have a fleet of boats. I could begin by giving up my flat. I've had it for three years. That's a chunk of time the way we've been living, mama and I."

" Travel? "

" Mama's idea."

" The world *is* large."

" So they say. Did you hear that mama is moving again? She's been complaining about the Florentine climate. She's taking a villa at Alassio. The place is full of old English beaux. I'm rather for it: the regime is getting tougher every month. When I was in Rome papa tipped me off: they're keeping an eye on her. She'd be much better off in a place near the border."

Mr James looked worried. " We can't have more trouble for Anna."

" I know! I should have liked her to go to Bordighera which *is* only a step from France, but didn't like to suggest it. I can't worry her. Flavia doesn't want to go. She's got an idea about school in England. She's working on it."

He said, " And what will you do with yourself? "

" It'll sort itself out."

He looked at her.

" What do you want to say? "

" My dear . . . Only that you might make some people very happy."

Constanza thought of the people she had loved most. " It hasn't quite worked out that way," she said.

Constanza gave up her flat. Doing this kept her in London later into the summer than was her usual way. It was hot, most of the people she knew were somewhere else; the streets, full of ice-cream papers and strollers in shirt-sleeves, had a dishevelled, faintly raffish air. Constanza, too, felt herself already a stranger. On one of her last days, a Friday afternoon, she had to go to a shipping office in the Haymarket to see to some arrangements. She was handed a bundle of

forms, asked for a pen and sat down at one of the low tables.
As she was writing, she became gradually conscious of
somebody looking at her. She looked up in her turn and
saw a big darkish man stand in front of her. He was burly
and at the same time glossy, he wore no hat and she could
see that he was rather bald. He stood quietly, smiling
down on her with a friendly, faintly ironic expression in
his eyes.

" Mrs Herbert, do you remember me? "

And then she knew who he was. " My co-respondent," she
said, and held out her hand. She had never seen him dressed
in anything but khaki. " Captain Ware. If it is still
Captain? "

" Neither," he said. " That was just a name I took. Now
I'm Crane."

" *Lewis* Crane? " she said.

With another smile, with full irony and pleasure, he
said: " Lewis Crane."

" Douanier Rousseau," she said. " You did it! "

Lewis Crane's reputation at that time—as a critic and
manipulator of the modern-art market—was far greater than
it is today when the painters he has made or helped to make
are household words and astronomical picture deals have
become commonplace. His dual role as distinguished writer
and *marchand amateur* shocked many and what was known
about him did nothing to soften or explain. He was reported
to be aloof and ruthless, living like a tycoon with the tastes
and language of an intellectual. If he wrote an article it
would appear in a quarterly; he did not contribute to the
Weekly or the Sunday Press. His books were few, authorita-
tive, original and, if one could discount the buying and
selling side, independent in judgement. They were badly
written. (All but the first one which showed patches of
style and grace.) His financial transactions were discreet
and very successful. He was much talked about and a

frequent figure in gossip columns, yet few people had met him. He did not live in England, did not consort with his fellow writers, was known only impersonally to dealers and appeared to have no clique or hangers-on.

He said, " Let's get out of here. There's no need for you to fill in all that stuff yourself."

Constanza obeyed. Lewis Crane put a hand on her arm and steered her to the door.

A clerk rushed out to him. " Sir——"

" It can wait till Monday. Send the lot to my hotel."

" But sir—your *tickets*, sir——"

They were through the door and in the street. " Let's sit somewhere. I want to talk to you."

Constanza said she had a flat quite near. " Full of crates and dust-sheets, I'm getting out of it next week."

They walked to her flat. It was in the state she had described. In the sitting-room, already off the wall, stood a large flamboyant canvas of a bright beast in the jungle.

Lewis Crane stopped in his tracks, hit by a second shock of recognition.

" So *you* have it! "

Constanza said, " One of the customs man's rum pictures. Did you know it? It was Simon's. It doesn't belong to me. It's my daughter's, he left it to her. That—and this one." She turned to a small, quite exquisite Juan Gris that was still hung. " I never knew he had them."

" He didn't like them much," said Lewis Crane. " They were not his period."

" So you do know about them? "

" Sure," he said. " I sold them to him. I sold them to him for twopence to do him a good turn. Simon's been a good friend to me."

" Tell me," said Constanza, her eyes on him.

" Simon had a very kind side." Oh, about the two pictures—that was quickly told. " I had to have a sum of money in 1917. Simon lent it to me. It was quite a big sum."

" He probably borrowed it from my mother," said Constanza.

" As a matter of fact he did. He told me so. When the Armistice came and I was able to lay hands on some of my assets, I was able to pay him back. It was also necessary for me to get out of the Army quick——"

" Captain Ware, D.S.O.? "

" That part was all right. Only Ware didn't stick. Simon was able to help again. He pulled strings and I got demobbed."

" Like Angelina's soldier," said Constanza.

Lewis ignored him. " I happened to have the pictures then and I offered to let him have them for what I'd paid myself some years before. Cash wasn't anything to Simon by then, anyway it was so little, so I persuaded him to take them as an investment. It was the best I could do for him at that time, and later we drifted apart. And now here they are."

Constanza told him about Simon's will.

" They won't stretch to an interesting life," he said, " but they'll make her a whopping good dowry. Does she need one—your daughter? "

" One never can tell," said Constanza.

He stepped to the canvas on the floor, ran a finger over it. " Could do with a light varnish," he said. " You are moving house: where're you taking them? Who's crating them? Who are your insurers? "

" I thought of having them shipped to my mother in Italy."

" Shouldn't do that. Italy's tricky. Might get torn up as decadent art. Store them in England or get them to America. I can do it for you."

When he left, he had arranged to call for her in an hour to take her out to dinner.

It did not occur to Constanza to say no. She had liked him eleven years ago, and she liked him now. She had found him attractive then, and she found him more attractive now. He had mildly intrigued her then, and he still intrigued her. He appeared a different man in various ways, and yet he did not; and this, too, added to the sense of double-vision she had floated in since that moment he first spoke to her in the shipping office. All this meant much, meant nothing—what exercised the magnet pull was the feeling he had for, the glimpse she had through him, of Simon.

In the course of their evening she learnt casually that he had been supposed to leave for Amsterdam that night. By next morning they had reached the stage of discussing where they could go away to for a few days. " I'm sailing from Cherbourg on Tuesday," he said and that, too, was the first she heard of it.

If you have three days in front of you on a Saturday in August, he told her, the best thing to do is to stay where you are. Less wear and tear. Less waste, less people. " Though we could fly to Paris."

Constanza said she had never really been to Paris. " A few times with my mother, at a Right-Bank hotel. I never got what other people have, what one knows they've got when one reads their books."

" It's still in front of you."

" Perhaps."

" Well, shall we go now? "

" Perhaps not."

" Right," he said. " We stay where we are. I don't want you involved with Paris. I want to be alone with you."

He asked her to move into the Savoy with him. " Separate rooms, *this* time. Separate suites." But Constanza said she

would rather stay on at her flat, camp at her flat. " I'm
practically gone. Nobody is going to disturb us."

They remained as she had said, moving invisible, alone,
in the high summer anonymity of London. He spent the
nights at her flat; disappeared early and came back in a
few hours after a slow morning at the Turkish baths. They
lunched at restaurants he knew that even now were cool,
uncrowded and not glum. The afternoons were best at the
Savoy, on a high floor, the blinds drawn, an electric fan hum-
ming. At night they dined on the river, strolled endlessly,
returned late in the hired, chauffeur-driven car. On Monday
Lewis asked her, " Will you sail with me tomorrow? "

" Why not," she said.

Right, he said; and not to think of anything. " I will
send my own packers to the flat, they'll do everything beautifully."

" Did you mention where we are going? "

" New York," he said.

" America! " said Constanza. Then she said, " I don't
know. It's too quick, too sudden."

" You *have* taken your time about it," he said.

" If I ever do go, I feel I ought to be more . . . prepared.
I'm sorry my being so untravelled is proving such a nuisance.
But you can understand? "

" No," he said. " But we do as you wish."

He was like that with her. Tolerant, unexacting.
Uncurious. He would ask, defer to, what she wanted; then
take over and see to it.

He put off his own sailing. A few cables, a couple of
telephone calls. The Île de France next Friday. There was
something almost ostentatious about his unencumbrance
with a secretary. All done by himself in a quarter of an hour,
simply but concentratedly. With, obviously, a great deal

of money, and disregard for money, behind it, and an entire
absence of anxiety, of nerves. Living with her mother, Constanza was used to a certain smoothness of the surface of
life. This was a different order of smoothness, on a different
scale. She found it inhuman, alien to her sense of
measure, but for the time being she suspended judgement.
She listened to Lewis, watched his dealings, and could not
decide whether he had reached a fine peak of all but subli-
minal swagger, or whether this *was* the man, wholly unselfconscious and not showing off at all.

It was the same with his self-assurance that had already
impressed her in Cambridgeshire, that also was, possibly,
too complete to be real. Yet there it was: solid, calm, even
modest. It was not conceit, there was nothing high-pitched
about it. It was sang-froid, Constanza decided, and she
liked it very much. Lewis had really loved Simon. Again
and again he told her how much he owed to him. During
their brief friendship that much younger man had been a
clarifying, even liberating, influence. It was Simon who had
provided the key phrase to the way Lewis later organized
his life: the separation of work and money, writing and
money. One should be able, Simon had believed, to write
as little as one must.

" And poor Simon never wrote . . ." said Constanza.

" He wrote my Douanier book," said Lewis. " The best
part of it. It was my material; his words. He said I wrote
like a quadruped. All that's a dead secret."

This was another angle that fascinated her: The things
Lewis came out with and the things he withheld. He never
volunteered a fact about himself until he was bang in front
of it, then out he came with it, square and straight enough,
but without a frill of trimming. There it was, take it or
leave it, as concrete and as unrevealing as a meteor. Once
he mentioned a son.

Constanza raised an eye-brow.

" I've got one."

" What age? " she asked.

" About the same as your girl's."

" Only child? "

" No."

" And the mother? "

" My first wife."

" No longer? "

" That's right."

" Lewis, have you got a second wife? "

" Not at present."

Something crossed her mind. " You weren't married by any chance in 1918? "

" I was."

Constanza pondered on the various aspects of that past situation.

" And you took that chance over my divorce? Madman! "

" There wasn't the slightest chance of her getting to know about it."

" She might have learnt it from the newspapers."

" She couldn't."

" Do you mean that she couldn't read? Or that she couldn't read English? " Constanza was beginning to feel conspicuous with her questions, but she was curious and she longed to know. " Please, Lewis. Or do you mean that she wasn't called Mrs *Ware*? "

" She could read."

" Oh, she was Mrs Crane," said Constanza.

" No," said Lewis.

Another aspect presented itself. " What *would* you have done, poor man, if I had said yes to you in 1918? "

" Divorced," he said blandly.

He was quite patient when once or twice during the next

days she brought the subject up again. " Where is this family of yours lurking now? The boy of Flavia's age who isn't an only child? "

" The boy's at Eton," said Lewis.

Constanza laughed so loud that everybody in the restaurant looked up.

When he had to sail they made an appointment to meet a few weeks later, in September, at Genoa. Constanza kept it, and when she met him things had changed between them: she was no longer searching for her past, she was meeting Lewis. Within a week she said very well she would marry him.

Again he took over. Marriage in Brussels at a *Mairie* in October. A fortnight in Paris. He had commitments that winter in South America and they would sail, if she agreed, for Rio de Janeiro after Christmas. They could come back by way of Peru, he would like to show her the Inca ruins. " We can go or not go to the United States."

" Don't you have to go a good deal for your . . . commitments? " she asked.

" They don't commit *you*," Lewis said. " I like independence. Your independence."

Constanza told herself that at last she was getting what she had wanted.

She sent for Flavia. " What if she takes against me? " said Lewis. " Would you throw me over? "

Constanza said she only wanted Flavia to be in on things, able to see for herself; she did not believe in springing things on people. " She's nearly grown-up, and I must warn you, she is very curious."

" Like her mother."

" Not at all. I never ask you where you come from. She may. So will my mother. She will ask *me*."

Flavia arrived, greatly pleased to be meeting Lewis

Crane. She submitted him to a well-laid set of questions. Did he have to have a particular setting to write in, or did he believe in writing as Hemingway was supposed to have said *in your head*? Did he make his own indexes? When did he meet Modigliani? Did he think it was possible to look at *one* picture for five or six hours on end as his *confrère* Meier-Graefe said to have done when he had himself locked up with the El Greco in the Escurial?

Lewis answered. He said that personally he found half an hour about his limit; he liked to leave a picture and come back refreshed. But he well believed that Meier-Graefe might have done so: " He has huge capacities, everything he does is on a large scale."

Flavia pocketed this with a look as if she had received sheer gold.

Lewis had immediately taken them to the excellent restaurant of their hotel. If he had a way with headwaiters, Flavia here was one up on him, being more voluble, more interested and more native. Lewis sat back while she and Constanza and the staff exchanged a liturgically divided dirge: Too late . . . . Too soon . . . . Alas . . . . So Brief . . . .

He caught the gist: White truffles not in season. " Do you think a French wine? " he addressed his guest.

Flavia's pleased look deepened.

" Shall we make it Burgundy? " he asked.

She spoke up. " Don't you think perhaps . . . claret? " Her tone was social, light.

Lewis gave back the wine-list to the waiter. " Choose us a good claret," he said in French.

Flavia's expression changed.

Constanza said, " Oh, leave it to her, Lewis. She'll do us very well."

Lewis signed to the waiter and the list was brought round to the girl. " Thank you," she said to all of them. She read with a happy smile, took her time, ordered. She turned to

Lewis apologetically. " It's more interesting this way. Of course I make mistakes. Inexperience. It needs years and years. Unfortunately wine is a very expensive——" she was at a loss for a word.

" Hobby? " said Lewis.

" More than that," she said.

Constanza was watching Lewis. He leant across the table and said in his most friendly, serious way: " I must tell you *how much* you remind me of your father."

Flavia lowered her eyes. " Oh, do I? " she said.

Lewis talked while Constanza ate, as usual, like a hungry country person and Flavia ate and drank with feeling. Later she said in her social tone, Constanza knew she used when her heart was set on something very much, " Could I possibly persuade you to come to the Gallery with me tomorrow? It would be such a treat for me to go with *you*."

Lewis said he was no expert on Old Masters.

Flavia said, " Oh, *cher maître!* " Then she asked him to tell her how exactly did one influence the art market? And could he also explain why people bought paintings as a safe investment when they were no last-ditch investment at all? " It puzzles me as much as the gold standard. What can you do with gold in a revolution or a famine, except fill teeth? The Germans, as you know, are backing their new currency with grain."

Lewis said she had something there and he was grateful that more people had not caught on. Financial practice was much more mysterious, he said with delight, and much less logical than would appear sound to a donnish mind. He ordered brandy and, to Constanza's amusement, began to tell them quite a lot (up to a point) about the workings of the international art market.

Next morning when they were alone, Flavia said, " I've

got great news, too, mummy. Mr James has found me a most interesting family in London: they both teach and they're going to coach me for the University Entrance. I'm going to live with them in their house at Hampstead. *Nonna* has said yes. I'm to go in two weeks." She added with relish, " For Michaelmas Term."

Constanza congratulated her. " It's always nice to know what one wants," she said.

" *Nonna* doesn't know *your* news, Constanza."

" There hasn't been much time, darling. Lewis doesn't want to meet her before we're married. I've decided how I can present it to her, I'm going to stop at Alassio on my very way to Brussels and tell her as a big surprise. Anyhow *I* couldn't stand a lot of fuss and dithering. I don't think I can like getting married. How does this plan strike you? "

" She didn't like his attack on Van Gogh," said Flavia, " the slashing attack as the papers called it. It upset her very much. Why did Lewis do it? "

" He doesn't like the Sun-Flowers and he thinks Van Gogh absurdly over-rated. Darling, can you keep your mind on human affairs for one minute? Mama didn't know then that we should meet Lewis."

" She longs for you to be settled again." Flavia fell into the principessa's voice, " Constanza's life has been a great disappointment to me——"

" Stop it. Does she talk so much about it? "

" It's getting worse."

" The move's been a failure," said Constanza. " She used to like a place at least at first."

" Mena says she's restless. Mena says——"

" Darling, Mena has been crying wolf about mama so long. You know what I am hoping for? That Lewis will brighten things for her. Think if we could persuade her to come on those long journeys with us—to South America—I can see her take to it."

Flavia said, " What are Lewis' politics, Constanza? "

" I wish I knew. Do ask him."

" I have. He said he was a spectator."

Constanza groaned.

When Flavia left them a few days later, all had been arranged. Constanza, who was moving on with Lewis to Milan and other places, was going to stop at Alassio in ten days' time, and spend twenty-four hours with the principessa then she and Flavia would start out together on their journeys.

" Lewis has booked for us on the Calais Express," Flavia said. " Mummy, I think he's reliable. He will look after you."

" Don't let your mother lose the tickets," he said, " I shall be counting on you that she catches her connection."

" *D'accord, mon père,*" said Flavia, " I'll see that she gets to the *Mairie.*"

They were on the platform, seeing Flavia off. Constanza said, " You don't happen to be a Catholic after all, Lewis? "

" No."

" I would have liked to show myself to my father as an honest woman for once. The *Mairie* will be no help at all."

Lewis let out, " There's been some red-tape hitch, we shall be married at the Consulate at Brussels."

Constanza said mischievously, " May I ask which consulate? I shall have to share your nationality."

" British."

She laughed and waited. There was nothing further.

" I do wish my ear were better," she said, " as *all* I have to go on is your accent. It isn't foreign, it isn't quite American; I can't place it in England. Dear Lewis, are you by any chance a South African, a New Zealander? A Colonial? "

He kept his friendly quizzical smile. " Perhaps."

" *Who's Who*, mummy. Or don't we stoop to that? "

Lewis gave them no sign.

" What if we find a blank, mummy? "

Constanza said, " If this is a game, Lewis, it is very uninteresting indeed."

From the first Lewis had made Constanza feel that she was the world to him. And that was the one solid thing between them. The rest, most of the rest was covered by Lewis' will. Milan was not like Genoa, the first days of Genoa; more and more Constanza found herself feeling in terms of plans, plans for her family. And perhaps this was best after all, she thought: at long last I shall have my *mariage de raison*. And she liked him immensely as a man, she liked him as a companion, a buccaneer side had always appealed to her; and most of all, most free of all, was that she liked him, was able to hold him in affection without that awful compassion she had for Simon, the compassion one comes to feel sooner or later for all living beings. Lewis, like the men of her earlier days, was her equal, her accomplice, her brother.

He was also still irreducibly Simon's dark horse. They had some high moments together; yet this remained nagging, and before they parted, a week before their wedding, they had another bout of the question-and-answer game.

Provoked at last, Lewis said, " Why do you want to know so much about me? "

" Why do you want to tell so little? "

" I thought you were a woman without prejudices."

" Then give me something to have no prejudices about. Wanting to know who a man's father was, wanting to know how he grew up is not prejudice."

" *Why* do you want to know? "

" Because it is part of the man. Because the whole is more true than a half. Because the truth is more interesting than mysteries."

He was silent.

" Because," and here she held his eyes, " the reasons for mysteries are often childish or shabby."

He met this well. " What if the truth is utterly irrelevant to the man? "

" Is it, ever? "

" Who has the right to another man's truth? " he said.

She accepted this. " Ah, but then—if the man wishes to separate himself from the truth, then I think he ought to provide some substitute."

" A jolly good lie? "

" A jolly *good* lie. A cover-story, well-cooked up, well-served. He ought to give up the pretentiousness of mystery, the teasing, the invitation. . . ."

He drew a red herring. " So you believe in lies, Constanza? "

" I've never been able to see how one can manage without them. We would hurt each other *too* much. *I* lie like a trooper; and for my own convenience. The thing is to remember one is lying. The truth is safe enough as long as one does that." Unlike my poor mother who even hesitates over the whitest of social lies. . . . This Constanza did not say aloud for Lewis was a stranger still to Anna and the problem of Anna.

He said nothing. Constanza had never learnt to cope with silence; she did not use it herself.

" Is it that you want the world to think you have been through romantic hardships? " She felt she had to do it, had to clear it up, as it was something in him which she could not accept and which might wreck them because she would not accept it, as Simon's jealousy had done. " I can't make out whether you want me to think you *are*, or whether you want to *hide* from me that you may be, the son of an anarchist Rumanian tailor? "

" I love you when you talk like that, Constanza," he said. It was no use; she got no further.

The next day she was on her way to Alassio, and that evening she told Anna. It was devastating. Anna ranted herself into a state of despair from which there could be no return by argument. Mena tried to keep her arms round her, Flavia left the room; Constanza stood, as she had so often stood before her mother, chilled, at a loss. She was aware that there were many things against her marriage from her mother's point of view (as well as things that she knew might please her), but there was nothing rational in that storm. Anna asked no real questions, listened to no answer. It was only late that night when Constanza was alone that she was able to see it as what it was, an out-cry against life. A cry of disappointment: Is that all you brought to me after these many years? all that is come of promise? all that was in store?

I am marrying Lewis Crane, a man full of life, who will give us all a new lease, the sense of a new lease. *Or*: I am marrying a middle-aged art-dealer who refuses to admit he is one, a critic with a shady reputation.

Constanza blamed herself; for lacking showmanship, for failing in imagination. She ought to have persuaded Lewis to appear: Lewis in the kind of Isotta he was apt to conjure up, bland and quizzical, laden with presents, alight with plans. Now it was a mess; perhaps irretrievable.

In the morning, Flavia said in a small voice, " Are we still going? " Constanza, determined, cold, answered, " What else? "

The principessa did not come down to luncheon; then suddenly appeared, stood in the door.

She pointed a hand. " You are even taking the child

from me! You are all a treacherous breed. I wish to heaven I had never set a foot on Europe."

Badly shaken they were driven to the station by the principessa's man. They were nearly late for the train. As they boarded it Constanza touched a hand to her ruby as it was her way.

Chapter II

The name of the French fishing port where they found themselves that night was St-Jean. St-Jean-le-Sauveur. For
the first few days circumstances propped her; afterwards,
unaided, Constanza pursued her instinctive course. She
refused to move.

They took the villa that had been so fortuitously offered.
It was a preposterous choice, as they learnt later on, at the
time it did not occur to them to look for any other. It stood
on the end of a narrow hill edging the sea, and it was exposed
to every wind. The hill which was called the Hill, *la
Colline*, was covered chiefly with stunted, shrubby pines, and
there were a few modest villas, all new, and all of them
already locked and shuttered against the winter. Half a
mile inland lay Mediterranean country—cypresses, olives,
vines, but the hill with the sea, the pines, the villas, offered
only a mélange of the grandly bleak with the suburban. The
only graceful thing on it was a Roman watch-tower at the
tip, white-washed and soberly converted into a place to live.
The tower, too, was shut up.

Lewis's telegrams subsided. He accepted Constanza's plea
to postpone, to wait. We have been rushing ourselves into
things, she wrote to him. Very well, if you wish, take your
time, he answered by telegraph. She had never had a letter
from him yet.

" Do you think *all* his books are ghost-written? " she said
to Flavia.

He did not offer to come to the South of France, but
suggested various meeting places. Her answer always was:
Later; not yet. At last he acquiesced.

"I rather think he has commitments at Stockholm at the end of the month," Constanza said.

She asked Flavia when *she* would be off. "Michaelmas term must have started."

Flavia had thought it over. "I think I'll stay on with you for a bit, if I may," she said lightly.

"Darling, your career!"

"I'm very young actually, I'll be able to catch up. We might write them to send me some books: I might try to do some work for them by correspondence."

Flavia did not know why she, too, now felt compelled to stay. There were several pointers: a chivalrous sense that she must not desert Constanza; a sense of something going to happen; curiosity.

Constanza had rather felt that to be alone—a rare state for her—was a prerequisite of the *reculement*, the retreat, she was seeking for herself; but she was touched and pleased, and she said yes.

"As long as you remember that you are not stuck here because I choose to be. There is still a Calais Express for you every day."

Their villa was new and clean and ugly, down to the coloured tiles. Except for the dining-room there was mercifully little furniture besides the wide brass bedsteads and the *armoires à glace*. The coal-stove in the kitchen was hard to light and smoked whenever the mistral blew, the windows were badly fitted and rattled in the wind, and the mistral that winter blew a very great deal. It is a hard wind, bringing swept blue, bitter days. Soon they were extremely cold. They lit *mi-russes* and kept them going and they bought a tinny electric fire with two bars, but the current was weak and regularly failed and their fire often fused. Flavia enjoyed mending it. The first-floor master bedroom had a glassed verandah overhanging the sea, and while the sun was on it this was the one warm room in the place. Flavia turned it into her study and had the dining-room table moved upstairs to work on. The drawback of this glass-house was that if one opened a window—which one was obliged to do now and again if only to gain respite from the rattling—in swept the wind and out whirled one's papers. There wasn't a drawer in the house and even the stones they used for paper-weights did not always avail, so at least once every day this happened and the only thing to do was to hurl oneself downstairs, scramble down the precipice and retrieve what could be retrieved off thyme and pine before it was blown into the sea. " *Mes œuvres!* " Flavia shrieked and Constanza, too, dropped everything and out they dashed on one more paper-chase.

They had no cook or maid. A *femme de ménage* washed up and cleaned; she was one of the best in the place but by their Italian standards, she was a slut. A woman who kept a fish-stall outside one of the cafés on the front, and who had been in service in her youth, was easily persuaded by Constanza to come up every day at noon and cook them a delicious mess of provençal vegetables or fish. Their dinner was cooked by Constanza. If the stove did not light, she would start a charcoal fire. On some evenings Flavia walked down to the village with napkin and bowl and brought back a *plat à emporter* from the *traiteur*.

St-Jean was a summer place, they found out; the painters still came, but also foreigners now and writers. One very eminent English man of letters indeed was said to be building next year; they did not quite believe this but Flavia pricked up her ears. The people they got to know that winter were French, local and middle-aged. The man and wife who owned the hotel, the *maire*, the man who ran the house-agency in summer and was trying to start a bus-line to Bandol, the man who ran the paint-shop, a retired wholesale grocer from Clermont-Ferrand and an old journalist who still wrote *feuilletons* for *L'Echo du Midi*.

These new friends sent them confitures, mimosa from their gardens, freshly caught sardines. Constanza was advised where to get wood, Flavia was given the use of a bicycle in good repair. They were asked to houses for *l'apéritif* and a game of *boules*, though most of their social life took place at the Café de la Marine. Flavia and Constanza went down there after dinner to play *belote* or dominoes. The French forgave Constanza's bungling play because she was so beautiful, and because she was animated and enjoyed what they had to tell. There were always stories—they were all articulate, all *raconteurs*—stories about food, about love, about politics, about funerals and money. On they went, with Constanza languidly putting the wrong trump on the wrong suit, about *les amours du médecin, le terrain du curé, les pots de vin du ministre* and *la mort de Madame Bontemps*. And of course about what to eat, where to eat, what to drink with what to eat, what one ate last night, where to eat next Sunday, what one drank, what one paid, what was said. What was said entranced Constanza most. In Italy, she told Flavia, she had been taught to express herself by exclamations, in London by a five-term code, " These people use *words*." Flavia, with the conservatism of youth, kept more aloof, but she did apply herself to learn proper French.

" *Sans accent*," they told her.

Immediately Flavia broke into her mother's Italian accent and after that into English French.

" She's a parrot," said Constanza. But when they were alone she encouraged Flavia to tell the stories back to her in meridional or genteel *pointu*.

At that season the café shut by half past ten. The *consommations, cafés arosés, demis de bière*, tisanes and rum grog for the jovial, had been settled in rounds by the men. Everybody shook hands and said *bonne nuit* and *à demain*. Flavia and Constanza had their pocket torches and thick overcoats.

Nobody lived their way, and together they set off on their walk home up the hill.

When they got there they would find the villa freezing. Constanza went straight to bed, Flavia in overcoat and trousers sat up with her. They drank Viandox, a concoction made with liquid bouillon essence and thermos water, which had the virtue of being hot. And they talked. Much about the French. How strange they were to her, Constanza said, and how familiar; they made her feel like an animal uncertain if it is its own image that is confronting it in the looking-glass. The French, she said, had a most unnerving effect on the Italians. *She* found them soothing and diverting—so much scepticism tied to so many certainties. " They are softer than we are *and* more stoical." Their losses in the war, she said, had been on a tragic scale and one still had a sense of national bereavement. Yet they had kept a glow on life, and she admired them for it.

She also said to Flavia what an unexpected relief it was to find herself here, in a neutral country, " where, thank God, nobody is Anglo-Saxon either," to have come to *terra incognita*, new ground.

They read enormously that winter, mostly in the mornings because the days were short and the artificial light so poor, and the books were French. Not Stendhal—*he* was another France, Constanza said—but Balzac of course, Zola and Maupassant and the Goncourt Journals; Jules Romains, Jules Renard, François Mauriac and Julien Green.

" No wonder we are so much simpler, *nous autres Italiens*, we haven't had so many people tell us what we're like."

They also read the polished idols of French literature, who were idols then, Jacques de Lacretelle, Abel, Hermant, Giraudoux, Valérie Larbaud. And Flavia also read Théophile Gautier's *Mademoiselle de Maupin*.

Every day in the afternoon they went for a walk to the tip of the hill as far as the Roman tower. An enclosure had been walled off in front of it and below those walls there was shelter from the wind and it was warm. So warm, that when they peeped inside they were not surprised to see a flourishing fig-tree. There was also a fountain, only a sketch of a dolphin spouting, a pastiche, a learned mason's joke, but here, in this region so poor in casual architecture, its presence moved Constanza and filled her with contentment.

Flavia peeped further. Through a chink in a shutter she saw a book-lined wall, a fire-place, something that must be a paraffin lamp. " Wise man." They knew now that the tower belonged to a Parisian, *un homme politique*, without, it appeared, party, following or office.

Now and then they spent the day at Toulon—by tram to La Seine, thence by ferry across the harbour—buying books, sailor clothes for Flavia, eating *coquillages*, but their real reason for going was that they liked to be there. One night when *Topaze* was on tour at the Municipal Theatre, the St-Jean house agent took them all *en bande* in his brand-new bus; after the play they had supper on the Boulevard, and getting the bus home was like collectively driving a whale.

There was a local cinema hall and it gave a performance on Sunday nights: a short silent film, a long silent film, static advertisements, a man at an upright piano. Down in the well sprawled the youth of St-Jean, in *berets basques*, whistling tunes, champing *cacahouettes*. The notables and villa people sat in the balcony upstairs. The whole place was blue with caporal tobacco smoke. Constanza and Flavia went regularly. The price of the grand seats was Frs 4.50, nine pence. It was an innocent life they had that winter, and they were very happy.

When they found out her address, London friends proposed themselves to stay. After they'd been discouraged they said, " Oh well, Constanza must be off with a new man."

" Oh, well."

" Flavia's with her this time."

" What *is* going to happen to that girl? "

" What will *she* turn into? "

" Join a cloistered order I daresay."

The real outside world was Lewis and the principessa. Constanza was surprised how easily, how plainly, she had come to a decision about Lewis. She could no longer imagine marrying him. False trails had misled her. One was simple enough: for a few days at Genoa she had believed it to be the *coup de foudre*. It was not; it was a mistake she made, and that was that. The other, irresistible, trail had been her own interpretation of portents: the sudden meeting with Lewis, the co-respondent, the key-figure of her divorce, during her last days of London in the mood of change (off with the old); Lewis almost wordlessly moving into her pattern; the dismantled flat; the discovery about Simon's pictures; all, all of it, sudden and condensed, pointed one way. It pointed: she mistook the direction. It was not to the new, it was not to the future; it had been a final going backwards, it had been the rounding of the past, the end, not a beginning, of the pattern. It had been in fact the last step in her off with the old. A narrow escape!

Flavia, very disappointed indeed but equable, asked her, " How does one break with a man? "

" I never found it difficult," Constanza said. " If you really mean to break; *and* do it. There's a natural breaking point, though it's always one who sees it first. If you allow things to mend—one does and they do—you get something different, a kind of artificial fibre, and then, well, misery begins. I don't find it at all easy to explain to you, my sweet."

" I'm learning," said Flavia loftily.

It was not easy with Lewis. St-Jean knew that the tele-

graph woman (it was an old woman in a black dress) once
more climbed that hill two or three times a day. Lewis would
not take no for an answer. At last he made a suggestion
which he was forced to send under cover of an envelope. He
wrote a letter. All right, he said, if it is marriage you object
to, will you allow me to establish you in a house or flat in a
European capital of your choice? Paris being of course the
most convenient.

Constanza roared with laughter. Dear Lewis, she said,
and it's always Paris. " Simon longed for us to go when we
were married. It was the war and we had to make it
Wiltshire."

" Does Lewis want to make you a kept woman,
mummy? "

" Yes, darling. No more, nor less, than in marriage. But
so much more flattering always."

At length, Lewis had to start for South America.

" Shelved? " said Flavia.

" Well, he *is* fond of cabling. That poor woman! Yes,
Flavia, it's shelved. Lewis isn't one to go after what he
cannot get."

In London they said, " Constanza's going to marry Lewis
Crane."

" She can't, he's been to Sing-Sing."

" That wouldn't stop her. As long as he doesn't get
jugged again."

" Anyhow, Crane's got at least five wives."

Someone else said, " Nonsense. I happen to know all
about Lewis Crane. I know his people."

" Oh? "

" *Is* he Rasputin's son? "

" I couldn't possibly tell you. The man once did me a
good turn."

" So *very* frightful? "

" So *frightfully* respectable."

From time to time Anna descended on them. She arrived with Mena, driven by her spoilt young Italian chauffeur, and they all got out of the car. Anna, slim, erect, dressed in sober and becoming silks, walked up the gravel path. Anna was nearly sixty and her beautiful soft hair was white. Her blue eyes were paler than they had been, and by her clothes and presentation of herself she was marked as an old lady, but her face was unlined, smooth, with the skin and features as finely fragile as they must have been at thirty. There was an unreal, waxy, artificial look about her, yet whatever it was it was not art. Mena and the chauffeur followed, having unloaded baskets of exquisitely chosen provisions.

" Mama, *cara*," said Constanza, and they kissed.

For a few minutes all went well. The presents were unwrapped. Then gradually it came back again. The principessa looked at the room with disfavour as if she were seeing it for the first time.

" Really Constanza, I cannot understand you."

" Yes, mama. I'm not as adept as you in choosing houses."

" We are as hideous as we're uncomfortable," said Flavia and giggled.

Mena meanwhile had gone off to sort and sew up Constanza's things. She did this every time. Anna fastened her attention on the door-knobs.

" What is their substance? "

Nobody answered her. She said, " White *porcelain*. I'm sure they come off in your hand. And the way these doors are set—how can you bear it when you have the *tramontana*? "

" The name of the prevailing wind is mistral," said Constanza.

Anna returned to where she started. " I cannot understand you. When I think of Somerset! We knew one or two old people in Rhode Island who made themselves deliberately uncomfortable. Can't you at least find a better house? "

" For one thing, I signed an eight months' lease for this one."

" I never let that worry me," said the principessa.

" Mama," said Constanza, and not for the first time either, " there's a depression on. Mr Baxter writes to me, too."

" The depression doesn't touch honest investments," said Anna.

Flavia snorted. She had come to feel very critical of her grandmother, even hostile.

In point of fact Mr Baxter had secretly written to Constanza on a reassuring note. Their investments had suffered relatively little (so far); dividends had dropped off and were bound to drop off further, yet as it happened the fund disposed of a capital sum to tide them over for some time to come. Nevertheless it would be wise to impress economy on the principessa.

" We're not in the work-house yet," she said. " As a matter of fact, Giorgio is doing very well."

" Tell us? " said Flavia.

" He's gone into partnership with some car-designer at Turin. He spoke to Colonel Robinson about it: they are putting an engine back to front——"

" Front to back," said Flavia.

" The colonel says it's quite an innovation. They're going to show it in Milan this spring."

" Not a new motor car? " said Constanza.

" Giorgio calls it his proto-type."

"He talked to me about something like that on the train."

"Was that the hare-brained scheme, mummy?"

"It sounded as if it required a round sum of money," said Constanza.

"Oh, Giorgio is only one of many partners," said his mother. "Wouldn't it be wonderful if after all he turned out——"

"Responsible? Very wonderful."

"And what are *your* plans?" said Anna.

The truth was that Anna was as disappointed by Constanza's backing out of marrying Lewis as she had been by the original plan. After the first wave, she had waited to be persuaded, tempted, won over; the blankness instead frustrated her. She could not bear Constanza's inactivity. She called it aimless, empty.

Constanza did not give way.

To Mena she said, "What *is* the matter?"

Mena answered, "She is tired of herself."

From Italian friends Constanza now received warning that her stay so near the border had aroused suspicion. It was known that she had been put on a black list and they advised her to cross into Italy as seldom as she could. It was not unexpected news and it put an end to Constanza's slightest usefulness. It also served her present resolution to stay put: no visits to Alassio. Flavia, with ill grace, went every other week.

"How was she?"

"She hardly eats. At least not at table."

"That *is* bad," cried Constanza.

Flavia, of a more ruthless and enlightened generation, said, "It's probably a pose. She wants to attract attention."

In February came news from Rome that shook Constanza

deeply. A letter from papa, she said to Flavia who was breakfasting by her bed. "My word—it's running to a second sheet. What can it be?"

She read quickly and tears began to flow to her eyes. "Flavia, Flavia, he wants her back. He is asking mama to return to Rome!"

What the prince had to say was this. He had learnt that Anna had been very indiscreet. If the fascists did not arrest her, they would put pressure on her to leave the country for ever. "The man at the head of Province Genoa is a bad man. Nothing can be done with him. She is too old to go into exile again. We are both old. She is my wife. I have been assured that if she lived with us in Rome she would be safe, nobody would touch her." He offered her the protection of his house and name. "If she will come, she will find a family. Carla and Maria have missed her. She has been gone a long time, it is right for her to come home now. We shall all forgive each other what there may be to forgive. For the rest, the palazzo will be as she left it. We shall accommodate ourselves to one another."

In a postscript the prince said that he had written to Anna in the same spirit, but touching lightly only on her danger from the fascists. "It is better so. It would only upset her."

Flavia said, "Giulia?"

"Giulia is old now. She was always a good bit older than papa; she is the eldest of the three of them."

Constanza took the next fast train to Nice. On the journey thoughts came. Only she had seen how much the prince and Anna had settled in their separate ways. The single man, hardly living at home, who had not noticed that the house had changed. The prince, too, was old now—he had aged quickly, slipped into an old man; it was one of the sadnesses Constanza bore. And Anna, with her energies still untapped, *she* was not softened, *she* was not pliable; she was too alive

288

still to glide into this twilight element of forgotten rancours, casual tolerance and resignation. If Constanza wished it, she could not see it.

They met in one of the large hotels on the Promenade des Anglais. In the ornate hall, she heard the principessa give her No. There was no raking-over this time, only a bare negation. Constanza thought her mother wore a strange look on her face that she could not interpret.

A flash of love compelled her to say: " I always knew how you suffered." Anna's face hardly flickered; and when Constanza kissed her there was no response.

" No soap? " said Flavia.

" *Something* moved her about papa's offer."

" Constanza, you know what I think? Only a doctor could help her—you know the kind I mean? "

Constanza faced this. " That there is something . . . abnormal? I've long known that."

Soon there was a promise of spring. The almonds were out, the days were longer, the mornings balmy. They opened all their windows; it was not a time to stay indoors and at noon they often took their food and wine to the watch tower and ate below its sheltering walls. They knew more now about the owner. He excited much speculation in local gossip; stories about him varied but he was always described as a man of parts hampered by a ludicrous probity. They called him *le député raté*. The most coherent account of him came from Frioulle, their journalist acquaintance.

" *Un garçon d'une excellente famille*, extremely intelligent, *Normalien*, Catholic agnostic, and all the rest of it. Honourable judicial career in front of him: but no, he must turn to politics. His people did not like it one bit, but they needn't have worried. When our man got to the water he refused to drink. He was actually elected—God knows how, as he made the kind of speeches one in ten could understand and declined to promise his supporters as much as a hand-shake—but elected he was. No sooner in, than he resigned. He'd discovered some irregularity in the ballot! He was with the Socialists to begin with, not with the Radical-Socialistes, nor the Socialistes-Républicains, with Léon Blum's lot. He left them, they must have been relieved to be rid of him in spite of his brilliance, and formed his own group with two or three other bright lads, *professeurs de lycée*, one of them a poet. Well, they're all in by now, one's at the *Quai*. You know——" he named him. " But not our man. There was something he couldn't swallow, some tinge of concession, and he dissolved the group.

" Now he's alone and writes books. He wants to reform the Chamber, he wants to reform the Bar, he wants to abolish the Prefectural System; and that's not all. He tells us that the first step towards sane government is the renunciation of war as an instrument of policy. *Tout bêtement* he wants us to send home *l'Armée Française*, neither less nor more. *Que voulez-vous, mesdames, c'est un homme à principes.*"

" Is that what he wants? " said Constanza.

" I can lend you one of his books. He writes extremely well."

Other people spoke of a private tragedy in the man of principles' life. He had married early, a girl from another family of *grand-bourgeois*, as arranged by the parents. His wife developed a nervous disorder and their life was hell. He bore it with great fortitude and patience for a number of years; recently they had separated. The wife was shut up somewhere, they said, but this may have been a St-Jean touch.

One morning Constanza handed Flavia a slim volume. " You ought to read this."

Flavia gave it a glance. " *De l'Administration* by Michel Something——? Not what I'd call a catch-penny title."

" It's by the man of principles. It's remarkable. So lucid, so dispassionate—so magnanimous. I wish *he* were Prime Minister. I wonder if he ever will? "

People pressed Constanza to look at a house inland that was to let. They went and found a low, ochre-coloured, seventeenth-century farmhouse, the kind called *bastide* in that region. It was flanked by cypresses and stood above terraced fields planted with artichokes and vines. Inside the house the floors were red-tiled and the walls were thick. Someone had built on a portico. Constanza liked it very much. " Shall we take it for the summer? " she said. But they told her that the owners insisted on a twelve years' lease.

Chapter III

It was already March and Flavia said that in a week they might begin to bathe, when the envelope addressed by Giorgio came.

It contained a receipt. Constanza stared at it quite stupidly for a moment then she cried, " The ruby—the ruby isn't lost! I'll be *blowed*."

The receipt bore the address of a Milan firm, gave a brief description of the ring and stated that it might be retrieved for a certain sum.

" The ring is coming back to us. Oh Flavia! And it was Giorgio, Giorgio all the time and we thought it was lost or stolen. What fools we were."

" We have nice minds," said Flavia.

" One up for Giorgio. The devil." Constanza laughed, delighted. " It *was* his turn to get some of his own back. He's got even. For once. He *may* loathe me less now."

" *How* did he do it? " said Flavia.

" *Yes*——? "

" He didn't pull it off your hand, mummy—you're not *so* absent-minded? "

" I was thinking of mama and our row, and I was scared at his turning up like this—I'm always scared stiff at that border. I was afraid the customs louts would think he was bringing me something to smuggle across and come back again."

" I can see how it was," Flavia said: " You must have pulled your rings off—like this—and had them on the table in front of you, you sometimes do when you are anxious. You always slip them on again. You don't notice."

" Simon did," said Constanza, " he used to tease me about it."

" Giorgio must have been pretty quick! I bet he hadn't driven down from Sestriere to steal your ruby."

" We're all quick," said Constanza with a touch of pride. " He came to borrow money for the car he wanted to build. He was furious when I turned him down. Well, good for Giorgio, I didn't know he had it in him."

" Does it mean *you* have to pay for the ring now, mummy? "

" Oh dear," said Constanza. " The *impudence*."

" It's a huge sum."

" Huge. Only mama could help us to lay hands on it."

" They're giving you three weeks. How is that? "

" It must be just under six months since Giorgio pawned the ring."

" Is that a pawn-shop? " Flavia said, looking at the receipt.

" Gracious no. No pawn-shop would have paid so much. They are very well-known jewellers at Milan. I went there with Lewis as it happened, he had his watch chain polished up."

" Mightn't they have arrested Giorgio? "

" I suppose he played it bold," said his sister. " Told them who he was: family ring, temporary money troubles. These grand firms are used to that kind of thing. Decent of Giorgio not to have sold the ring outright. Well, *that* might have been bad luck."

The day was fine and Flavia said they had to celebrate. But when they arrived at the tower, the shutters were open and a car was standing outside, a high, old-fashioned touring car with beautifully polished head-lamps.

" The man of principles must have arrived," said Flavia.

" That's the end of our picnics. Those French professorial types are apt to be awfully stuffy."

Back they turned and ate their tunny-fish and olives on

their own windy door-step. " You know what, Constanza? "
Flavia said in the middle of it, " If Giorgio hadn't snatched
your ring you would be married now to Lewis."

Again Constanza arranged to meet the principessa at Nice.
They sat in the same hotel hall. Anna did not take the news
in Constanza's way.

For a time she said nothing at all. She sat as though she
had been turned to alabaster. At last she made a sound.

" So my son is a thief."

Constanza spoke; pleaded; assembled another picture.
She spoke against her mother's silence and against the
presences and movement of a public place. From off, came
palm-court music. The tea they had ordered was brought.
Constanza knew she was failing.

" What you have always lacked is a sense of proportion,
mama."

Suddenly Anna gathered momentum. " You two are a
chip off the same block. . . ." The need to keep her voice
down made the words come out in a hiss. " All, all of a piece
throughout . . . Everything you touched has come to naught
. . . Waste! Nothing but waste. . . ."

Constanza, captive, endured the tirade. Anna was unable
to end it.

". . . You were too selfish, too frivolous even to marry—all
your men, one after the other, led on, led on with empty
promises. You never thought of *them*——"

From Anna, this was too much. Blazing, clearly, looking
fully at her, Constanza said: " At least *I* went to bed with
them."

After Anna recovered, she said, " This is *not* true? "

But Constanza was now riding her own wave.

" Didn't you know? " she flung out. " You must have
known. Oh, mama, *be* your age."

Anna was always supreme in showing when she was struck. Now she rose, slowly, swaying like a statue in a dream. Upright and small, she walked down the pilastered aisle and out of the hotel.

Constanza sat on for a moment. When she was about to follow her mother, the waiter stopped her with the bill. By the time she had reached the fore-court, the car had just moved off.

She had an impulse to follow by train into Italy. Hesitated; told herself she was losing her sense of proportion as well. She returned to St-Jean-le-Sauveur. Next day she tried to put through a call from the café. This, as they had learnt before, was a frustrating business. When she got some connection, Mena at the other end, never at her best on the telephone, kept shouting one word through: *tranquilla*. Whether it meant they must keep calm or that the principessa had calmed down, Constanza could not make out.

Four days later in the very early morning they were awakened by a knock at their gate. It was the postmaster, a message had come through from Alassio. Anna was dead.

Constanza dressed, put some things in a bag and was down again. " Are you ready? " she said.

Flavia, with darkened eyes, not looking at her, said: " Have I got to come? "

Constanza did not hear, and Flavia had to repeat the question.

" No. Not if you don't want to."

They were standing in the road, when they were approached by a slim, slightly-built man in mechanic's overalls. He wore a beret. Flavia's first thought was, they've managed to send up a taxi.

He went to Constanza swiftly, kissed her hand and said,

"*Je crois, madame, que nous sommes un peu voisin*—can I be of some use to you?" It was said socially but with great gentleness.

Then Flavia saw his face. It was a very French face of a certain period, such as one might see in a portrait by Clouet: a well-shaped nose, a curved mouth, thick brown hair, deep-set eyes, alight with mind. It was essentially an intelligent face, of noble structure; yet there was also an expression reflecting other things: kindliness, humour, persiflage.

Constanza said, "We have no car, no telephone——"

In a few minutes he had the Delage at their door, ready to catch the express at Toulon. Constanza accepted unseeing; but Flavia had caught on that it must be the man from the tower.

At Alassio, Constanza was met by an English colonel who named himself and said he had been a friend of her mother's.

They shook hands. The colonel muttered.

"Where is my mother's maid?"

The colonel said, "She's been most helpful, you know." As a matter of fact it was she who had found the principessa before dawn this morning. Very sensibly, she had called him, their nearest neighbour, and he had called the doctor. "The English doctor. We had the Italian fellow in later on. He signed the certificate. The maid's explained everything—how badly your mother's been sleeping for some time, her loss of appetite, the sleeping pills on top of her weak heart——"

"Sleeping pills?" said Constanza.

"Veronal, don't you know? Shocking how much of the stuff you can get out here without prescription. You might call it an overdose, the maid says it was just too much for the principessa's heart, *she* had no idea how strong they were. And if you ask me, that's what it was."

In the car the colonel said, "I telegraphed the family in

Rome. Your mother's sisters-in-law are arriving tonight with their husbands. I understand the old gentleman himself is not up to the journey."

" Have you known my mother long? "

" Only a few weeks," said the colonel, adding some words of appreciation. " And you will of course come and stay with us, my wife is expecting you. We've asked the women servants at your mother's villa to sleep at our place."

" You are very kind," Constanza said. " But I shall be with my mother. I expect the others will want to stay, too. You see, we are all Italians."

She arrived. The two women rushed into each other's arms. Constanza had been prepared to uphold Mena, instead she found her composed and tearless. The tiny woman was holding herself stiff, like a watch-dog at bay.

When they were alone, Constanza said, " And *you* found her. *Oh, Mena.* What were you doing in mama's room in the middle of the night? "

" I sleep lightly. I get up to look at her. I told so to the *colonnello.*"

" What made you specially anxious? "

Mena's face stayed shut. " I always went to see she was all right. I have no-one else to look after."

" *Did* mama take sleeping pills? "

" Sometimes."

" Veronal? *You* would have known if she took that? "

" I may have known."

" There was no letter? No word for me? "

" Nothing," said Mena.

Later in the day Constanza asked, " Where? You would know best."

" Rome! " Mena said at once. " She must go to Rome."

" Yes, that would be what she wanted. My father will do everything that must be done."

In the evening Carla and Maria and their men arrived. They made much ado and cried a good deal, which Constanza could not, but she was glad they had come, she found that it was right.

They said to her, " Aren't you going to send for your girl? " No, Constanza said, she did not want her to go for the first time like this. She did not tell them that Flavia was terrified.

In due course they took Anna to Rome. She was buried from the palazzo. There was a last hitch when Mr Baxter cabled from America that Anna had left instructions with him many years ago. The principessa wished to be buried in the Foreigners' Cemetery, the cemetery by the pyramid of Cestius.

" It *is* the most beautiful cemetery in Rome," the prince said, " and the Americans who go there will see her grave. We must not forget to put Howland, also, on the stone. But *Dio*—how like Anna! "

Constanza took his hand. " How like mama to want to make the best of all worlds." For the cemetery where Keats lies, the cemetery at the Pauline Gate by the pyramid of Caius Cestius, is a Protestant cemetery.

" Perhaps it can be arranged," the prince said. " Perhaps Catholic foreigners go there? She would have known: she knew Rome so well."

When Constanza returned to St-Jean-le-Sauveur she brought Mena with her. Now that the principessa was buried, Mena gave herself to unstinted grief. Flavia was drawn to listen to her lament; it eased her, too, and she minded it less than being alone with her mother.

She suggested their asking Mr James to come. No, Constanza said, it was a long way for him. Then she said, perhaps yes. " He may like to be with us. He must be very sad."

Mr James answered that he would come as soon as he could;
they arranged for him to have a room at the hotel at
Bandol.

Fortunately Constanza was kept busy and away from the
house a good deal. Anna's will was being proved in America,
the estate had to be settled; Mr Baxter, unable to come over
just now himself, was dealing with everything through a
lawyer attached to the American Consulate at Marseilles.
Constanza had to go there frequently for signatures and consultation. Marseilles was some forty miles, with neighbourly
courtesy the man from the tower drove her.

After a time Constanza became more herself. Flavia
thawed. She was able to ask, " Why is it so different this
time? Why are you so——"

" So what? "

" Rigid? "

" It must be shock. I cannot take it in. All my life whenever I looked up there was mama. For better and for
worse."

In herself she knew that she had not begun to come
to terms. It might take a long time; it might take for
ever.

When she began to talk more, she said one day to Mena:
" Now that mama is safe, you must tell me. Did she mean
to do . . . what she did? "

" Who can tell," said Mena. " She is at peace now."

" You saw her come back from Nice? "

" Yes."

" Well then? "

" She was very angry. Like many other times. I'd seen
her worse before."

" Is that true, Mena? But the other thing——? "

Mena, with her shut face, said: " That as well. That
happened before. It began in London when the prince did
not come for her. *Before*, I was always in time."

Constanza said slowly, " *Is* this true? Can I believe you? "

" You ask as your mother asked. What use are questions if you don't want to believe."

At Marseilles, Constanza was being let into figures and facts. "This, as you know, was your mother's annual income. Before the recession that was."

They were seated in a cubicle. The American lawyer behind his desk, Constanza in a small armchair in front.

" This can't be right," she said. " Mama had only just over half of that."

" I was speaking of her income before the deduction of what went to her husband, the prince in Rome."

" Will you say that again? " said Constanza.

" You were not aware of this arrangement? " said the lawyer.

At the end of that interview she said, " How is it possible that after all there is so much? "

The lawyer became almost human. " Well, Mrs Herbert, it was always a pretty solid fortune. Then, as you may not recall, the investments were changed in 1914, a transaction that led to some eminently satisfactory results. To put not too fine a point on it, Baxter succeeded in more or less doubling the estate."

" We had no idea."

" There *was* evidence that your mother never read her financial statements. She never knew that she was a very rich woman."

Constanza did not suppress a smile. " She *read* Mr Baxter's letters."

The lawyer smiled, too. " Ah," he said, seeing her to

the door, " Baxter's always been a careful bird. Well, I hope he didn't keep you all *too* short."

The man of principles' car was at the door. So far, Constanza had accepted her neighbour's services absent-mindedly. He drove fast; she was able to keep silent. She was a woman who had just lost her mother, he had the Latin directness and simplicity with death.

What she had heard that day, led her into talk. " I learnt something about my mother," she said on their drive home, " I thought she could not surprise me. But she did."

" You've been with the lawyers, so it must have to do with money."

" It has."

" People always surprise one about that," he said.

She said, " You know, I've read your books."

From the wheel, he sketched a slight ironic bow. " Madame, you do me too much honour."

" Not a bit," she said. " You have a style like Anatole France with a modern twist. And you know, your idea about selecting our rulers by controlled tests was brought up—very rudimentarily—by a Labour man in 1912. The Fabians would have none of it. But I heard Birkenhead talk about it as a future possibility. For me the snag is still *quis custodiet*, who's going to devise those tests? "

The man of principles took his eyes off the road and gave her a quick glance.

"We shall have to learn to co-operate with one another so completely," he said, " that we can afford to play it lightly—democracy without equality."

" You might get misunderstood," she said.

" I have," he said, and laughed. He added, " Social justice can only be had by trying to be just in new ways over

301

and over again; you can't leave it in a set mould once and for all."

At the villa, he vaulted out of the car to open the door for her. Flavia had come out to meet them.

" You don't move much like a professorial type," she said.

" Oh, I used to ride a bit." He did not tell them that until only a few years before he had been show-riding for France.

Constanza went in, he was turning the car; Flavia saw the long look with which he followed her mother.

No sooner in the house Constanza told them: " For twenty years mama has been giving nearly half her income to my father."

" It was to keep the palazzo repaired," said Mena, " and they must never sell it."

" So you knew it? "

" I knew it," said Mena. " But she didn't like anyone to know."

" So that was the ' drain on her income ', that was what she had done for Giorgio. She used to blush when I spoke of papa's financial position; I thought it was because she was ashamed of having left him badly off. *What else did you know, Mena?* "

Mena said, " I knew everything."

It was from then on that she and Constanza began to go over the past. In the weeks that followed they talked; in snatches. If only we had not left Rome, was Constanza's theme: if this had not happened in quite such a way, if that had never been said. . . .

" Why did nobody shut up Mrs Throgmore-Wylie. If only we had stopped *her* from talking."

" My love, it wasn't la Trommo who told her. La Trommo knew nothing."

" What was it then that she spread? "

" Oh that. Something she got into her head after we'd been to Cortina d'Ampezzo. I told you La Trommo never knew anything worth knowing."

" But what was it? " said Flavia.

" It was rubbish. She told people that your grandmother had already turned against the prince after Constanza was born and that was why there were no more *bambini*."

" And then Giorgio came and mama carried on so frightfully. Was it because it made her look a liar? "

" La Trommo soon thought it was the prince who'd been a brute."

" Then *who* told mama about Giulia? "

" Some *giovanotto*," said Mena and described him.

" Oh, that ass Milly. My Latin tutor. Oh God: *I* started *that*, too. I never forgot how I snubbed him when he tried to tell me some tale about papa. I told him that whatever it was, mama knew nothing about it. And *he* never forgot."

Flavia said: " How is one to live—if every step leads to another? "

" Like that," said Constanza.

Mena said, " Don't fret yourself, my lamb. That young man didn't tell her anything she did not know. One day many many years before, when the old principessa was still alive, your mother opened a door and saw them, the prince and the Marchesa Giulia."

" And where was that? "

" In the long room at Castelfonte."

After a pause, Constanza said, " Mama never liked that house."

" She had arrived unexpected, it was about one of her schemes, she shut the door again and walked away to the other side of the house and came in by the terrace. She did not know I had followed her. She never knew that a soul had seen her. But *I* saw the prince look up and *I* knew that he, too, had seen."

Presently Constanza said, " I understand his letting her go without much of a fight. Why did he let *me* go? At that time I thought that he loved me very much. Why didn't he tell me? If I had known the truth, if I had known that my mother had arranged it so that I could not go back to him, I should not have left. I would have put my foot down and stayed. But he did not tell me."

" You are wrong there, too," Mena said. And she told of the plan they all had hatched to keep her, and how the prince would have none of it for her sake.

Constanza only said, " This is too much. Too much now."

And then one day Mena said there was something else. She lowered her eyes. Out of her dress she produced a manilla envelope. " The Signora Principessa asked me to give you this," she said formally. " ' Give this to my daughter,' she told me, ' and tell her that I know she will understand.' "

Constanza drew back. " When did my mother give you this message? "

Still looking at the floor, Mena said, " The day after she came back from Nice."

" The last time? "

" Yes."

" Why have you waited so long? "

Mena now met her eyes. " She was not herself then. You had too much to bear. She did not tell me *when* I was to give the envelope to you."

" Do you know what is inside? "

" I do not. I can guess. Angry words. Something that

had better been forgotten. But *she* told me to give it to you;
it is my duty, I must."

" Yes, Mena. And thank you. Mena—when I think of
you, when I think of the life you have had with us—the life
you have not had! "

Mena drew herself up. " *I?* I have had the best of lives!
I was with her. I loved her. She was always good to me.
My man left me when the *bambina* hadn't been born two
months. He told me there wasn't enough to eat and cleared
out. He wasn't wrong there. The *bambina* died. I never set
eyes on him again. How can you ask me what life I should
have had without her! She took me into service at the
palazzo and I knew nothing. That Cosima wanted me to
stay down in the scullery, but the Signora Principessa said
she liked my face and taught me to look after her. Since
then it has been nothing but, ' Mena, you are not working too
hard? Mena, shouldn't you take the day off? Mena, are
you comfortable? are they looking after you all right?
have they given you a good room? are your sheets dry? '
The best wasn't too good for *me*. When we travelled she
thought of me first. She didn't even make me go among the
snakes. You know what she was, the way she would get, the
things she could say. Yet to me, in thirty-five years, she
never raised her voice, I never had a harsh word. How many
can say *that* of themselves! "

Constanza took the manilla envelope and went to her room
alone. It did not contain abusive words, it contained a will.
It was brief, efficiently worded, dated, witnessed, signed.
It left everything the principessa stood possessed of to
Giorgio.

Constanza, the same day, told Flavia.

" We must cable Mr Baxter, as this changes everything.
Yes, darling, it's a blow. I must get used to it." She added

quickly, " Now listen, my sweet, *you* don't have to worry for yourself."

" *I*'m not worried," said Flavia, and it was true. To boys and girls of her age the world, the future, appears both wide open and unreal.

" We'll get you to Oxford and all if I have to borrow from Mr James. And I'm sure papa can help."

" You forget I was going to get scholarships in any case," said Flavia. Then she asked, " When did she make this will? "

" Last month, in March, it is dated three days before she died."

" Who are those witnesses? "

" Two garden boys, near illiterates; I engaged them for her myself."

" I suppose it *is* valid? "

" Oh, yes. I learnt enough from Simon's books for that."

" So have I," said Flavia, " I'm beginning to be interested in the Bar. Valid, *unless*— Constanza, we all know, including that colonel at Alassio from what you told me, that you could easily prove, well . . . unsound mind."

Constanza said, " Don't, Flavia. Let her rest in peace."

" She did not think of you."

" I see it as her money. When she was alive she spent it, on all of us. She had a right to leave it as vindictively as she pleased. She was a very unhappy woman and she always tried to express it. At last she has found an effective way."

" But *why* Giorgio, after the ring and all? If she was so angry with both of you why didn't she leave it to your Uncle Jack's children, or some charity as people do? Can you understand it? "

" *She* thought I would. She expected me to. It was a gesture of total destruction. She knew I knew she thought

that with Giorgio it would all be gone. Dead waste. She
must have wanted just that."

" I see. And you, Constanza? What will you do? "

" I haven't had much time to think. When women of
my age lose their money they try to become secretaries, or
do translations. I can't even spell in Italian. And farm
labour isn't very adequately paid."

" Giorgio would *have* to have you live with him in the
palazzo later on, wouldn't he? Isn't that expected? Your
father had *his* sisters live with him."

" Darling, let me get off that cable before I have second
thoughts."

Flavia prevailed on her mother to go through Anna's papers
before cabling. The contents of Anna's desk at Alassio had
just been sent in a large sealed packet by her friend, the
colonel.

" There may be something else."

" How can there? " Constanza said. " Those are the
papers that were in her desk downstairs. They can't have
anything to do with her last days."

Flavia said, " They were sent by Colonel Robinson. How
did it come about that they were in his possession? "

Constanza said she understood that Mena had taken them
across to the colonel's house immediately after the discovery
of Anna's death.

" *Before* the doctor or anyone arrived? "

" Apparently."

" Why should Mena have done that? if these were just
old papers in *nonna's* desk? "

" I see now," said Constanza. " Mena cannot read
English, at least not quickly and with certainty. She *may*
have found something upstairs."

" Yes: and not being able to make out what it was, and

not being sure if it ought to be found, and not wanting it destroyed, she put it with the papers in the desk and took the lot to the colonel. Don't you think we'd *better* go through them, Constanza? "

Constanza said she did not want to find anything more.

They took the packet with the papers upstairs to the verandah that served as Flavia's study.

There were letters, bills, more letters. " Here *is* something."

What they read was a letter from a high official at Florence, a surface fascist, who used to come to Anna's house at Fiesole. It was written in English and it was a warning. It advised Anna to leave the country within the next weeks, there was certain information that her arrest was imminent.

" That too! "

" Something else that Mena did not know," said Flavia. " Do you think this was what she found by *nonna's* bed? "

" I almost hope so," said Constanza.

The next thing was a second will in Anna's hand. It was as brief as the first which it revoked. It left everything " as in my previous will deposited in Providence Rhode Island to my beloved daughter Constanza."

Flavia spoke, " So *she* had second thoughts. It is all right."

" *My beloved daughter*."

" We can forget all about it, mummy. You need never milk goats."

" Signed and everything, I suppose? "

" Everything. The same witnesses."

" Did she do it on her last day? " asked Constanza.

" Yes—no—actually it is dated on the first. How very odd— Good God! it is dated the first of October."

" October? "

" She must have made a mistake. October first Nineteen-twenty-nine."

For a while they floundered in bewilderment.

" The same gardeners witnessed it—those boys hadn't even come to Alassio in October—a sheet of the same writing-paper as that of the first will—there can be no doubt that this is her latest will."

" She mistook the date. But how? "

" I think I can answer that," said Constanza. " The first of October was the date on which she left Rome twenty years ago. She always remembered it; it was a particularly difficult time for her each year, so Mena told me."

" So when she was so very unhappy again——"

" Yes, Flavia."

" But this *is* her last intention and will? "

" Oh undoubtedly."

" But not valid? "

" Not valid at all."

" Couldn't the witnesses speak up? "

" What could they have to say, poor illiterate louts."

" Morally it is valid," said Flavia. Then she added herself, " Tell that to Giorgio."

Constanza said, " There is one thing I can do: I can burn the first will. That is what I shall do; now that I am certain of mama's intentions."

" Isn't it a crime? "

" If it's found out."

" Oh, mummy, you will be breaking the law."

" I'm going to take the law into my own hands," Constanza said. " One only lives once."

" Would the man of principles do it? "

" Not he," said Constanza. " But do stop calling him by that silly name."

" Michel," said Flavia.

" I *shall* burn it."

Constanza looked about the room. It was full spring and there were no more stoves or fires in the grate. Neither of them smoked. There was not even an ash-tray. Downstairs in the kitchen Mena and the new French cook were busy with the dinner. To Flavia's surprise, her mother got up, put the wills on the table under a stack of letters, weighed them down with a stone and left the room. In the door she said, " Such things have to be done properly. I shall see to it first thing tomorrow."

Flavia now had her clue: " She does not like it; she is putting it off." She went downstairs, strolled into the kitchen. " What are we having tonight? May I peep? Oh, and Mena, will you cut us some lemon and some ice for our vermouth? Oh, I didn't see the tray, sorry." When she was out of the kitchen, a few French phosphorus matches were in her pocket. A few sticks, not the box; they would miss nothing. She returned to the verandah, locked the door—such things have to be done properly—struck a match on the sole of her shoe and over a saucer set light to the first will. When it had smouldered into a thin black curl, she struck another match and burnt the second will. She scooped the remains into a sheet of newspaper and took them out of the house. She went down by the side of the road and scattered and trod and rubbed them into the earth. It was still light enough for her to see that there was left no trace. As she was coming up again, the man from the tower went by in his car.

He stopped when he saw her. " Flavià, *bon soir—Bon Dieu, ce que vous aviez les mains sales.*"

" Haven't I? " she said. " Perfectly filthy hands—I've been doing dirty work. *Bon soir, à demain.*"

" *Ciao,*" he called as he had learnt from her.

Flavia went indoors, cleaned the saucer, washed her hands. All evening she said nothing. In the morning she got up early: she opened all the windows in her study, then sat waiting. When she heard her mother call for her breakfast tray, she went in.

" Constanza, I've been thinking of something. What will you tell Mena afterwards? She will expect to be told what was in the envelope she gave you."

" I cannot tell her the truth. I cannot put that kind of thing on her. As it is, she has enough on her mind."

Flavia said very deliberately, " We must substitute a perfectly harmless envelope."

Constanza did not catch the reference to the incident in her daughter's childhood which had left its mark.

Flavia now produced a manilla envelope. " What Mena will find inside it, is the letter from Florence that warned *nonna* to leave Italy."

" That is a good idea," said Constanza.

" And now, mummy, I've got something to tell you. Something rather awful's happened. I've just come in from a paper-chase. The wills, both of them, blown out of the window."

" But I left them under a weight."

" I am sorry. That was my fault. I had been looking at them again."

" You went after them? "

" Of course. Not a trace. I think they must have been blown right into the sea. I don't think they'll turn up again."

Constanza said, " They may. Or they may not. It is best so. I am glad. It's been left in the hands of the gods."

Flavia said, letting this pass, " Which reminds me: your ring? "

" Mr Baxter has sent the money he's advancing me. He thinks it's for a pressing debt. He wrote me a very stiff letter; he hopes I am not falling into mama's footsteps. The ring ought to be here any day."

" And so will Mr James, mummy."

Constanza had the grace to look confused. " Would you do something for *me*, darling? "

" I *might*," Flavia said amiably.

" Would you mind looking after Mr James for a bit? He always enjoys the youngest generation. Would you mind looking after yourself for a bit? You see, I think I should like to go away for a time; perhaps a change would be best."

" *Già*."

Constanza took a breath. " I thought I might go to Paris."

" Paris, Constanza? "

" It *is* rather absurd at my age not to know it properly."

Flavia lifted a piece of fruit off her mother's tray. " Oh quite," she said. " Well, the Calais Express: It is for *you* after all, Constanza."

But Constanza said: " Actually, I thought I might *drive* up. It would be pleasant to see something of the country."

" How not! And those big open touring cars are so convenient for that."

" Michel has very kindly offered to take me. He asks if you would like to have the key to the tower while we're away? You will find a book or two in the house."